Apparition of Desire

Pinned beneath the chair that had fallen on her leg, Amanda stared startled at the window of her room. She had heard that spirits of the departed walked the night at Sommersby Castle, but never did she expect to see such a shining specter—the figure of a magnificent man emblazoned by moonlight.

The window swung open. The intruder stepped into the room. He stood fierce and tall, the most beautiful man Amanda had ever seen. His bare, rippling chest muscles paid tribute to all that was primitive in male power, and his corded arms effortlessly managed the weight of his massive, unsheathed sword.

"I hope I did not frighten you," he said, as he bent to free her. "I am Sommersby."

He was no ghost then, Amanda thought, this man who was pledged to wed another but who now caressed her with his gaze even as his hand stroked her ankle. He was flesh and blood. Which made him far more dangerous. . . .

The Perfect Bride

by

Eileen Putman

A SIGNET BOOK

SIGNET
Published by the Penguin Group
Penguin Putnam Inc., 375 Hudson Street,
New York, New York 10014, U.S.A.
Penguin Books Ltd, 27 Wrights Lane,
London W8 5TZ, England
Penguin Books Australia Ltd,
Ringwood, Victoria, Australia
Penguin Books Canada Ltd, 10 Alcorn Avenue,
Toronto, Ontario, Canada M4V 3B2
Penguin Books (N.Z.) Ltd, 182–190 Wairau Road,
Auckland 10, New Zealand

Penguin Books Ltd, Registered Offices:
Harmondsworth, Middlesex, England

First published by Signet, an imprint of Dutton Signet,
a member of Penguin Putnam Inc.

First Printing, October, 1997
10 9 8 7 6 5 4 3 2 1

Chapter One

"My wig, Jeffers, if you please."

"The gray or the brown, Major—er, my lord?"

"I believe I shall require the hoary privileges of age for this particular mission."

Jeffers nodded and carefully removed the gray wig from a stand on the massive oak chest. "Do you wish a mustache as well, my lord?"

There was a brief, contemplative silence from the figure in the large wing chair. "The cursed things are a nuisance," came the response, "but I should not care to chance exposure."

From a drawer, Jeffers removed a matching gray mustache that he proceeded to tame into a neat military style. When he offered it for inspection, his employer frowned.

"Too rigid. Something more casual, perhaps with a bit of a droop to gain the young lady's sympathy. I mean to disarm the target, Jeffers, not frighten her."

The batman smoothed the mustache into a less prepossessing appendage and was rewarded with a slow smile from the figure in the chair.

"Perfect."

Jeffers preened under the compliment. The man who had commanded his loyalty and service for half a decade dispensed few enough of those.

"Did you procure the clothing?" his employer demanded in the rich baritone that had compelled instant attention on the battlefield.

Jeffers opened the mahogany wardrobe and removed a pair of trousers, waistcoat, and jacket. The frayed edges of the dimity twill betrayed its years, but the suit was impeccably clean.

With a critical eye, the figure in the chair studied the costume. "Where did you obtain it?"

"From an impoverished bank clerk who was only too happy to have the fifty pounds."

A rare smile spread over uncompromising features that had consigned many a foe to his doom. "I cannot imagine how I devised my disguises without your assistance in the early years of the war."

"It was my good fortune that our paths crossed, sir—er, my lord," Jeffers insisted, flushing with pleasure.

"Nonsense." Briskly dismissive, the baritone voice dispensed with Jeffers's heartfelt declaration. "You would have bested that French bastard eventually. I merely hastened his demise."

Jeffers kept silent, knowing that above all things, his employer disliked praise. Still, nothing would ever persuade the scrawny batman he could have defeated the Frenchman who weighed nearly twenty stone and who ambushed him that day near Bayonne. Fortunately, the tattered "beggar" who had come along as Jeffers made his last prayers possessed extraordinary fighting skills. The French soldier breathed his last in the pauper's lethal embrace.

A rustling of paper from the wing chair indicated that his employer's attention had moved on to other things. "Three names. That is the best you could do?"

Jeffers bowed. "Your requirements were exceedingly stringent, my lord."

A mercurial gaze held his. "You believe I demand too much from my future bride?"

Jeffers took note of the warning tone. "It is not my position to express such a view."

"But it is your opinion, is it not?"

The batman had long ago learned that a strategic retreat could be more valuable than a frontal assault when dealing with his employer's unyielding nature. Silently he returned the worn suit to the wardrobe, making a great show of arranging the garment so as to avoid wrinkling it. Reaching for a polishing cloth, he donned a preoccupied air as he rubbed the ancient suit of old armor that stood next to the wardrobe as if in a constant state of battle readiness.

An impatient sigh filled the chamber. "Your silence does not fool me, man. I know what you think of my methods."

Jeffers stared at the ancient broadsword that hung on the wall next to the armor with all manner of other fighting implements. "I merely find them . . . methodical, my lord," he replied carefully.

"Method has served me well enough in the trenches and out of them," came the brisk reply. "I defy you to think of a better way to select a bride."

Jeffers cleared his throat. "Some allow the heart to be their guide," he ventured.

"The same people who marry in haste and repent at leisure, no doubt," scoffed his employer. "I do not think it is the heart that guides them so much as another part of their anatomy."

Jeffers bowed. "As you say, my lord."

"Enough of this idle chitchat."

"How do you mean to begin?"

"As with any mission, Jeffers," came the impatient response. "Reconnoiter and reconnaissance. A wife is no different from an enemy target. Both must be chosen carefully and taken from a position of strength."

"Yes, my lord." As his gaze settled on a particularly lethal-looking cudgel from the twelfth century, Jeffers cringed.

"What a masterful figure! It is too bad you did not have more of his gumption, Edward."

"You know that Edward has not spoken to us in nearly five hundred years, my dear."

"Hmmph. He always could hold a grudge."

"Be reasonable, Isabella. We had him deposed. And roasted alive."

"I still say five hundred years is too long to nurse a grudge. It gets lonely up here."

A hurt silence followed this remark. *"You used to say that I was all you needed, Isabella."*

"After five hundred years, even your presence becomes wearing, Mortimer. I need something to occupy my time."

"Time is meaningless when one has eternity to atone for one's sins."

"But you do not see, Mortimer? Time is all we have."

"What are you planning, Isabella?"

"We must do something about our tenant. He is missing the passion to which he is entitled in his lifetime."

"I would prefer not to get involved, if you do not mind."

"But I do mind, Mortimer. Our hearts have always beaten as one, have they not? Or so you always said."

"Yes, Isabella. That is what I have always said."

Felicity Biddle, daughter of Sir Thomas Biddle, adjusted her spectacles. "Only think, Amanda! The fearless warrior rescued the princess from the phantasm without a care for his own safety." She sighed. "I cannot imagine any of my admirers braving an apparition in the name of love."

Amanda Fitzhugh regarded her young cousin with a critical eye. "Since phantasms exist only in your exceedingly fertile imagination, it is not necessary to put any prospective suitor to such a ridiculous test."

Felicity pursed her heart-shaped mouth, which had already provoked many eager young swains into declaring undying love. "You would rob the fairies of their fairy dust, Amanda. Is there not a fanciful bone in your body?"

"No more than there are fairies." Amanda walked over to the hearth in the Biddles' parlor and briskly stirred the fire. "I have lived long enough to understand that fairy tales and dreams derive from wishes, not fact. I am most thankful for the exceedingly practical nature I have developed over the years."

Miss Biddle closed her book, put aside her spectacles, and studied her cousin with brilliant violet eyes. "You speak as if you are past praying for, when you have but twenty-eight years. You are still a remarkably handsome woman, Amanda. You could have your pick of husbands."

"Only if they are doddering widowers with a clamoring brood to raise." Amanda shot her cousin a wry smile.

"Not so! Why Mr. Merson was most particular in his affections last year, and he is neither doddering nor a widower. I thought him quite appealing."

"He is a reprobate and lecher," Amanda declared bluntly. "You had best clean those spectacles of yours. They must be fogged to see so poorly."

Felicity gave her cousin a reproachful look. Her spectacles were the one aspect of her appearance that she fervently wished to change. Of what use was a pair of exquisite violet eyes if one must hide them behind thick spectacles? She never wore them in public. No lady could captivate a suitor if she could not bat her exceedingly long lashes without the obstruction of thick lenses.

"I only make the point that you would have been wed long ago if you had shown the slightest willingness to entertain offers." Felicity's rosy lips formed a pout.

Amanda bestowed a tolerant smile on her young cousin. "I have no desire to wed, as you know. I could not be happier with my little spinster's cottage by the sea. I shall stand in for your mama this Season, see you happily betrothed, and then return as quickly as I can to Kent."

With a resigned sigh, Felicity shook her head. Sympathy lent her violet eyes a velvety sheen. "I am sorry, Amanda. I have been insensitive. It is all because of that nasty Lord Ramsey, is it not?"

This untoward statement brought a severe frown from her cousin. "I have long since forgotten about the marquess, but since you raise the subject, there is no more apt example of how fanciful notions can lead one astray."

Felicity held her breath. Amanda had never spoken at length of the scandalous incident in her past, and she knew she had been wrong to mention it. But Amanda had evidently decided that a purpose was to be served by her cautionary tale, for she fixed Felicity with a stern eye.

"I was no more than a girl when I allowed myself to fall prey to a man I imagined to be the hero of my dreams. Instead, he proved to be a scoundrel of the worst sort, as everyone but me knew to begin with." Her lips thinned grimly. "I wish I had had someone to warn me at the time, but I do not suppose I would have listened, any more than you are listening to me now."

Felicity blushed at her cousin's description of the scandal that had barely been avoided when Amanda had been discovered reclining on a bench in one of the darker paths at Vauxhall, her bodice askew and her skirts pooled above her knees. Knowing her cousin as she did, Felicity could scarcely imagine that the unsentimental Amanda could have been carried away by anything as impractical as passion. Nevertheless, it seems she had.

Fortunately, it had been Felicity's father who found Amanda in Lord Ramsey's embrace, so the discovery went no further. Despite being heir to a dukedom, the marquess was deemed so beyond redemption as to make a disastrous choice for a husband. Thus, Sir Thomas did not press the man to do the honorable thing and offer for his niece's hand. Amanda had abruptly ended what was otherwise a promising Season and beseeched her uncle to take her away to the country. In the eight years since, Amanda had retired to Kent, firmly closed the door on all prospective marriage offers, and become a relentlessly practical woman.

"I respect your opinion," Felicity replied, "but I could not live as you do. There is no harm in seeking a husband who inspires one's fancies."

"To say that Ramsey inspired my fancies is an understatement," Amanda retorted dryly. "And look at the disaster that nearly occurred."

Felicity pouted. "I am not you."

"No," Amanda agreed, laughing. "I am firmly on the shelf."

"By your own choice."

"Nonsense. I know my assets, or rather lack of them." Amanda smiled. "I am a long Meg, whereas you are charmingly petite. My eyes are ordinary brown; yours are violet jewels. My face is plain, and I have neither your delightful curls nor your angelic countenance. Your hair is the color of spun gold. Mine is rather like the dishwater Mrs. Simmons throws out at the end of the day. I do not begrudge you your considerable assets. Indeed, they would only prove an inconvenience for one bound to live alone for the rest of her life."

Felicity sighed. Her cousin was determined to don the oppressive mantle of old age long before she reached that deplorable state. Even though Amanda was past her first blushes, she was still quite attractive for a woman of twenty-eight. And since that long-ago indiscretion, Amanda had conducted herself with such modest propriety and decorum that Felicity's mother, Lady Biddle, suffered no qualms in charging Amanda with the responsibility for Felicity's come-out, although Sir Thomas had stroked his chin thoughtfully before agreeing to the proposal.

Lady Biddle had brought out Felicity's five elder sisters with stunning success, as all were married to men of wealth and title. Now, however, the prospect of another London Season seemed to weary her. When she tumbled from her horse and severely sprained her ankle a month before the start of the Season, Lady Biddle immediately— and rather happily, Felicity thought—summoned Amanda to step into the breach.

Delighted to have Amanda's company, Felicity never-theless worried that her phlegmatic cousin might take her chaperone responsibilities so seriously as to depress the at-tentions of any true romantic. Amanda eschewed sentiment with such fervor that Felicity shuddered to think of the fate of any suitor who dared quote the poets or offer a fulsome compliment in her presence.

"Cheer up." Amanda regarded her younger cousin affec-tionately. "I am not a dragon. I promise not to chase away any lovesick gentlemen. Unless," she added with mock severity, "they try to do battle with phantasms."

A vague image of a fearless warrior astride a white horse, churning up the dirt as he raced to Felicity's side, caused the younger woman to sigh in longing.

Amanda's brow furrowed thoughtfully as, unbidden, an image appeared in her mind as well. It was of Julian LeFevre—Lord Ramsey—in all his satanic glory, looking down at her with gleaming midnight eyes that promised a wild paradise of sinful delights.

A shiver rippled through her, even though the fire still blazed warmly in the hearth. Thank goodness, she no longer believed in fairy tales.

His pitifully thin collar provided scant protection against the rain, but Major Simon Hannibal Thornton had never had the luxury of minding the elements. Downpours that had left his fellow soldiers shaking with cold and cursing the heavens had never affected him. He had simply slid under his clay-smeared blanket, made a pillow out of straw, and slept.

Rain was blessed, life restoring, and it held off the battle to come. Better to sleep whole and miserable in a quagmire than to rot senseless under the sun in a field of broken bodies. It was what followed the rain one always had to watch out for.

A betrothal would likely follow this rain, a tedious foray into the frivolous world of the Marriage Mart with a woman he had not yet met. She would hold him accountable for her protection and happiness, and he would provide those things for her because that was what he did.

Facing Napoleon and his entire Imperial Guard paled in comparison to this onerous duty of finding a wife.

Jeffers was partially to blame for his foul mood. The man had outdone himself in procuring a broken-down horse to fit Simon's masquerade. Surely even an earl's impoverished cousin could afford a better mount than this nag. The gray would not make Mayfield by dusk. Simon could not imagine that Sir Thomas would welcome the delay of his dinner.

The real cause of Simon's dour spirits, however, was the fact that his mission had already suffered several setbacks.

Lady Serena Fielding had possessed considerable beauty, youth, and the requisite large family. Her reputation was spotless, her dowry considerable, her reading skills superb. But she had proven to be a snob. Though she had treated him with the respect due an earl's emissary, she did not trouble to hide her disdain at his frayed collar. He could have told her that it was not wealth or clothing that made a man, especially on the battlefield, but he elected not to bother. He would not spend the rest of his life with a woman who would not welcome a down-on-his-luck soldier for dinner. He crossed the Lady Serena off his list.

The Honorable Harriet Dunham had no such pretensions. She read voraciously and displayed an egalitarian spirit. Her birth and breeding were unexceptional, her dowry superb, and she possessed a sufficient number of siblings to raise no doubts as to the breeding abilities of her family tree. Even at nineteen, her looks had nothing to commend them, but she had a friendly smile and a way of engaging a man in conversation that made the time pass pleasantly.

She had, however, articulated the shocking view that a woman had no obligation to provide her husband with an heir, and even hinted that intimate relations ought to be solely a matter of mutual pleasure. Simon did not hold with such radical notions, which he suspected were but an excuse for a roving eye. Nor would he suffer a woman who would shirk her breeding responsibilities.

That left only Miss Felicity Biddle. A baronet's daughter, she was the lowest-ranked candidate on his list, but her father possessed sufficient means as to guarantee a perfectly adequate dowry. Not that Simon needed the money; the earldom had brought him great wealth. But a woman's family ought to contribute to the marriage. It enforced the principles of duty and obligation, which had guided his undertakings on the field of battle and elsewhere.

Youth was on Miss Biddle's side—she was but eighteen. She had five sisters, but no brothers. Simon wondered whether the Biddle women could only produce girls. That would not do, as he must have an heir. Still, she seemed the most tolerable of the three ladies whose names Jeffers's research had produced. If Miss Biddle were sufficiently biddable, he might take a calculated gamble on her ability to produce a son. When one scattered enough grapeshot, one was certain to hit the target.

Miss Biddle was said to be fond of literature, and although poetry bored him—he favored political treatises and military dispatches for his reading material—Simon was gratified to know that she understood the importance of reading and would see to the education of their children.

Sir Thomas had sent a letter welcoming Lord Sommersby's emissary and inviting him to stay at Mayfield to discuss the potential suit and business matters that marriage to the earl would involve. The baronet was obviously inclined toward the alliance. If Miss Biddle proved adequate, the courtship could be conducted during the Season, and a wedding held immediately after.

His tedious mission would be accomplished with satisfying efficiency.

Chapter Two

Amanda stared at the man Sir Thomas introduced as Mr. Thornton, secretary and cousin to the Earl of Sommersby. An uncommonly tall figure in a worn and somewhat ill-fitting suit, he surely must be all of fifty, as his hair had gone completely gray and his mustache wore a tired droop. Mr. Thornton's jawline had held surprisingly firm for his years, however, and his keen gaze indicated his wits had lost nothing to age. The eyes themselves ran to neither blue nor green, but seemed to change with the light. They radiated a coolly assessing air, and Amanda had the distinct impression that beneath Mr. Thornton's politely respectful exterior lurked a rather arrogant nature.

His proudly erect bearing seemed perfectly in keeping with a man in the employ of such a war hero as the earl was reputed to be. Were it not for his age, he might have been a soldier himself. His shoulders spanned the breadth of the doorway and appeared quite capable of bearing the entire weight of the door frame, if need be. Never once did he slump to accommodate Sir Thomas's diminutive form; he was quite at ease towering over his host, as if there was nothing out of the ordinary about his proportions. Amanda wondered why a man of Lord Sommersby's wealth did not pay his employees well enough to procure a decent suit. Such a form as Mr. Thornton's demanded quality attire.

Mr. Thornton displayed no embarrassment at his frayed lapel and worn collar. Instead, there was a subtle confidence about his demeanor, Amanda observed, as the party gathered in the drawing room after a late dinner. Moving with a grace and agility surprising in a man of his size and age, he surveyed a room with hawklike eyes as he filled it with his considerable presence. And though he was clearly a man of lesser means, there was nothing subservient about his manner. Obviously, Mr. Thornton was a man to be relied upon. Amanda suspected that Lord Sommersby allowed his secretary a great deal of authority.

Lady Biddle's ankle was troubling her, and she retired early. Sir Thomas assisted her up the stairs, charging Felicity and Amanda to get to know Mr. Thornton, as they would be spending no small amount of time in his presence.

Her uncle's cryptic statement confirmed Amanda's suspicion that Sir Thomas favored a match between Felicity and the earl. Over dinner there had been talk of a visit to Sommersby Castle so that Felicity and Lord Sommersby could meet before the whirl of the Season began. That meant the Mayfield party would probably leave within a few days, as it was no inconsiderable distance from eastern Sussex to the west Dorset coast. Amanda never doubted that Mr. Thornton was quite capable of escorting them. The man radiated efficiency and poise. Indeed, the only awkwardness he displayed came when Felicity, in high spirits over the prospect of meeting such a noted war hero, began to question him about his employer.

"Is it true that Lord Sommersby's brilliant distraction of French troops on the Peninsula enabled Wellington to win at Salamanca?" Felicity flushed in anticipation of hearing tales of the earl's cleverness.

Mr. Thornton stiffened. "'Brilliant' is an inflated assessment," he replied in a clipped voice. "The credit for the Peninsula strategy is Wellington's, of course."

Felicity's eyes grew dreamy. "But even Wellington accorded Lord Sommersby a hero, did he not?"

Shifting uncomfortably, Mr. Thornton regarded Felicity as if she had just said something extremely unpleasant. "The true heroes of that mission," he corrected with a pained expression, "were our ships, which held their positions and forced the French to maintain a cordon defense around the entire perimeter of the Peninsula."

"What?" Felicity blinked. She was not accustomed to being contradicted by any member of the male gender and, in any case, had not truly comprehended Mr. Thornton's words.

Amanda wondered why Mr. Thornton was so reluctant to sing his employer's praises, which had already been trumpeted by Wellington himself and even the Prince. Still, his point was well taken. "Mr. Thornton means that the threat of sea landings forced the French to leave no area undefended, greatly diminishing the number of French troops left to fight in reserve," she told her cousin.

Felicity showed no interest in the finer points of military strategy. "I believe I will just fetch a shawl from my room," she said, and left.

Mr. Thornton shot Amanda a surprised look. "You seem to grasp the principles of war quite adequately, Miss Fitzhugh."

"My father fought on the Peninsula," Amanda said quietly. "I followed the events most avidly."

His eyes searched hers, and Amanda again noted their peculiar, changeable color—now more green than blue. They held a question, but he did not ask it.

"He is buried at Busaco," she added, instinctively comprehending the reason for his reticence.

"I am sorry." Surprisingly, compassion glinted in his eyes.

"Thank you. Some people do not understand why I have so little enthusiasm for the celebrations that have overwhelmed England in recent months. Many families lost loved ones, of course, but I cannot bring myself to celebrate the end of something I wish had never begun."

Somberly, he nodded. "War is nothing to celebrate. And yet, a nation must fight."

"Must it?" Amanda challenged. "I cannot see that the sacrifice of so many lives serves any purpose other than to forever separate them from their loved ones."

An assessing coolness in his gaze chilled the air around them. "Would you have handed the Continent to Napoleon, Miss Fitzhugh?" Beneath his neutral tone, Amanda sensed the accusation.

"It is one thing to defend one's home," she replied, angered by the implied slur on her loyalty, "and quite another to cross the seas to interfere with a tyrant whose overweening confidence would have led him to destroy himself eventually in any case."

"Do you mock the sacrifice of thousands, madam?" Though his words bore a sting, they were delivered in such an expressionless voice Amanda was seized by an urge to shake that implacable restraint.

"Not at all, sir," she said, for once glad of her height, which made it easier to stand up to Mr. Thornton's looming presence. "But I do not believe war serves any end except the causes of those who decree it. And while the soldier, the man whose life is forfeit, pays the price, the King and his ministers see little change in their comfortable existences."

A silence ensued. Amanda sensed his condemnation, but his expression betrayed nothing of the distaste she suspected he must feel. He merely studied her for a long moment before quietly observing, "There are those who would take such talk as treason."

"There are those who dismiss any opposing view as treason," Amanda retorted. "That does not dissuade me from my principles. Were I a man, I might have held forth in the taverns and meeting places and stirred the people with my seditious talk—and no doubt would have been clapped in irons long ago." She paused to fling him a self-mocking smile. "I suppose it is fortunate that I am a woman."

His brows rose. Oddly, they displayed no hint of the gray that had overtaken his hair. Amanda flushed in sudden embarrassment. She had spoken these thoughts to no one. Why had she blurted them out to a man who—given his employer—could have no sympathy for such a position?

But it was not his silent disapproval that made her uneasy. It was the clear gaze that, without seeming to move at all, studied her from head to toe—as if to confirm her last statement.

Mr. Thornton was assessing her femininity. Of course, he would find her wanting, but surely he would not be so rude as to mention that she was uncommonly tall for a woman or that her features were not small and delicate like Felicity's. His eyes narrowed thoughtfully, and Amanda grew warm under his inspection. For all that he was old enough to be her father, Mr. Thornton did not possess a particularly fatherly air.

Though he made no comment, the silence between them

was in itself a thunderous commentary. Amanda supposed she ought to steer the conversation into more amiable channels.

"I understand that we are to journey to Sommersby together," she said politely, unable to bring herself to convey much enthusiasm over the prospect.

"It is a pity that Lady Biddle will be unable to come," he replied, accepting her change of subject with an equal lack of fervor, "but Sir Thomas appears to have every faith in your skills as a chaperone."

Despite his polite response, shards of ice glinted in his eyes. Amanda decided that anyone unwise enough to cross Mr. Thornton was to be pitied. On the other hand, she thought irritably, who was this tall stranger to judge her convictions?

"That is because I am known to be incorrigibly practical, Mr. Thornton," she retorted. "I am not one to be swayed by sentiment, nor do I scruple at plain speaking. Ideal qualities for a chaperone, do you not agree?" Amanda could not keep the cross tone from her voice. "I fear I will not be counted a lively addition to the earl's gathering," she added defiantly.

Something volatile flickered in his eyes before vanishing in the cool blue of newly calmed seas. "The party will be quite small, Miss Fitzhugh. And I should perhaps warn you that a practical nature fares best at Sommersby Castle."

"Oh?" Amanda eyed him curiously.

"The castle is very old—rich with history, but plagued by a rather dark reputation. I have spent only a little time there, but—"

"Come, Mr. Thornton," Amanda interrupted, unable to keep a sardonic note from her voice. "*People* have reputations. Buildings merely have names."

Whatever irritation Amanda imagined that she saw spring to his gaze in sudden flecks of green immediately disappeared in that maddeningly cool blue. "I merely suggest that Miss Biddle should be prepared."

"For what, pray? Is the place haunted?"

"Not at all." There was not even a glimmer of humor in his eyes. "But the castle is not in the best condition, and its reputation has made it difficult to secure servants. It seems that over the centuries, the castle's dungeons were responsible for a considerable decrease in the local population. Political disputes, I understand."

"I see." Had Mr. Thornton cast some sort of gauntlet before her? "Dark reputations do not frighten me," she replied crisply, "nor do I believe in ghosts. Miss Biddle has a rather more fertile imagination, but I will be certain to keep her occupied with other matters." Her eyes were challenging. "Is there anything else we should know before our visit? I trust the place is not unsafe?"

"You may count on the earl to see to your safety."

"I do not believe that answered my question, sir," she said, wondering how she was going to stand two more minutes in this maddening man's company, much less the two weeks at Sommersby Castle.

At that moment, Felicity returned with her shawl and insisted on taking the night air, the rain having stopped. Reaching for her own shawl, Amanda buoyed her spirits with the hope that Mr. Thornton might not remain at the castle during the entire visit.

Eager to take in the fresh scents of the newly dampened garden, Felicity immediately dashed out onto the terrace, leaving Mr. Thornton little choice but to offer his arm to Amanda. As Amanda placed her hand lightly on his sleeve, a little jolt shot through her fingertips. It was nothing, really. Nevertheless, it drew from her an involuntary gasp.

"Is something wrong?" He frowned.

"Of course not," she replied briskly, trying to cover her embarrassment.

For one brief moment, he turned his full attention to her with eyes that bore all the acuity of honed steel. Then he looked away, his hand slipping lightly to her waist as he propelled her out the door toward Felicity.

This time there was no spark, no tiny jolt of electricity. Nevertheless, in the heavy air that instantly brought the sweet smells of the garden to her nostrils, Amanda was acutely conscious of his touch. Abruptly, she halted, feeling silly—and unexpectedly dizzy with the garden's heady perfume.

"Are you ill?" His voice held a note of impatience, and

Amanda guessed that a man of his cool bearing had no tolerance for female hysterics.

"I am perfectly well," she assured him. As he eyed her skeptically, Amanda found herself wondering exactly how many years Mr. Thornton had on his plate and why a man of his age should provoke her into such childish behavior.

Undoubtedly, she had been away from Kent too long.

"Sommersby will be the making of her." Lady Biddle sat forward to allow her husband to plump up her satin pillows, then reclined again and smiled. "I have never met the earl, but one can only admire his accomplishments. Even Wellington has published his praises far and wide."

Sir Thomas studied his wife. Although she hated the fact that age had eroded the graceful definition of her cheeks and jawline, he thought the pleasing plumpness that time had lent her features softened what had been an uncompromising sharpness. The fiery red hair that had driven him wild so many years ago had acquired a silvery patina that in no way mitigated his passion. But as the years had left their unmistakable imprint on her once-fresh beauty, his wife had become dispirited about the prospect of abandoning her youth and had grown more and more remote. Perhaps the enforced separation they were about to endure might serve to reawaken the spark between them. On the other hand, the prospect of leaving his wife alone in the country for nearly three months was disquieting. His recent business trips to London, though frequent, had been of much shorter duration.

"I cannot help but wish you could accompany us," he said.

"Perish the thought! Amanda will have things well in hand. I daresay my fall was a blessing in disguise. Having fired off five daughters, I am entitled to this little respite—though I shall miss the opportunity to see the famous Sommersby Castle. A duke was murdered there, was he not?"

"A king," he corrected. "With the connivance of the queen and her lover."

A dreamy look appeared in Lady Biddle's cornflower-blue eyes. "How exciting. I would dearly love to see the place. To think that Felicity is to be mistress there!"

Sir Thomas gave an exasperated sigh. "Felicity's head is filled with outlandish notions, Eloise. She needs a steady hand. You see how she has turned away one suitor after another. With all that talk of warriors and heroes, I despair of forcing her to see things sensibly."

"Then it is fortunate that a hero has fixed his interest on her," his wife shot back. "I daresay Sommersby will not disappoint."

"No man can live up to the unrealistic expectations of such slavish adoration," Sir Thomas warned.

"Felicity has not a slavish bone in her body."

A fleeting grin of appreciation of his wife's ready wit lightened Sir Thomas's somber features. It was quickly replaced by a look of concern, however. "I cannot help but wish Felicity had Amanda's sense to see a man for what he is, not what she wishes him to be."

Lady Biddle eyed him sharply. "Amanda did not always possess such wisdom, my dear. Look what happened with Ramsey."

"She was very young at the time."

"Two years older than Felicity is now."

Sir Thomas eyed her in consternation. "And yet, you are happy to put our youngest daughter into her hands."

"Amanda is beyond all that, Thomas. She is a spinster. The lesson she learned has purged her of foolish notions. A woman does get to the point in life where a pretty phrase and a devilish eye no longer turn her head."

"Does she?" An odd light illuminated Sir Thomas's gaze.

"Of course," Lady Biddle assured him. "And I have every faith in your ability to manage the situation."

Sir Thomas stroked his chin. "Just what do you plan to do with the time you will have on your hands, Eloise?"

Lady Biddle stretched languorously. "Oh, I shall do a bit of reading, perhaps some gardening if my ankle can manage. And there will no doubt be callers to help me while away the hours. Spring is a lovely time in the country."

A shadow darkened her husband's features. "What I have always believed," he said softly, "is that spring is a time for lovers."

Lady Biddle closed her eyes, and her mouth curved

dreamily. "Then Felicity and Lord Sommersby shall do very well indeed."

By all rights he should have been riding outside the carriage with Sir Thomas, rather than sitting in the confines of a rattling coach with two chattering women. Or rather, *one* chattering woman. Miss Fitzhugh could in no way be called loquacious, having scarcely spoken to him all day. Miss Biddle, on the other hand, had not ceased talking since they left Mayfield.

"You must tell me more about Lord Sommersby," she pleaded. "I understand that he single-handedly fought off an entire French battalion at Vitoria."

"Good God, no!" He stared at her. "A battalion is a rather large number of men."

Miss Biddle regarded him with her enormous violet eyes. "But the earl is very strong, is he not? And clever? Wellington said he is very clever. And fearless. He *is* fearless, is he not, Mr. Thornton?"

More than ever he wished to be riding outside with Sir Thomas. But his nag had not been up to the task, and Sir Thomas had seemed happy to keep to his own company, which is why Simon had to suffer Miss Biddle's relentless quest to hear the Earl of Sommersby lauded like some Greek god.

"I am afraid you have an inflated notion of the earl's accomplishments, Miss Biddle," Simon began patiently. "He served with Wellington in a number of capacities, but can in no way claim the accolades people would bestow upon him. Sometimes he did little actual fighting—except for at Waterloo. He was more of a . . . messenger in disguise."

"A messenger? Disguise?" Miss Biddle frowned, then her brow cleared. "Oh, you mean a *spy*! Why, that is even more daring, is it not?"

Gently, Miss Fitzhugh touched her cousin's arm. "I believe we are becoming a trial to Mr. Thornton. Perhaps we might speak of something else, dear."

Miss Biddle merely smiled and squinted out the window at the passing scenery. The poor girl obviously needed spectacles, though it was not difficult to guess why she had not obtained them. He had to admit that Miss Biddle possessed an unusual set of violet eyes. She had obviously put vanity ahead of her eyesight. Ridiculous, to be sure, but what else could one expect of the female sex?

Shifting his long legs to the other side of the carriage, Simon was careful not to brush the feet of the ladies sitting across from him. Like most women who possessed only a superficial understanding of the world, Miss Biddle had not the slightest inkling of what it meant to daily risk one's neck, to engage in mortal combat with a foe who had nothing to lose but a life that offered no great pleasure to begin with. Miss Fitzhugh was a more sober sort, having lost a father to war and fully understanding the risks, but her loss had led her to ignorantly condemn the cause for which her parent made his noble sacrifice. Did she think that a man took lightly the decision to lay his life on the line?

Women inhabited a strange, frivolous world. Unfortunately, he was going to have to spend the next months immersed in that world, with its fancy gowns and glittering balls. But then every mission had its drawbacks. Every victory came with a price. As a prospective bride, Miss Biddle met all of his requirements; moreover, she was not a snob like Miss Fielding, nor a determined bluestocking like Miss Dunham, who would withhold her favors on a whim.

The amiable Miss Biddle would willingly provide him with the brood he must have to secure the line. It was his duty to see that the title and its wealth did not disappear, as it very nearly did until the late Lord Sommersby's solicitors discovered that the ninth earl's second cousin had somehow survived the maelstrom at Waterloo and was available to assume the title.

He had not wanted an earldom. It was very different from soldiering, and its chief tasks—preserving one's assets and keeping one's wife breeding—seemed trivial by comparison. A soldier's world was defined by the turf he commanded, the weapons at his disposal, and the mission of the day. When resources were short, he made do with those at his disposal. Honor and self-reliance, those were the keys to success. In the end, they were all a man had. He would not claim a hero's crown merely for doing what had to be done.

The military was simplicity itself. Courtship, on the other

hand, was a complicated business to be tolerated for as short a period as possible—until a decent interval had passed and a wedding could be held. Jeffers, who seemed to know about such things, had insisted that one must afford one's betrothed a Season to bask in the attention due a young lady of breeding and beauty. Enduring a few months of social frivolity was one thing, but tolerating Miss Biddle's blind adoration was another. That nonsense must stop.

"Lord Sommersby is a very ordinary man, Miss Biddle," he said sternly. "You will be very disappointed if you allow your imagination to run amok."

These words had absolutely no effect on Miss Biddle, who continued to wear a rapturous air. Miss Fitzhugh, however, tilted her head consideringly. "To those of us who remained at home with the comfort of a roof over our heads and food on our table, the men who endured war are not ordinary at all."

"Putting one's life on the line is extraordinary, to be sure," he conceded, "but Sommersby's feats have been exaggerated in the telling. The valiant souls he commanded are the ones who deserve the country's deepest respect."

She nodded, and he wondered whether she was thinking of the once-proud soldiers whose injuries and lack of employment turned them into beggars after the war. It was a sad postscript to their brave service.

There was a steadiness about Miss Fitzhugh that no doubt stemmed from the loss of her parent. He gathered that her mother was dead also. Idly, he wondered why she had never married. Although she did not possess her cousin's devastating beauty, she was by no means unattractive. Her commanding height imparted a certain regal air augmented by the elegance of her long, tapered fingers. Her chin had a proud, uncompromising line, and her eyes reminded him of the deep, velvety brown of rich earth.

With her noble profile, he could almost imagine her as Queen Boadicea leading the troops into battle. Strangely, the comparison seemed not at all absurd.

Other matters commanded Simon's attention, however, as the party arrived at the Bard and Bed Inn, the midpoint on their journey. Sir Thomas quickly disappeared to the taproom, where he looked inclined to remain for quite some time. It was just as well. Sharing a room with a sober man might prove difficult. Simon had little confidence that, in the throes of deep sleep, his wig would stay in place and his mustache remain attached to his lip.

The burdens of disguise were many. Still, it served him to continue his masquerade, at least until he was more certain of Miss Biddle. People were more likely to let down their guard around a mere secretary than they were an earl.

There was no substitute for thorough scouting before any contest, martial or marital. It was essential to know one's opponent beforehand.

Chapter Three

"Amanda! Wake up! Someone is at the door!"

Opening her eyes, Amanda discovered Felicity shaking her so vigorously that the room spun.

"Stop it, Felicity! I declare my teeth are rattling in my head. Whatever is wrong?"

Clutching the blanket, Felicity pointed mutely to their door. The stout oak shuddered in protest as someone out in the hall pummeled it relentlessly.

From the cot under the window, the maid accompanying them sat up with a start. "Oh, miss!" she cried. "'Tis a ghost, I know it!"

"A *ghost*!" Felicity's violet eyes grew wide as she fumbled for her spectacles. "Oh, *do* something, Amanda!"

Amanda frowned. "There is no more a ghost on the other side of that door than I am Princess Charlotte. Some harmless castaway has mistaken our room. I daresay he will move on when he realizes his mistake."

But the presence out in the hall did not seem altogether harmless. Indeed, a sudden enraged shout indicated his growing impatience.

"Open the door, Meggie!" came the slurred command. "I saw ye sneak off with that Captain Sharp. Promised the night to me, ye did, and I mean to hold ye to it!"

"Dear lord," Amanda muttered as she flung the covers aside. "The man is raving drunk."

Plucking some dipped rushes from a bucket at the hearth, she lit them from the dying embers. An unpleasant odor of grease wafted through the room as she placed the rushes in a tin lantern, which cast a garish light on the walls. Felicity and the little maid huddled close to each other as Amanda strode to the door.

"See here," she declared sternly through the keyhole. "You have the wrong room, and we would very much appreciate it if you would go on about your way."

The ensuing silence lasted but a moment. "Do not think to fool me by disguising yer voice, Meggie!" the man roared. "Best come out before I break down the door!"

"Oh, no!" Felicity cried. The little maid scrambled under the bed and immediately set up a loud keening. In spite of herself, Amanda felt a surge of fear.

"There is no need to break anything, nor make such a fuss," she insisted. "Your friend is not here."

A thunderous crash was the only response as the man heaved himself against the door.

"Help!" Felicity shrieked. "He is breaking it down!"

"If he does, he will certainly see that his Meggie is not here," Amanda replied, forcing her voice to remain calm. "I daresay we shall be perfectly safe."

Her words conveyed a certainty she was far from feeling. Amanda had little experience with senseless drunkards, but she suspected they did not listen to reason, even when the evidence was right before their eyes.

The door gave a mighty shudder as the man rammed it like an enraged bull. An ominous crack split one of the panels. It was clear that the door would not take much more punishment. Amanda wondered that the commotion had not brought the proprietor, but perhaps he was as castaway as his guest. Her gaze flew to the window, but it was too small and too high above the ground to offer escape. They would just have to hope that the man exhausted his strength before he exhausted the oak that barred him from them.

With rising panic, Amanda braced herself for the next charge.

It never came.

Instead, three short, peremptory raps broke the ominous silence. "Miss Fitzhugh? Miss Biddle?" demanded an imperial baritone. "Is everything all right?"

"Mr. Thornton?" Amanda asked, incredulous. "Is it you?"

From the hall came the sound of a throat clearing. "Yes, ma'am," he said in a more modulated tone.

"But what has happened to the other man?"

"He will not bother you further."

"Is he gone?" Amanda persisted.

"Not precisely," came the slightly impatient response. "But he is harmless. You may go back to sleep."

Felicity sighed in relief. The little maid crawled out from under the bed. Overcome with curiosity, Amanda opened the door a crack.

Mr. Thornton stood in the darkened hall, wearing a claret velvet dressing gown. Sleep had apparently proven a rather turbulent exercise for him, as his gray mop of hair stuck out from his head on all sides, and his mustache curled erratically. He might have cut a comical figure, had he not worn such a somber expression.

There was no sign of their drunken intruder.

"How did you get him to leave?" Amanda tried to imagine how a man of his age dealt with an enraged young lout. "Did you give him money?"

"Money?" His brows arched in surprise. "No, I did not give him money."

A low groan sounded somewhere behind him. Amanda stepped farther out into the hall. A large figure of a man lay on the floor in a crumpled heap. Even prone and nearly senseless, he looked strong enough to have broken down ten doors. Amanda swallowed hard as she realized how close to disaster they had come.

Her eyes flew to Mr. Thornton's face. In the shadows, his expression was unreadable. It did not seem possible that a man of his years had bested such a sturdy young man, but she could not think of any other conclusion.

"Did you . . . *hit* him, sir?" she demanded, incredulous.

He frowned. "Surely you do not object, Miss Fitzhugh. The man was within an inch of breaking down the door."

"N-no," she stammered. "I do not object. I . . . we are in your debt, Mr. Thornton."

"You are in my protection," he corrected stiffly, "Sir Thomas being indisposed at the moment. Since you are my responsibility, there can be no debt incurred."

The notion of Mr. Thornton protecting three defenseless women from a robust country lad half his age should have been ludicrous. Oddly, Amanda found the notion comforting.

"Thank you, sir," she said gravely.

Without another word Mr. Thornton turned and, in one fluid motion, heaved the senseless man over his shoulder. As he disappeared with his burden down the narrow stairway, Amanda blinked at this display of extraordinary vigor. The earl's secretary was a most unusual man.

And he wore an uncommonly fine dressing gown.

Sommersby Castle reigned over land and sea like the king's stronghold it once had been. Perched on the edge of a steep cliff, the stone pile towered majestically several hundred feet above the rocky Dorset beach. With sheer drops on three sides, the castle looked to be impregnable from the sea. By land, a twin-towered gatehouse, its dark windows regarding them like unfriendly eyes, greeted the visitors as they passed under the portcullis. Amanda had no doubt that this fortress had seen triumph more often than defeat over the years.

The ancient stronghold might have been grand in its day, but that day had been several hundred years ago. Daylight might afford a more charitable view, Amanda reasoned, but the dusk that accompanied their arrival brought out Sommersby Castle's uncivilized side.

Stark stone statues of satyric beasts guarded the gateway, fierce sentries whose menacing smiles extended no true welcome. Beyond the stone-curtained walls, a glassy lake that must have served as the castle's chief source of water over the centuries glittered in the encroaching darkness. The massive wooden door that opened into the bowels of the castle looked strong enough to have withstood any number of assaults. Inside, kerosene lanterns sent smoky trails wafting upward; the odor of tallow candles also permeated the air.

The draft that ushered them into the Great Hall brought with it a glowing sense of doom, not at all offset by the pallid fire flickering in the hearth. Wind rattled at the bare windows, whistling like a restless soul searching the shadows for surcease.

But the most disturbing aspect of Lord Sommersby's

castle was yet to come. As Amanda's eyes adjusted to the dim light, ominous shapes began to condense on the stone. When at last they spurred a spark of recognition, she gasped in astonishment.

Fearsome weapons of all stripes hung from the walls, their burnished metal gleaming in the eerie light like predatory creatures. Suspended in time on gray stone, the ancient swords, rapiers, muskets, rifles, and bayonets waited as if for long-dead warriors to take up their arms. A great cannon, its once-deadly mouth yawning and empty, stood threateningly in one corner.

"Dear lord," Amanda murmured, "the place is an arsenal."

Felicity's eyes grew wide. "Well," she ventured uncertainly, "the earl *is* a war hero."

"Lord Sommersby is a peer of the realm, Felicity, not some warring Norman conqueror," Amanda pointed out. "Yet it appears he anticipates imminent attack."

Felicity smiled, and Amanda could see that she was beginning to take to the notion of living in an historic castle with a noted man of war. "I expect he is merely eccentric, Amanda. Heroes are, you know."

Amanda rolled her eyes. "The only thing you know about heroes is what you have read in books. You heard Mr. Thornton. Lord Sommersby is quite ordinary."

But as she surveyed her surroundings, Amanda doubted very much that was the case. No ordinary man lived here. For the first time, she began to have doubts about the suitability of a match between Felicity and the earl. Her cousin did not belong in such a setting, where her fanciful dreams would wither in the portentous darkness.

Immersed in the inspection of an old musket, Sir Thomas appeared to perceive nothing amiss in their surroundings. But then he had been largely silent since their trip began. Doubtless he missed Lady Biddle. Amanda sighed, for the first time feeling the weight of her responsibilities as chaperone.

They waited in the Great Hall for some time, Sommersby apparently having few servants, as Mr. Thornton had warned. Finally, a diminutive man appeared and soon had them seated with glasses of sherry in a nearby room so different from the Hall it might have been dropped into the wrong castle.

Brightly burning candles, their light reflected in the gleaming windows, dispelled any hint of gloom. The room looked to have been newly redone. Gold braid trimmed the rich green damask of the only curtains Amanda had yet seen in the castle. An enormous chair upholstered in chocolate leather beckoned invitingly, and lush tapestry pillows on a plump claret-and-gold sofa offered welcoming comfort. A soft carpet of royal blue and burgundy adorned oak planking the years had burnished to a mellow brown.

A handsomely carved Adam mantel occupied one wall of the room. No wan fire flickered in its deep hearth; instead, enormous crackling logs sent brilliant white and blue flames licking up the chimney walls like the lazy tongue of a well-fed cat. A majestic walnut secretary presided over one corner of the room, where stacks of bookshelves soared to the vaulted ceiling.

Stunned, Amanda could only stare at her surroundings. Warmth radiated from every corner, in eloquent contrast to the drafty Great Hall. Lord Sommersby, it seemed, was a man of contradictions.

"The earl is not available until tomorrow," Mr. Thornton said, his tone vaguely apologetic.

It was odd that a man who had invited them to be his guests was not to greet them until the morrow, Amanda thought, eyeing Felicity uneasily as a rapt expression spread over her cousin's face.

"Is there a portrait of the earl in the castle?" Felicity asked, clearly eager to view a likeness of her future husband, if not the man himself.

"Certainly not." Mr. Thornton's curt tone prompted Amanda and Felicity to look at him in surprise. He cleared his throat. "I meant to say," he added more temperately, "that Lord Sommersby does not indulge in vainglorious displays."

Felicity frowned. "But surely a portrait of him in uniform is not excessive. Has no thought been given to commissioning such a picture?"

"The earl would view such a portrait as a frivolity," Mr.

Thornton said, very nearly scowling his own disapproval as well.

"But now that the war is over and Lord Sommersby has assumed the title, it is his responsibility to honor that part of his heritage," Felicity persisted. "There are some exceptional painters about," she added.

Mr. Thornton stiffened as Felicity chattered on helpfully. "Sir William Beechey is the queen's favorite, but Mr. Hoppner is considered to possess greater talent with male subjects. I have heard that they are somewhat less expensive than Sir Thomas Lawrence, who is said to charge more than four hundred guineas for a full-length portrait."

At Mr. Thornton's appalled expression, Amanda thought it best to intervene. "I gather the earl is a man of simple tastes," she said diplomatically. "Perhaps you might tell us more about him. Does he enjoy speaking about his years on the Continent?"

He turned toward her. Amanda felt rather than saw the reproof in his eyes. "I think not. War is quite serious, Miss Fitzhugh. The earl does not consider it a fit subject for drawing room conversation."

"I lost a loved one to war's embrace, sir," Amanda rejoined quietly. "You need not educate me on that score."

The blue of Mr. Thornton's eyes suddenly gave way to a velvety green. "I did not mean to be insensitive to your loss."

"No offense was taken," Amanda replied, shifting a bit as those steady eyes held hers. "Would you care to tell us about your cousin now?"

"My cousin?" he repeated blankly.

"Lord Sommersby," Amanda prodded, wondering why she found it impossible to look away from his gaze. Age had in no way robbed those mercurial eyes of their keen spark, nor did his drooping mustache hide the sensuous curve of lips that pursed thoughtfully as he studied her. Amanda tried to imagine what color his hair had been in his youth. Blond, perhaps? Or would he have possessed a mane of rich brown? Not with those sandy brows, she decided, then flushed as she realized that she had been staring at him for some time. It was not like her to daydream. No man could spark her fantasies. Certainly not anymore.

"What do you wish to know?" The husky note in his voice made Amanda feel inexplicably girlish.

As she sipped her sherry, its bracing warmth restored a bit of her equanimity and a measure of common sense. Perhaps it was merely Mr. Thornton's imposing physical presence that made her feel so off balance. She stepped away from him and managed a polite smile.

"We were intrigued to see the earl's weapons," she said. "How came he to have such a collection?"

He appeared to consider the question as if it had never been asked of him—as if having an arsenal hanging from one's walls was commonplace.

"The Thorntons are military men," he explained after a bit. "The last earl was the first in generations to die of old age, not battle. Thorntons have always collected the implements of war as a reminder of our heritage. The present earl had weapons from the recent war added to the collection." He paused. "Do you like it?"

"Like what?" Amanda echoed, caught by the hint of pride in his voice as well as the tentative tone of his question. It was almost as though he sought her approval.

"The collection, of course." The suggestion of a smile under that sagging mustache made her inhale sharply. Mr. Thornton had straight, white teeth and the merest suspicion of a dimple in one of his cheeks. "Though I suppose it is not the sort of thing to appeal to a woman."

Felicity, who had been studying the bookshelves, smiled. "I should think it fascinating to live among monuments to one's military triumphs."

"Monuments?" he repeated, frowning slightly. "Yes, well." He looked away. "You will wish to refresh yourselves. I will have someone show you to your rooms."

Amanda rather hoped that her chamber resembled this cozy parlor instead of the rest of the house, but she feared that was too much to ask. Following a silent housekeeper up the stairs, she was filled with curiosity about the Earl of Sommersby.

Was he the cold descendant of some fierce, warfaring clan that cared only for the implements of power and destruction? Or was he, like the comfortable parlor they had just vacated, capable of warmth and kindness?

And, finally, was he as attractive as she imagined his enigmatic cousin Mr. Thornton once had been?

"The devil take it, Jeffers. I cannot abide this mustache any longer!"

Simon ripped off the offending article and tossed it to his long-suffering batman, who placed it carefully in a small pouch. "How did I let you talk me into that thing? A neat, military trim would have been far more preferable."

"I believe you thought a slight droop would disarm the lady, or some such, my lord."

"Well, it is dashed inconvenient trying to keep it out of my soup, not to mention the brandy." Simon refilled his glass from the bottle on the table next to his chair.

Jeffers sighed. His employer had been in a rare taking since dinner, and if he did not miss his guess, it had something to do with the arrival of the company from Mayfield. "Miss Biddle seems all that is pleasant, my lord," he ventured.

"Indeed," Simon snapped. "She is a veritable paragon. I have no complaints, other than that her head seems to be filled with foolish notions about my war record and plans to immortalize me on canvas. It is that *other* woman who is getting on my nerves."

"The chaperone?"

Simon nodded darkly. "Miss Fitzhugh is a distraction to the mission."

Without comment, Jeffers laid out the earl's dressing gown.

"She asks too many questions and studies me far too closely. I do not think she suspects my identity, but it is altogether unsettling. I cannot remember when I have had such difficulty concentrating." He paused. "I believe I need something to clear my head."

Jeffers stifled a groan. Such a statement could only mean one thing. But in the next instant, his employer drained the second glass of brandy and yawned.

"Perhaps I make too much of this. Tomorrow I shall send Thornton on his way and let the Earl of Sommersby court Miss Biddle in earnest. I imagine that Miss Fitzhugh will cease to prove a difficulty. Come to think of it, Jeffers, what I need most is a good night's sleep."

With a relieved sigh, Jeffers visibly relaxed.

"Ah, now it begins."

"What begins, Isabella?"

"The business of educating that young man. And now that I think on it, those two young ladies as well. That chaperone is far too grim."

"She has a difficult history, I believe."

"You are referring to the nefarious marquess, I assume. She makes too much of it. In our day, we thought nothing of a brief tumble on a park bench."

"Oh, I am not so sure of that. Edward had Lancaster executed for his excesses—remember?"

"Lancaster never learned subtlety. He might have taken a lesson from you, dear Mortimer."

"Everything that I learned, dearest, came from you."

"Oh, surely not everything!"

"Perhaps not. But back to our tenant. What do you mean to do to him?"

"Nothing unpleasant, Mortimer. I seek only his happiness."

"The possibility of your seeking anyone's happiness besides your own is about as likely as our leaving this cursed castle."

"You need not be unkind, Mortimer. I see nothing wrong with having a little fun."

"May I remind you, my dear, that your idea of fun was torturing Edward to death?"

"Shhh! You will set him off again. You know Edward does not like to be reminded of that episode."

"He cannot have forgotten, Isabella, even in five hundred years."

"Well, this is nothing like that. This time I mean only good."

"And I am Saint Peter."

"Hush! Do you want to bring down the wrath of the heavens upon us?"

"I should think, my dear, that blasphemy is the least of our crimes."

Chapter Four

Faint tapping awoke Amanda from a restless dream in which warriors wielding ancient swords and shields waged a fierce battle for Felicity's hand. Balancing on the edge of the crumbling parapet, one of the swordsmen toppled into the moat, only to face a diabolical crocodile holding a large cannon. A man who looked remarkably like Mr. Thornton tossed the warrior the ends of his drooping mustache to use as a rope. Watching the entire episode was a trio of wispy eminences, perched like clouds on the turret above.

"Stuff!" Amanda grumbled sleepily as she pulled the blanket more tightly around her. She was on the point of wondering how Mr. Thornton managed to grow such a long mustache when the tapping grew more insistent and Felicity's voice pierced the fog surrounding her brain.

"Amanda! You must come right away!"

An eerie creaking punctuated Felicity's words as the door between their rooms swung open on hinges that evidently had not been oiled in years. A solitary candle provided the only light as Felicity stood motionless on the threshold like an angel of doom.

"What is it?" Amanda demanded.

"I heard noises!"

"Nonsense." But she sat up in bed quickly.

"I did!"

A sudden gust of wind kicked up the leaves on the balcony outside her window, whirling them in a mad little dance and rattling the windowpanes like some ghostly hand. Sommersby Castle certainly provided ample inspiration for a rampant imagination like Felicity's, Amanda thought, groaning wearily. One had only to look at her own room.

Rubbing her eyes, she brought the chamber into focus for the first time since retreating into the blessed oblivion of sleep. Evidently, the Thorntons' thirst for blood went beyond merely displaying ancient weapons in the Great Hall. The same martial air permeated Amanda's room. The heavy walnut wardrobe opposite her bed seemed to glare at her with knotty black eyes. A vivid painting of a bloody battle overlooked the dressing table. At the fireplace, a carved mantel depicted grotesque figures in various stages of torture. Outside, a balcony ran the length of the wing; even a practical woman might be forgiven for imagining what nocturnal creatures might creep in through the full-length window. No wonder her dreams had been grotesque.

Amanda shivered as her bare feet touched the cold stone floor, but one look at Felicity's face banished any thought of stopping to find her slippers. As Felicity held up her solitary candle, the ghostly light illuminated her cousin's fearful eyes. Amanda hurried to her side.

"I daresay whatever you heard was only a vivid dream," she reassured her. "I have had some rather colorful dreams myself tonight."

Felicity shook her head. "I distinctly heard a noise coming from my wardrobe."

Stepping through the adjoining door into Felicity's room, Amanda noted that her cousin's chamber was not half so gruesome as hers. The heavy wardrobe matched the one that had stared at her so relentlessly, but there were no wild paintings to conjure images of war and death, no bare floors to chill the feet. A comfortable rug covered a large portion of the stone floor, and several beautiful quilts adorned the bed. Blue damask bed hangings matched flowing draperies at the balcony window.

Amanda frowned. "I cannot see what is so troubling, Felicity. Your room is vastly more peaceful than mine. Why, you should see the painting on my—"

"Hush! There it is again!"

A faint scratching sound met her ears. Amanda forced her pulse to remain steady, but Felicity's nervous state was contagious. "I daresay these are but the customary nighttime noises in the castle," she said with a confidence she was far from feeling.

"I do not think so. I believe it came from the wardrobe."

"Mice, no doubt." Taking a deep breath, Amanda threw open the wardrobe doors.

Felicity's gowns, hung neatly by the maid earlier, proved to be the only contents.

Relieved, Amanda turned to her cousin. "It is nothing. Our surroundings are a bit unusual, I will grant you, but I expect that when you get accustomed to the castle, your fears will vanish."

But Felicity was staring in horror at a point above Amanda's head. "There! Something moved!"

Amanda whirled. There was indeed a slight movement on the top of the wardrobe, although the piece was too high and the room too dark for her to see what caused it. Her pulse racing, Amanda looked frantically around until her gaze settled on a heavy chair.

"Hold the candle up a bit," she commanded, dragging the chair over to the wardrobe.

"Be careful," Felicity cautioned as Amanda hitched up her nightrail and climbed onto the seat.

"I daresay it is nothing to be concerned about." But Amanda extended her hands over the top of the wardrobe with no small trepidation. "Hold the candle higher, dear. I cannot see a thing."

Suddenly her groping fingers met something solid, furry, and very much alive. An ungodly wail emerged from the thing as it charged, toppling Amanda backward onto the floor. Felicity's scream pierced the night.

For Amanda, the next moments were a rush of blurred impressions—from the fleeting small shadow that raced by them to her wrenching spasms of pain and Felicity's hysterical cries. Rubbing her aching head, Amanda tried to gain a measure of control over her pain, her senses, and the stocky chair that pinned her solidly to the floor.

Abruptly she caught another movement, this one at the window. Amanda's heart leapt to her throat as a masculine figure came sharply into focus.

Like a ghostly apparition summoned from the night, the figure stood on the balcony, silhouetted in the window. Shadows obscured his face, but Amanda could distinctly see the enormous sword he held, poised at the ready.

Moonlight lent the weapon an unearthly silver radiance, suggesting it had been forged by some celestial hand.

Responding instantly to his touch, the window swung open. The intruder stepped into the room.

Felicity's terrified shriek could have waked the dead, but Amanda felt no fear, only a riveting thrill as he paused to regard them silently. Even in scant candlelight, he was the most beautiful man she had ever seen.

Bare, rippling chest muscles paid tribute to all that was primitive in male power. He stood fierce and tall, as grand as Zeus in the moment before wreaking vengeful justice on some hapless mortal. The massive sword looked to have demanded the strength of two men, but his corded arms effortlessly managed the weight.

Slowly, the flickering candle unveiled his features. Amanda drew a sharp breath at the clean, uncompromising jawline, piercing crystalline eyes, and fiery red hair that framed the shadowed contours of his face. Thick and untamed, his windblown mane stood in stark contrast to the still discipline that radiated from every tensed muscle in his body, as if wild passions warred with steely control.

Not Zeus, Amanda amended. *Ares.* A warrior, bred to the bone. Primitive. Bloodlusty.

For an assessing moment he stood motionless, balancing on the balls of his feet, capable of reaching any opponent with the lethal tip of that luminous broadsword he wielded so easily.

Then, in one masculine stride, he closed the distance between them and lifted the heavy chair off Amanda as if it were a feather. Laying the great sword beside him, he knelt down to assess her injuries. Amanda felt every muscular fiber of his fingers as they moved over her battered legs.

As Felicity watched mutely, Amanda remained motionless, pinned by the heat of his sure, probing fingers and the unabashed intimacy of his touch. He unleashed something in her that she did not think even existed any more. Robbed of rational thought, she stared at him, marveling as what was left of her mind spun all sorts of uncharacteristic fantasies. Truly, he might have been a god, come down from the heavens to rescue them from their nocturnal demons. As he worked over her limbs, she drank in every movement of those perfectly shaped muscles, giddy in the unexpected pleasure of him.

When his fingers reached her ankle, however, she winced. He looked up.

Their gazes held. In the depths of those mesmerizing green eyes, Amanda's pain vanished. Where his hand rested on her ankle, her skin burned in a delicious fire as painful in its own way as the injury he had discovered.

A spark leapt the space between them and caught her fast in its relentless pull. Amanda could scarcely breathe. Her vision grew strangely cloudy; it was as if a great haze had enveloped his features, leaving only his velvety gaze holding hers with all of its awesome power.

"I hope I did not frighten you," he said at last. His voice was low, mellifluent, and it resonated with an intimacy meant only for her. "I am Sommersby."

Dazed, Amanda could only blink in amazement while the wispy haze spun around him in a seductive dance.

And I, she thought weakly, *am your devoted slave.*

Like Pack at Quatre Bras when the French calvary moved in on his flank bound for the crest at Waterloo, Simon felt utterly exposed. Among all his Royals and Highlanders, Pack could only muster 1,400 bayonets, and Simon's solitary sword stood as an equally insubstantial weapon against the strangely overwhelming force that emanated from somewhere behind Miss Fitzhugh's eyes.

Perspiration dotted his arms. His pulse pounded wildly. His breathing grew labored. Battle-readiness did that to a man, and though he had not faced fire in months, some things a man never forgot.

Like confronting a murderous brigade of French cuirassiers with only rum-soaked Dragoons at his back. Like the look in a woman's eyes that threatened a discipline hardened by charging Napoleon's twelve-pounders and taunting death more times than he could count.

Bursting half-naked into the room, brandishing the ungainly relic of a sword hurriedly snatched from his bedside wall, Simon knew he had scared her senseless. It was certainly not the usual manner in which one met the chaperone of one's prospective bride. No wonder Miss Fitzhugh looked at him so strangely.

"*Sommersby?*" she stammered.

There was something different about her. It was not just the fact that her usually neat hair fell so wildly around her shoulders. There was a look in her eyes, a misty dewiness that projected an almost sensual vulnerability.

"We were not expecting you, that is, not until tomorrow . . ." Her voice trailed off, and she stared from him to the window and back again. Her lips parted slightly as her gaze dropped to his hand—which, Simon belatedly realized, still lingered on her ankle.

Jerking his fingers away, Simon heard her sharp gasp. He disciplined his own uneven breathing into a slow, steady rhythm. Slow and steady, that was the key. Men who panicked died in battle. Men who disciplined themselves stood a chance.

"I did not mean to startle you," he said in a low, controlled voice. "I heard screams and followed the quickest route from my room, along the balcony."

A dazed look was her only response.

Picking up the sword, he rose and placed a respectable distance between them. The heavy broadsword felt good and solid in his hands, although it would have been as cumbersome as a cudgel in a real attack. Since leaving the army, he no longer slept with his efficient sabre at his side and had simply seized the nearest weapon at hand.

Simon was acutely conscious of his lack of appropriate clothing as Miss Fitzhugh regarded him silently from her position on the floor. She still had not regained her powers of speech, but Miss Biddle quickly found hers.

"We are indebted to you for coming to our rescue, Lord Sommersby," she said. "When Amanda climbed up to investigate a movement on the wardrobe, that . . . *creature* jumped at her." She pointed, and Simon saw a tail twitching restlessly back and forth under the bed, where a large orange tabby had taken refuge.

A minute ago Simon would have judged a response beyond Miss Fitzhugh, but now she regarded him with clear eyes. "That is quite enough, Felicity," she said, reaching for her cousin's hand. "I am certain Lord Sommersby wishes he were back in his own bed. Help me to my feet, please."

Miss Biddle wore a vague gaze, and the delicate hand she blindly extended was not up to the task for which she intended it. Quickly, Simon laid his sword down again and lifted Miss Fitzhugh into his arms.

In the moment he brought her against his chest, he knew he had committed a grave error. The room's shadows had obscured the fact that she wore only a thin nightrail. The gauzy fabric settled around her like a caress. What of her feminine curves it did not reveal to his eye were readily apparent to his touch as he held her. Her hair flowed over her shoulders in waves, and some of the silky tresses clung to his face as they settled into place.

Miss Fitzhugh seemed not to know what to do with her hands, but after an awkward moment apparently decided that the only logical choice was to place them around his neck for balance. In such an intimate embrace did they remain, two relative strangers, until Simon had the presence of mind to ask her whether her ankle could bear any weight.

"Oh, yes, I imagine so," she quickly replied. When he lowered her to the floor, however, she grimaced in pain.

Much as he had carried wounded soldiers off the field, he carried Miss Fitzhugh to her bed in the next room—acutely aware, however, of how very unlike those soldiers she was.

Her weight was nothing to him; nevertheless, breathing suddenly proved difficult. A slow fire, instantly recognizable as desire, built in his veins. That a scantily dressed female would provoke such a response seemed logical, and Simon set his disciplined mind about the task of willing his desire away.

To his horror, the more he tried to suppress that heat, the more it seethed within him and threatened to escape the fortified boundaries of his iron will. It was an almost primitive force, akin to that which had made it possible for him to kill and to take what was necessary for survival in war. It stripped from him all but the urgent need to possess, and to win.

Simon was not proud of the raw, uncivilized side of himself, for it sometimes warred with honor. He had always controlled that side, never allowing it to interfere with the mission or turn him into one of those bloodlusty soldiers driven to rape, plunder, murder. Years of battle had taught him that discipline could be had for a price, and that he was willing to pay that price.

But he was not at war anymore. Miss Fitzhugh was the spinster cousin and chaperone of his probable bride-to-be. As such, there was no reason for him to be experiencing a raging, primal desire as he gingerly set her down upon the bed. Nor was there reason to contemplate the way the fabric of her gown fell into place around her as she lay back against the pillow, her strong chin and high cheekbones giving her anything but a fragile appearance. Despite the somewhat dazed manner in which she regarded him, Miss Fitzhugh radiated strength.

Strange how feminine strength could be so stimulating. Simon allowed himself to contemplate how her strength might complement his in a moment of physical intimacy. Then—ruthlessly—he willed the image gone.

"Your ankle is not broken," he said, tension lending his voice a harsh note. "I will send for the doctor in the morning. He will probably instruct you to keep off it. In the meantime, I will wrap it in a light bandage."

"*You*, my lord?" She eyed him in surprise.

"I have bandaged enough injuries in my time. You may depend on my skills."

"Yes. Of course," she murmured.

Jeffers was quickly summoned, with his kit of bandages and salves, and a dressing gown for his employer. Simon worked rapidly, and his finished work was pronounced quite excellent by the batman and Miss Biddle. He was pleased to see that his patient had not descended into hysterics; though her ankle obviously pained her, she bore it well. She said very little but continued to regard him steadily from those dark brown eyes.

As Simon was congratulating himself on his handiwork, his gaze wandered from the bandaged ankle to her calves, which had been unavoidably exposed for the procedure. The deep heat flared anew within him.

It was past time to retire, he decided, turning quickly to

bid Miss Biddle good night and taking comfort in the knowledge that tomorrow the mission of courting his bride would go forward. Miss Biddle possessed everything he required—youth, beauty, breeding, education, and almost certain fertility.

Nothing would stop him from securing his target—certainly not some uncivilized urge. He had long ago mastered the art of control.

"Has it occurred to you how often a member of Lord Sommersby's family has rescued us?"

"What?" Felicity peered up from Mr. Wordsworth's latest volume of poems. Her brow cleared. "I collect that you refer to the earl's appearance last night and Mr. Thornton's timely arrival back at the inn." Adjusting her spectacles, she smiled. "The Thornton men are certainly reliable, are they not? It is comforting to be in such capable hands."

Not comforting, Amanda thought, recalling Lord Sommersby's hands as they ministered to her ankle and Mr. Thornton's unreadable countenance as he effortlessly tossed their intruder over his shoulder at the inn.

Disturbing.

"What did you think of the earl?" she asked casually.

Wrinkling her brow, Felicity considered the matter. "He is handsome in a rough sort of way, as befits a warrior." She hesitated, blushing before adding, "I cannot say, however, that I have ever seen a man so . . . exposed."

Remembering how it felt to be held against that naked chest, Amanda swallowed hard. "Nor I," she agreed.

"He is quite large, is he not? I shall have to strain to look up at him, I fear, but I daresay we shall manage."

"I daresay," Amanda murmured, wondering whether her young cousin was up to the challenge of a husband as fierce as Lord Sommersby.

Thank heavens *she* would not have to spend day and night with him. She could not imagine what primitive appetites a man like Lord Sommersby possessed, but she wondered whether Felicity would find them acceptable. Had Lady Biddle prepared her for the marriage bed? How would her sweet, romantic cousin manage a man of such raw power, who looked as if he could easily bend a woman to his will?

Amanda closed her eyes as that mortifying night at Vauxhall came to mind with Julian LeFevre's sensual, mocking face. He had possessed that power, and it had taught her that it was the woman who suffered when lust ruled. Nothing in her life had been so shameful as being caught by her kindly uncle in such a disgraceful situation.

Julian had given her no spirits, no powder to rob her of her sense of propriety. Nor had he plied her with promises or flowery terms of endearment. She had simply been no match for a handsome libertine's cunning ways. He had sought her out all Season, and Amanda had allowed herself to believe his flattering attentions indicated he cared for her. Little had she realized that he was merely setting a trap. Young and naive, she had been unaware that a man's sensual nature could be so overwhelming.

Amanda had vowed never again to be so witless. In eight years, she had seen no reason to break that vow.

Until last night.

She sighed. Felicity's fanciful imagination must be catching. Lord Sommersby might be an impressive figure of a man, but nothing could make her abandon the practical resolve she had achieved in the years since Julian had made her tremble in desire and shame. There was no reason to feel the stab of longing that had, for a few magic moments last night, held her enthralled.

In any case, he was to be Felicity's husband.

"It is worse than we thought. Both of them are incorrigibly practical."

"Not incorrigibly so, my dear. Not with your genius."

"But there is not a practical bone in my body, Mortimer. I wonder if I know how to proceed."

"There are no bones at all in your body, Isabella. No body either, for that matter."

"This is not the time for levity, Mortimer. That young man and woman are headed for dull lives if they do not come together. Everyone is entitled to a little passion in his time, do you not think?"

"*Ah, passion. Now there is a subject in which you possess a true genius.*"

"*Do you really think so, Mortimer?*"

"*I should know, my dear. Your charms proved my undoing.*"

"*Yes, well, you always were a bit faint of heart, dear.*"

"*Not at all. I have always followed your lead. With a woman like you, Isabella, it is that or die.*"

"*But you died anyway.*"

"*Because your son's dastardly soldiers ripped me from your bed.*"

"*Oh, Mortimer. I am so glad we have eternity together— just the two of us.*"

"*And Edward.*"

"*Oh, yes. And Edward.*"

Chapter Five

Simon enjoyed fencing. The rules were defined, the targets clear. It was a civilized contest, nothing like warfare. One's opponent did not die, either.

That was fortunate for Jeffers, who never managed to look anything but resigned to his doom when he faced his employer at foil. Invariably the batman chose the longest blade to compensate for his short arms. No matter that Simon repeatedly warned him that the extra inch of reach came at the expense of precision, Jeffers stubbornly insisted on wielding a weapon that left him at a disadvantage in balance and control.

In a ritual as familiar to him as breathing, Simon extended the tip of the foil toward the floor. Jeffers followed suit. Simon brought the blade up to his chin, then pointed it at his opponent. The salute exchanged, Simon gracefully moved his front foot forward and cocked his left hand behind his head at a precise right angle.

"En garde."

Sighing, Jeffers did likewise.

A civilized sport for civilized men.

Yet Simon did not feel civilized tonight. His first day spent with the ladies as Lord Sommersby had brought only frustration. The doctor had been summoned, examined Miss Fitzhugh, and decided that while the ankle was not broken, it must be rested—with the result that Miss Fitzhugh had not come downstairs all day. Miss Biddle, after greeting him cordially over breakfast, declared herself unable to think of leaving her cousin's bedside. Thus Simon had spent most of the day with Sir Thomas, discussing the latest agricultural methods and the baronet's breeding plans for his new chestnut stallion.

It had been a day that made Simon itch to be back in the battlefield, testing his stamina, using his strength for a purpose instead of stewing helplessly in a moldy castle awaiting a young lady's pleasure.

Not that he enjoyed war. It had claimed too many friends and ruined too many lives. Action—that was what he missed. The sudden surge in his veins that pitted his life force against the unknown, against any enemy fate might throw his way. The knowledge that his destiny was in his own hands. The raw thrill of sensing that existence boiled down to this: standing in a cornfield face-to-face with a tyrant demented enough to think he could rule the world. And knowing, deep in his bones, that he, Major Simon Hannibal Thornton, would prevail.

Not the Earl of Sommersby, not a lord with a fancy title and a king's wealth. He wanted no useless trappings of nobility. He wanted the contest, the battle, the confirmation that he was alive—when so many were not.

Perhaps that desire was the source of his restless need to test his strength, against even so ineffective an opponent as Jeffers.

Simon had never cared for protective devices like the padded jacket and cumbersome wire cage Jeffers insisted on wearing. Simon preferred to keep his skills sharp, primed, as if every contest were the real thing. Speed and alertness served a man better than padding—which is why he now had Jeffers in retreat. The batman had dropped his forward shoulder during an ill-advised lunge, leaving himself open to attack.

Deftly, Simon took advantage of the open line. Jeffers's weak parry brought their blades together, a useless maneuver that set up Simon's disengage.

In one smooth, continuous motion, Simon whipped the point of his foil under Jeffers's blade and lunged in to score on his opponent's shoulder. Like steel lightning, the foil proved quick and true. Triumph was his.

There was no blood. Jeffers had nary a scratch. In a true battle, however, the wound would have been mortal.

"My lord," Jeffers gasped, leaning against the wall in the narrow portrait gallery that served as their field of play, "you have killed me five times over. Surely it is time to leave off for the night?"

Peeling off his leather glove, Simon absently stroked the tempered blade. Cold steel could not assuage his restlessness, but its sure, steady strength had provided a brief respite.

For a few moments, his destiny had been in his control again. Major Simon Hannibal Thornton had prevailed.

Unfortunately, the man who minutes later strode from the picture gallery was once more the Earl of Sommersby.

The crutches Jeffers brought her made Amanda want to kiss the little batman. She had no desire to spend two weeks in Sommersby Castle in bed with something as silly as a sprained ankle. Felicity needed a chaperone, and *she* needed to get out of her gloomy room with its images of death and war. Hobbling downstairs for the first time since her accident two days ago, Amanda's spirits rose.

Until she encountered Lord Sommersby, who was showing Felicity a particularly vicious-looking instrument that looked capable of tearing a man to shreds.

"An old Italian war hammer," the earl was saying. "Few men could master it, but those who did possessed a nearly invincible weapon with the power to rip open plate armor."

"How delightful," Amanda muttered dryly. Her cousin turned.

"Amanda!" Felicity smiled in delight. "I did not know you meant to come down today." Her brow wrinkled. "Are you certain you are not rushing things?"

"Not at all." Recalling that she had been in her nightgown the last time she met the earl, Amanda could not prevent a blush that deepened with the sudden, unbidden image of him ministering intimately to her bare ankle. "I am not certain that the topic of lethal weaponry is one that a young lady needs to study so extensively," she said sternly, to cover her embarrassment. "Good morning, my lord."

Lord Sommersby bowed. "I am pleased to see you about, Miss Fitzhugh," he said coolly. "I regret that you do not approve of the subject Miss Biddle and I were discussing."

Amanda wanted to curse her bluntness. She had meant to set him at a distance, not to alienate him. A man who thought nothing of displaying instruments of bloodshed on the walls would undoubtedly find her squeamish attitude offputting.

"Years ago, a woman required fighting skills," he continued, pointedly meeting her gaze. "Often she was the only one at home to defend herself and her children from marauding invaders."

Amanda eyed the massive instrument he held so easily. "I am certain I could never wield that hammer, my lord, even in self-defense. It looks far too heavy."

His gaze roved over her, and Amanda was surprised to see a speculative look in those unsettling eyes. She breathed a sigh of relief when he turned away, set the great hammer aside and picked up a flat little knife with a quartz-encrusted handle.

"Perhaps you would find the skean-dhu more manageable," he said. "'Tis a Highlander's weapon, small but effective. Men customarily carried one in the top of their stockings. Would you care to examine it?"

Without waiting for a response, he placed the knife in her hand. Fluted brass edged its flat pommel, made smoky by the dark quartz. It was surprisingly lightweight, but looked capable of inflicting substantial damage.

"Oh, Amanda, it is the cutest thing!" Felicity trilled. "Would you not adore one?"

"I do not think so," she replied uneasily, regarding the earl. He was dressed impeccably in a claret coat and buff breeches, but Amanda saw only the wild, barechested warrior who stood so fiercely at the window that night.

Today he was all cool, remote civility, despite that flaming hair. His stern demeanor made him look older, but Amanda guessed he was not above thirty. She knew she had started off on the wrong foot with Felicity's intended and would very probably stay there. A man like Lord Sommersby would have no use for a woman who opposed war and shuddered at the sight of its implements.

But then the earl only had to like Felicity, not her chaperone. That was fortunate, for Amanda had never encountered a man with whom she had less in common.

To be sure, that magnificent warrior had had a profound effect on her sensibilities the other night. She had thought of little else as she lay in bed, resting the ankle he had bandaged with those strong hands.

Thank goodness her disaster with Julian and years of spinsterhood had left her beyond the reach of a mesmerizing gaze, cleanly chiseled jawline, singularly broad shoulders, and powerfully muscled arms. Lord Sommersby might possess an impeccable military record and extraordinary physical assets, but he was just a man, after all. And men could be beastly. Amid foolish daydreams, it was important to remember that fact.

"You look lonely, Papa."

Smiling, Sir Thomas patted his daughter's arm. "It is only natural to miss one's home, I suppose. And I cannot help but wish your mother were well enough to help with your Season."

Felicity sidestepped a rock in the path they were following around the edge of the cliff. Normally she would not have seen such an impediment, which is why her father had a tight hold on her arm. But this afternoon she felt free to wear her spectacles, Lord Sommersby having excused himself to attend to some estate business. Amanda had retired to her chamber to rest her leg, and Felicity did want to see the view from Sommersby's west front.

She was glad she did, for such beauty deserved to be appreciated. As the sun slipped lower in the horizon, the wispy clouds took on an orange glow, almost as if some great hand painted them right there in the sky. A dreamy look settled over Felicity's features.

"I hope that my marriage is as happy as yours and Mama's."

Sir Thomas did not reply.

"I mean to marry for love, you know," Felicity added in a quiet voice.

Sir Thomas studied his youngest daughter. "That is a worthy goal, to be sure," he said carefully. "I would not have you marry where you did not wish. But even the most blessed of unions has its moments of . . . disillusionment."

"Disillusionment?" Felicity frowned.

"Love is an ephemeral thing, daughter, as well it should be. One cannot live every moment in a state of exalted longing for one's spouse. It is just not done. Husbands and wives do not sit in each other's pockets."

She smiled. "You really do miss Mama, do you not?"

"I do not begrudge her the rest she needs."

"I did not say anything about a grudge, Papa."

Sir Thomas's face reddened. "No. Of course not. Your mother is well-occupied at Mayfield. She needs her rest and her . . . other activities."

"Still, I know she would love to see Sommersby Castle," Felicity replied. "I would think she could defy Dr. Greenfield this once."

"Dr. Greenfield is very thorough," Sir Thomas said with a little cough.

"I think he is a nuisance. I am sure we were better off before he moved to Mayfield with all of his airs."

"Airs?"

Felicity sighed in disgust. "Have you not noticed, Papa, how he affects the manner of a poet? Always spouting lines from others' verse. Mama thinks it is charming. She does not realize he almost always gets the lines wrong."

Sir Thomas shot her a sidelong look. "He does?"

"Oh, yes. The man does not know a sonnet from a sauce boat."

Her father's mouth twitched. "A sauce boat, eh?"

"And he should not wear his hair so long. It only underscores how thin it is on top."

"Dr. Greenfield is a widower. I do not imagine he has the benefit of a female who will set him to rights about his appearance."

Felicity rolled her eyes. "He would not listen, in any case. I believe he thinks he cuts a dashing figure, though I do not suppose he is so very much younger than you."

Sir Thomas did not reply.

"His eyes are nice enough, but I cannot imagine why he must look at one so . . . *intensely*. Do you know that I danced with him at the Harvest Assembly last fall?"

"You did?"

"Yes. Immediately after the set he forced Mama into."

"Your mother has never been forced into anything in her life."

Felicity sighed. "It is too bad you were in London, for I

declare, Dr. Greenfield has positively haunted the house since then."

"Yes."

In silence they watched the amber glow stalk across the sky and merge at the far horizon with the deep blue of the sea. It was a breathtaking sight.

"'Like a departing thief,'" Felicity recited softly, "'entrusting its jewels to night until dawn reclaims the treasure in the brilliance of renewed day.'"

Sir Thomas eyed his daughter. "Another of your poets?"

She flushed. "It is something of mine."

"I did not know you wrote poetry, daughter."

"I merely scribble down thoughts that occur to me now and then." She smiled sheepishly. "They are nothing of consequence."

"Everything has consequence, my dear." Sir Thomas's gaze wandered from Felicity to the horizon. After a moment he turned to her. "Lord Sommersby has spoken to me."

Felicity's eyes widened. "About . . . about me?"

Her father nodded. "The earl did not mince words. He told me that you are exactly what he wants in a wife and that I would honor him by looking favorably on a match between you. He realizes that you expect a Season, and he is prepared to accompany us to town and announce a betrothal at the Season's end. It is a generous gesture, as I do not imagine the earl is the sort of man who has much patience for parties and routs. I gave him permission to speak to you, which he indicated he would do very soon."

"My goodness." Felicity expelled a great breath.

Sir Thomas studied his daughter. "Surely this cannot come as a surprise."

"Not precisely. I knew when we accepted the invitation to Sommersby that this would likely happen. It is just that I do not know him very well."

"That is what this time here is for, my dear. And the entire Season, if need be. But such decisions do not require an eternity. Sometimes they happen overnight."

"Is that how it was with you and Mama?" Felicity asked.

"How what was?" Sir Thomas frowned.

"Did you fall in love overnight?"

His color deepening, Sir Thomas recalled precisely when he discovered he could not do without Miss Eloise Herrity. He had persuaded her to elude her dragon of an aunt and accompany him on an afternoon outing to Richmond in a closed carriage. The afternoon had one unplanned consequence in the conception of his eldest daughter, Elizabeth, but had he not compromised Eloise so thoroughly, he would have married her anyway. Her red hair was not her only fiery aspect, he had discovered to his great delight. That, of course, was quite some time ago. Things were different now.

"I am not talking about love, daughter," he said briskly. "I am talking about a suitable spouse. You must not confuse the two."

"But you and Mama are admirably suited. That is why you miss her so. I want to get to know Lord Sommersby as well as you did Mama before you wed."

Sir Thomas's brows rose in alarm at the image of his youngest daughter cavorting with the Earl of Sommersby in a closed carriage. "You will know the man well enough by the end of the Season," he quickly replied.

As he took his daughter's arm, Sir Thomas spared one last glance for the waning sunset and one final, fleeting thought for the foolish hopes of the young.

"That is another one who needs a push or two."

"You cannot meddle in everyone's life, Isabella."

"Nonsense, Mortimer, you must not begrudge me my amusements. There have been precious few these last hundred or so years."

"I realize the castle may have lost its appeal for you, my dear, but . . ."

"Why does Edward never speak? All he does is scream. I declare, he drives me mad."

"That is his way, Isabella."

"He was ever one to carry a grudge. Vain, and stubborn, bluntspoken . . . not an ounce of tact in his body."

"Ah, back to that are we? The corporeal state."

"Does it not bother you, Mortimer? Never being able to touch each other? Or anything else for that matter?"

"It is the way of our world."

"*But five hundred years without the touch of flesh . . . it is not to be borne.*"

"*I suspect it is our punishment for having allowed the appetites of the flesh to lead us astray.*"

"*You have regrets, then?*"

"*I accept what is.*"

"*That is the trouble with you, Mortimer. You accept too much. At least Edward put up a fight.*"

"*That he did, and I have the scars to prove it. Or did, anyway.*"

"*I used to love to run my fingers over those scars.*"

"*And I loved your caresses, Isabella.*"

"*Oh, Mortimer? What are we to do?*"

A sigh, lonely as a whining wind, filled the tower.

Chapter Six

Amanda pulled her shawl tighter as a chilly gust swirled through the stone corridor. Going downstairs on crutches provided adventure enough without the wind tugging on her clothing like some mischievous spirit. The little ungainly hop-skip movement she had devised effected a steady descent—although at times her precarious balance depended solely on the unwieldy crutches.

Her efforts to nap had come to naught. Something about Sommersby Castle invaded one's peace of mind. Perhaps it was the unsettling decor in her room or the keening of the wind outside. Whatever the source of her unease, it had finally driven her from her chamber, if for no other reason but to escape her own thoughts.

No one else seemed to find the castle oppressive. But except for that warm and inviting parlor that was now her goal, Amanda had seen little else in this pile of stones to like. She wondered how Lord Sommersby could spend his time in such a place, with weapons peering at him from every wall and the wind whining at every turn.

There must be all of a hundred rooms. She wondered whether he had inspected all of them. He had only come into the title after Waterloo, so perhaps he had not yet had time. Had he seen the dungeons Mr. Thornton had mentioned? Did he mind that people had died in this castle, doubtless unheard beyond the thick stone of their dark cells?

How morose, Amanda thought glumly. The oppressive atmosphere was beginning to absorb even her sensible mind. She must try to remember that while the castle might be a bit drafty and thin of company, it was home to a man known for his courage and battle prowess. Who could possibly feel anxious in such a setting?

"Good afternoon, Miss Fitzhugh."

Startled, Amanda looked up just as the crutches took her full weight on the last step. Like an ungainly fledgling who had not yet mastered the art of flying, she teetered briefly before her balance failed altogether.

At the foot of the steps, Lord Sommersby regarded her with horror as she pitched forward into his arms.

For a fleeting moment Amanda wondered whether they would both go crashing to the floor and whether she would ever recover from the embarrassment. But there was nothing like being caught against that broad chest once more to drive all practical thought from one's head. As the earl's arms closed around her, their solid strength generated a wave of longing to remain within that powerful circle rather longer than necessary. His warmth banished the drafty chill, penetrating whatever mechanism controlled her internal temperature—which had escalated quite suddenly.

With a sigh, Amanda inhaled the faint smell of sandalwood that clung to his clothes. Something undefinable but purely masculine made its way into her senses, triggering a feeling that vaguely resembled a stomachache, but infinitely more pleasant.

That feeling tugged at her memory, knocking on doors that she had firmly shut years ago, until it made itself known as the foe she had long thought vanquished in that fumbling, humbling experience with Julian LeFevre.

Desire.

Easily identifiable, now that she thought about it, and truly appalling.

Gamely, Amanda smiled up at Lord Sommersby, hoping to cover her discomfiture. His unreadable expression made her hasten to set herself aright again.

"I do beg your pardon, my lord," Amanda stammered, reaching for the crutches he had caught with the hand that was not wrapped securely around her waist.

He did not immediately release her.

Instead, and to her great surprise, he tucked the crutches under one arm and lifted her quite effortlessly. Ignoring her shocked gasp, he carried her down the hall to a door that was partially ajar. With the toe of his gleaming Hussar boots, he pushed it open. Inside the room, he set her on a divan, placed the crutches at her side, and turned toward a small table that held several decanters.

He had said not a word.

On the divan, Amanda shifted uneasily and glanced quickly around the room, which appeared to be his study. A massive oak desk surrounded by dozens of book-laden shelves filled one end, while the divan and two comfortably worn leather chairs framed a small fireplace at the other. The tone of the room was decidedly masculine, but it was just as appealing as the parlor.

Regarding her silently, he handed her one of the glasses he had poured. Accepting it, Amanda felt exceedingly foolish at the fact that he had twice been called upon to rescue her from an ungainly accident. Now she—the chaperone, no less—sat alone with him in his study, drinking spirits. He must think her so desperate for masculine attention that she hurled herself at every man within reach—even her cousin's intended.

To cover her awkwardness, Amanda took a sip and discovered a fine old sherry that conjured up images of oaken barrels gently aging their treasured contents over the centuries. Taking another sip, she savored the slightly woody taste and the bracing liquid heat as it slid down her throat. Perhaps, she thought giddily, there was something to be said for ancient castles after all.

Amanda shot him a bright, detached smile.

"Thank you for your kindness, my lord. I must confess that it is mortifying to find oneself in need of rescue so often. I am an independent woman accustomed to doing for myself and not normally so clumsy."

The look he bestowed on her was nothing if not dubious.

"Truly," she insisted, wishing that she could stop chattering like a magpie. "I cannot remember when I last fell down the stairs. As for the accident with the chair in Felicity's room . . ."

Her voice trailed off. Towering over her with that impressive physique and penetrating gaze, he looked like a man who did not suffer fools. Or giddy women.

Even his clothing made no concessions to frivolity. His dark green jacket had a rolled collar that gave it a vaguely military air, and it was tailored against the constrictive fashions of the day to allow room for easy motion. His serviceable Hussars rose to a slight point to protect the shins without restricting movement. Amanda guessed that he had worn them in the war and that, like other military boots, they were shod with iron.

Iron was a perfect metaphor for the man, Amanda decided, recalling the finely sculpted muscles that lay beneath that heavy superfine and the rigid strength of those corded arms. Clean-shaven, his face bore a slight indentation near his mouth that might have been a dimple, had not the possibility been unthinkable in such a man. The only thing at odds with the controlled image he projected was the unmanageable shock of red hair that suggested a tantalizing wildness beneath his restraint. With that fierce mane and crystalline gaze, the Earl of Sommersby was a man to make any woman swoon.

Except her. Sternly, Amanda told herself that this would not do.

"Lord Sommersby," she began again, her tone brisk, "I fear we may have gotten our acquaintance off on the wrong foot, so to speak. Our initial meeting was rather . . . awkward."

She colored at the image of that night in Felicity's room, but went on. "I also realize that my blunt comments about your weapon collection may have given offense, for which I do apologize. I hope you will allow us to start anew, as surely we both have Felicity's happiness in mind."

His uncompromising expression did not alter. Indeed, he seemed scarcely to have noticed her words.

"Is it your habit," he asked at last in a severe tone, "to climb upon wobbly chairs and to navigate a crumbling stone staircase on crutches without summoning assistance?"

Surprise and indignation surged through her. "I am a woman, my lord, not some frail creature."

Regarding her steadily, he frowned. "Miss Fitzhugh, I am at a loss as to how to prevent you from harming yourself in my home. This castle is a relic that years of neglect have not improved. It does not boast the staff that is needed to assure the comfort of every guest, and for that I apologize. I can only say that refurbishment is one of my goals, but it is a piecemeal task at best. For now, I must insist as your host that you exercise more caution. While you are under this roof, you will call upon Jeffers or myself if you need assistance."

It was a command, from one accustomed to issuing them.

"I am not an invalid," Amanda protested, appalled at the notion of summoning the earl or his manservant to move her from one place to another. She was here to help Felicity, not to be a burden.

The frown disappeared, and the barest hint of a smile took its place. Was that a dimple in his cheek after all? "Not yet, madam. But I would not wager against your chances."

Against her will, Amanda laughed. "Touché, my lord. I suppose I have given you reason enough for that."

Lord Sommersby eyed her thoughtfully, then abruptly sat in the chair nearest her divan. "I would like to ask your advice on a matter."

In the act of sipping the last of her sherry, Amanda paused in surprise. "My lord?"

"I am accustomed to solving problems in the most efficient way possible," he began. "Wasting time appalls me. I like to have a plan and follow it."

Amanda nodded uncertainly. The earl drained his glass, set it on the table with a thump, and shot her a pained look.

"I am more comfortable on the battlefield than in occupying a position in society, but I have been dealt this hand and must live with it." He hesitated. "I would not trouble you with this matter, but I have no other females to consult."

Unable to imagine any delicate female matter on which she could advise him, Amanda swallowed hard. "Yes, Lord Sommersby?" she said politely.

Rising to his feet, he poured himself another sherry, absently taking Amanda's glass and refilling it as well.

"I am told that a woman of breeding is entitled to a Season." This time he sat next to her on the divan, wearing a preoccupied expression. "Yet it seems an utter waste of time. If one has decided upon a wife, then why spend months dashing about to parties where the goal is to match young ladies to their future husbands?"

"You would rather just carry her off and be done with it, I suppose," Amanda said, unable to keep the amusement from her voice.

Solemnly, he considered her words. "Yes, I would."

The image of Felicity slung over Lord Sommersby's shoulder like some prize he had just won in battle made Amanda laugh out loud. "My lord, there must be some concessions to polite society."

"Must there? Sir Thomas has made it clear that Miss Biddle must have a Season, and so I have promised to accompany her to town. But I do not see the point in it, if we are agreed to have each other."

"She has accepted your offer, then?" Somehow, the thought was instantly sobering. Gulping her sherry, Amanda wondered why Felicity had not mentioned the fact.

Draining his own glass, Lord Sommersby shook his head. "I have spoken only to her father. Assuming Miss Biddle agrees, we leave for town within a fortnight. I will spend the next months escorting her to as many parties and balls as she wishes to attend." He frowned. "But I simply do not understand the need for such frivolous rituals."

Amanda could well imagine why Felicity would enjoy being the center of attention in the company of such an esteemed war hero as Lord Sommersby, but she could also quite understand why a man of the earl's disposition would view such a prospect with reluctance, if not loathing. She hesitated. "A young lady of breeding is raised to expect a Season. It is an exciting time that marks her social acceptance. Though it may well result in a suitable match, a Season is also enjoyable and amusing in itself."

"Did you have a Season, Miss Fitzhugh?"

The question took her aback. "Yes, my lord."

"But you achieved no 'suitable match.'" He eyed her thoughtfully.

Amanda managed a smile. "I think it is safe to conclude that I did not take."

"There was no one for whom you formed a tendre?"

"No." Other than the scandalous Lord Ramsey, she thought ruefully. "I do not regret my single state, my lord," she added. "I am entirely content with my little house in Kent."

He arched a brow. "It begins to sound as though you too have little use for the rituals of society, Miss Fitzhugh."

"My feelings are not at issue here, my lord," Amanda noted pointedly. "I believe we were speaking of Felicity."

Lord Sommersby sighed. "Forgive my personal inquiry, Miss Fitzhugh. It is just that I have much to do here at the castle. Workmen are scheduled to report soon. Already, a young scholar has begun cataloguing the weapons and the contents of my library. Servants must be hired, tenants must be dealt with. There are many other business matters I must manage. Dancing attendance on a woman who has already agreed to have me seems an absurd waste of time."

"Then perhaps Felicity will refuse you, my lord," Amanda retorted, suddenly quite out of sorts. "Mayhap you will truly have to work to win your bride. I daresay it is not as difficult as winning a war, or even having your vast weapon collection catalogued."

Grabbing her crutches, Amanda lurched to her feet. "You will excuse me. I feel the need for some air."

Too much sherry spoiled her grand exit. The floor was not quite where she expected it. As she swayed precariously, Amanda felt a strong pair of hands instantly grasp her waist and hips from behind to steady her. Rising, Lord Sommersby quickly transferred his grip to her elbows, but for Amanda the damage was already done.

The nascent desire she had so firmly banished after toppling into Lord Sommersby's arms at the foot of the stairs bloomed into something far more potent. With this new intimate contact—fleeting though it might be—the butterflies in her stomach took wing. As he stood, clasping her arms, Amanda desperately fought the urge to lean into that large, masculine frame.

"You must not move so quickly," he reprimanded. "You will injure yourself again."

But she scarcely heard his warning for thinking of what a fallen woman she must be. Had the experience with Julian left her so thoroughly beyond redemption that she could feel desire for a man who belonged to Felicity? Was she to find herself weak in the knees every time she came near him—or any attractive man?

"Thank you for the reminder, Lord Sommersby," Amanda forced herself to say. "I will be on my way to the parlor, where I was bound when I tumbled into you." With grim determination, she fumbled with her crutches.

"Allow me to assist you."

Alarmed to see that he was prepared to carry her once more, Amanda shook her head violently. "No, my lord. I prefer to manage for myself." When he seemed about to resist, she hurriedly added, "I promise to summon someone if I need to take the stairs."

That seemed to satisfy him and, with a sigh of relief, Amanda hobbled out of Lord Sommersby's study. Long afterward, however, she felt the touch of his arms about her.

His proposal to Felicity Biddle went smoothly. Although Simon had never before offered a woman marriage, it was not at all difficult. One had only to state one's admiration, make a straightforward declaration of intentions, and wait for an answer. Gracious and blushing, Miss Biddle consented immediately. It all went precisely according to plan. His mission had been successful. While a trying few months in town lay ahead, Simon breathed a sigh of relief that the future was now settled.

Miss Fitzhugh had made him see the importance of the Season to Miss Biddle, and Simon was prepared to endure London as he had endured any number of unpleasant situations during the war—as minor inconveniences on the way to achieving the larger goal. Miss Biddle would make him a fine wife. Their sons would have his discipline and strength, their daughters her pretty violet eyes. Generations of Thorntons would thank him for securing their future and their heritage.

That knowledge, and the fact that his goal had been achieved in such a civilized fashion, brought a smile to Simon's face as he stood at the dinner table and offered a toast to his lovely bride. Sir Thomas beamed, Miss Biddle blushed prettily, and Miss Fitzhugh smiled approvingly at him over the rim of her glass.

It was important not to be distracted by the flecks of

amber in Miss Fitzhugh's dark eyes, or to be reminded of the way her form fit so perfectly against his when she had tumbled into his arms. Most especially, it was important not to recall that moment of weakness in his study, when he was swept by a desire so strong that he had mentally tossed her down on the divan and ravished her before he even realized that the thought had occurred.

He could not imagine why he felt lust for Miss Biddle's prim chaperone. She was not wildly beautiful. Her hair stood somewhere between brown and fair, though it had shone quite gloriously without its many pins the night she injured her ankle. To be sure, from the first he had appreciated the classical nose and high cheekbones that gave her a nobility of profile. And though there was nothing frankly sensual about her mouth, he wondered whether an ardent kiss or two would change that.

Simon gave himself a mental shake. So what if under those sedate spinster frocks lurked enticing curves and—as he had accidentally discovered in the study—a tiny waist and softly provocative hips? It was entirely natural to wish to explore the matter further, but that did not mean there was anything special about Miss Fitzhugh.

Fortunately, he possessed an iron control. From now on, Miss Biddle would be the recipient of his primitive urges, although he could not imagine feeling anything so base for his genteel betrothed. Still, he had chosen well. His bride would bear him the family he needed to secure Sommersby and to set down the roots he had never known in all his years in the military.

A man's duty was to a higher goal than the satisfaction of lustful appetites. Lust belonged to the uncivilized part of him, the part capable of warring and wenching and unleashing urges inappropriate to a man of title with a family to think of and a birthright to secure for his children.

Besides, Miss Fitzhugh was an independent sort. She had chosen to do without men in her life and apparently was managing very well. Indeed, he did not know of another female who would think nothing of scrambling up on a chair to investigate a strange noise or hobbling downstairs alone on crutches. Her demeanor suggested she did not need a man, or anyone else for that matter.

Simon could understand that, for he had been happy enough on his own for years. On the other hand, he could not remember a time when he had not been responsible for somebody—either his men or, before that, his widowed mother. He had always taken care of his own. He supposed that marriage was not much different.

He would be a good husband and father. He would transform his castle into a comfortable home. Moreover, he thought, draining his glass in satisfaction, he had an excellent wine cellar.

The woman exactly resembled his mother. Though she had been dead for years, she stood in his bedchamber now—looking as she had eighteen years ago when she read his father's name off the lists of soldiers killed fighting Humbert's invasion at Killala. Until then, Ireland had been only a faraway place that kept his father from home.

Simon blinked. His mother's face was lined and worn from the strain of her growing pregnancy and the babe she would lose in the agonizing grief that followed the loss of her husband. At twelve, he had understood enough to know that his mother needed something he could not provide. Almost overnight he had become a man, but he could not shield her from the bill collectors who wanted their due, or the other men who wanted far more. When she died in his fifteenth year from a sickness of the body and heart, he had been powerless to prevent it. There was nothing left but to go, like generations of Thornton men before him, and fight the Frenchmen who had killed his father.

And though he had long carried the image of his mother in his heart, never had he encountered her standing in front of the fire in his chamber, looking as if she had something important to say. Simon sat up in bed and rubbed his eyes. His imagination had run amok, undoubtedly because he had drunk too much, first celebrating his betrothal with Sir Thomas after dinner, then finishing in solitary the brandies Jeffers had brought to him later.

But when he looked again, his mother was still there. Or *something* was. In the dim glow of the dying embers in the hearth, the image grew indistinct.

His vision might have been affected by the spirits he had

consumed, but Simon began to consider the possibility that there was some foolishness afoot. Reaching for his dressing gown, he briefly turned his attention away from the fireplace. When he looked again, he froze.

His mother's face had lost its weary lines and now looked almost girlish. As she smiled, Simon held his breath. Only in the dimmest recollection of his childhood had he ever seen her so happy and carefree. Another image appeared next to her, that of a young man, a soldier. As the image grew more distinct, Simon saw that it was his father. The two people rushed into each other's arms, and Simon felt unaccountably pleased.

Suddenly, the images blurred. Then they were no longer his parents but two people dressed in the clothing of another century. A voluminous train indicated the woman's high rank. Her bodice was tightly wrapped and cut in a deep decolletage. The man wore pointed footgear, clinging hose, and a short jacket with heavily padded shoulders.

These images did not last either, disappearing in a smoky haze that quickly condensed into two naked lovers wrapped in each other's arms. Frantically, the couple tried to consummate their lovemaking, and the hazy fog that swirled around them grew more and more agitated as the wild dance of sex escalated.

Something was wrong, however. Fascinated, Simon stared as the lovers faded in and out, then evaporated into gray wisps that swirled restlessly in the smoky hearth before disappearing up the chimney. As an erotic dream, the vision had failed miserably, for the images of the two lovers had existed only fleetingly, and a sense of frustration lingered in the room long after they had vanished.

What a strange dream, Simon thought, yawning. He wondered whether by the time he awoke in the morning the dream would have played out to a more successful conclusion.

For the lovers' sakes, he hoped so.

As his head hit the pillow once more, Simon's thoughts were filled with the frantic lovers and their desperate passion.

Chapter Seven

"I wonder where Mr. Thornton has got to," Amanda said. "We have not seen him since our arrival."

Felicity looked up from her book. "I expect he is away on some business for Lord Sommersby." A smile flitted over her heart-shaped mouth. "Do you miss him, perchance?"

Amanda colored. "I merely wondered about his whereabouts." In truth, even the difficult Mr. Thornton would prove a welcome diversion. They still had a week remaining of their visit, and it seemed that everywhere she looked, there was the earl in all his magnificence.

"But you did enjoy his company, did you not?" Felicity removed her spectacles and eyed her cousin thoughtfully. "I suspect Mr. Thornton would be a kind companion."

"Just because you are betrothed, you think that every other female should do likewise." Amanda bristled.

Felicity ignored this remark. "Mr. Thornton is a bit older than your previous suitors, but that need be no disadvantage. Age has not left him infirm or enfeebled, and I do believe he must be wise about a great many things that a younger man may not."

"Mr. Thornton is *not* a suitor," Amanda protested, aghast. "Where did you get such a notion? We but exchanged a few words on the journey here. I declare, Felicity, your imagination is something to behold."

"I merely want what is best for you, Amanda," Felicity persisted. "I would not like to see the experience with Lord Ramsey ruin your life. Not all men are like that. Why, I imagine that Lord Sommersby will be a very pleasant and gentle husband."

Having herself been hoisted by those powerful arms,

Amanda hoped that for Felicity's sake she was right about the earl's gentleness. "Ramsey did not ruin my life," she insisted. "The man merely opened my eyes to the baser side of the masculine nature, and I have chosen to avoid any repeat exposure."

"But, Amanda! Not to have children, or to know a husband's embrace . . ." Rapturously, Felicity closed her eyes and murmured: "'A heavenly paradise is that place wherein all pleasant fruits do flow' . . ." She broke off, blushing. "I have been immersed in this book of poems. A nice young man helped me find it in Lord Sommersby's library."

"I did not know there was anyone else here."

"Mr. Frakes is cataloguing the earl's books and weapons. He is a student of medieval texts, but he was very familiar with the works of Campion and Herrity. He found a beautiful wedding song for me. Only listen"—Felicity adjusted her spectacles and read—"'I sing of brooks, of blossoms, birds, and bowers; Of April, May, of June, and July flowers. I sing of Maypoles, Hock-carts, wassails, wakes, Of bridegrooms, brides, and of their bridal cakes.'" She sighed happily. "I intend to have it read at our wedding."

Amanda doubted very much whether Lord Sommersby's notion of a wedding included a homage to Maypoles. And she was quite sure his thoughts were not inclined toward the pastoral. "Perhaps the earl may have other ideas," she ventured.

Felicity waved a dismissive hand. "He has left everything up to me. He does not care what sort of ceremony we have, just as long as we are wed by the end of June. He says there is no sense in wasting time now we have agreed to have each other." She blushed. "It is quite flattering to have such an eager fiancé."

After her recent conversation with Lord Sommersby, Amanda feared that the earl's eagerness stemmed not from any ardent desire to have Felicity as his bride—they scarcely knew each other, after all—but from a determination to have the thing over and done with. She studied her cousin, wondering at the degree to which her feelings were involved. It would be tragic if Felicity fell deeply in love with her future husband, only to encounter his indifference once they were wed. Her tenderhearted cousin would be shattered to find that her romantic impulses were not returned. And something told Amanda that romance was the farthest thing from the earl's mind.

"I imagine that you will want to take as much time as possible to get to know Lord Sommersby," Amanda said carefully. "The whirl of parties and balls in town afford little opportunity for that. There is no substitute for going into a marriage with one's eyes wide open."

"Oh, my eyes are open, Amanda. You need not worry. Papa says that married people do not sit in each other's pockets, and I know he is right. I shall enjoy the flurry of parties, and then I shall retire with my new husband to discover the secrets of marital bliss." Felicity smiled mischievously. "I expect that we shall fall in love and live happily ever after, like Papa and Mama. It will not happen overnight, perhaps, but it will happen."

"But what if it does not?"

Felicity eyed her sternly. "Lord Sommersby is everything I have wanted in a husband." She sighed. "It is a fairy tale come true. The handsome hero has stepped off the pages and into my life. I am very lucky to be chosen by such a man."

"I thought you considered him fierce."

Felicity frowned. "I do not recall thinking that. Still, I imagine that a man who has known and survived war must needs be fierce, Amanda. But fierceness bespeaks passion, does it not? And passion is the breath of life to love."

"Where did you hear that?"

"It is true," Felicity insisted. "You have only to study the poets to know that passion and love are inexorably entwined." She looked down at her book and read: "'What is a kiss? Why this, as some approve: The sure, sweet cement, glue, and lime of love.'"

"Lord Sommersby has *kissed* you?" Though the question was impertinent, Amanda could not stop herself from asking it.

Felicity colored. "Of course not! We do not know each other well enough. I imagine the earl is not one to take liberties, even with his betrothed."

"Perhaps you had best give him an opportunity. You will be sharing this man's bed for the rest of your life, my dear.

You had best find out if that much-vaunted passion is glue enough."

"Amanda!" Felicity stared at her cousin, shocked. "You are my chaperone. I cannot imagine you advising such a thing—especially not after your experience with the marquess!"

"It was my experience that taught me how superficial was the passion between us," Amanda said. "Ramsey was very clever. He took advantage of my inexperience and used his own . . . magnetism to lead me down a road I did not even know existed. I was quite unprepared. When I realized that he held no feeling for me, it was too late."

Felicity shuddered. "What a dreadful man! But Lord Sommersby is not like that, Amanda. He is honorable."

"Of course. Still, you have only three months in which to get to know him. This visit is an ideal opportunity, absent the crowds and the distractions of town. Why are you passing an afternoon with me when you should be spending time with your intended?"

"Lord Sommersby has been very busy. He is approving plans for restoration of the castle."

"Then get him to take you round with him. I should think you would jump at the opportunity to tour this ancient pile."

Felicity fingered her book of poems. "He did take me to his library. But then he left me there. I did not mind, as Mr. Frakes was quite helpful. Anyway, I do not want to trouble the earl today. He seems much preoccupied with his work. And I believe he is expecting a guest. He gave the housekeeper a long list of supplies and the like, and ordered her to prepare another room." Felicity cocked her head. "I do not believe Mrs. Hathcourt is accustomed to receiving such precise instructions as the earl is wont to give. She appeared rather overset."

"A guest?" Amanda brightened at the prospect of a new face added to the castle's thin company.

Felicity nodded. "Mrs. Hathcourt says he lived at Sommersby Castle as a boy. I believe he is a relative of the late earl's wife."

"I see. I wonder why he is coming."

"I do not know. Mrs. Hathcourt was in such a flurry that

I did not wish to trouble her with any more questions. I believe she is in a dither with so many extra people at the castle."

"But there is not even a handful of us," Amanda protested. "In its day Sommersby Castle must have had guests by the dozens. Unless," she added broodingly, "the previous earls were all too busy polishing their weapons."

"Do you remember the party we had to celebrate your birthday? Half the kingdom was here. There was revelry for a week."

"Yes. Edward ruined it by threatening to remove Sommersby as keeper. Poor Sommersby. His only fault was asking Edward to share in the cost."

"Be reasonable, Isabella. Edward had a civil war on his hands. And disastrous harvests. You should not have expected him to pay for a party for three hundred people."

"I always suspected that you sympathized with him, Mortimer."

"Sympathized with him! How can that be? I helped roast him on that spit. All for you."

"For us."

"Anyway, you had your revenge, Isabella. You outlived him by thirty years."

"Which is why he looks so much younger than I. As do you, for that matter."

"My earthly life may have been cut short, but in the context of five hundred years, I did not have to wait long for you to join me."

"No, but what of it? All we have done since then is whistle through the rafters."

"I cannot help it if the spirit form is less than satisfying, Isabella."

"We almost managed it the other night. I thought we were onto something. For a moment I felt almost human."

"I fear the plan was flawed. How could we hope to experience the delights of the flesh when the forms we sought to take were themselves no longer flesh?"

"It was nice seeing you again in your court clothes. I had forgotten how stimulating a codpiece could be."

"And you were beautiful as ever I remembered."

"Hmmph. I rather imagined you had taken a liking for the dear departed Mrs. Thornton."

"The earl's mother? She was pleasant enough, but nothing compares to you, my dear."

"I believe you were onto something a moment ago, Mortimer. Do you think if we tried to inhabit the forms of people who are still alive, we could manage it?"

"You are speaking about our tenant?"

"The very same. And the prim chaperone."

"He is betrothed to the other, a comely lass, to be sure. Why try to change what already is?"

"Mortimer, you know me better than that. Besides, the one with the violet eyes needs no help. She understands passion."

"I thought her rather innocent."

"There is innocence, and then there is innocence. That one will manage quite well. It is the other who is the true innocent."

"The tall one? The chaperone?"

"Yes. But the real problem is that our tenant has too much discipline over his passions. It will take some doing to stir them. I believe our little scene the other night at least had him considering just how much he owes his conception to the very thing he shuns. But we must work fast. They mean to depart soon for London."

"I do not see how you can hope to change our tenant, Isabella. He is an honorable man."

"So were you once, Mortimer."

For a moment, the wind merely whistled idly through the cobwebs of the tower's vaulted ceiling.

"You know . . . I have never made love to such a tall woman before."

"The earl's proportions are more than ample, Mortimer. You will enjoy inhabiting them."

"How is it that you are familiar with such details about the man, Isabella?"

"The fact that I am no longer alive does not mean that I am dead to appreciation of the finer things in life, Mortimer."

The problem of Miss Fitzhugh continued to preoccupy Simon as he went about the castle, approving the various renovations his architect had suggested. He did not for a moment suspect that she would adhere to her promise to seek help in negotiating stairs and other parts of the castle that could prove difficult on crutches. She was the most stubborn and independent woman he had ever encountered, rather like one of his men hell-bent on returning to the battle before a wound healed.

That she was not one of his men was quite evident every time he encountered her at the dinner table or in his parlor, which occurred with maddening frequency. It irritated him that she was determined to play the dried-up prune of a spinster, pulling her hair into a tight bun and dressing in high-necked gowns that hid a perfectly good figure.

She seemed to say whatever came to her mind, as if it was her right as a woman who no longer had a reason to dress up a thought in pretty packaging. Although Simon found such directness refreshing, her blunt-spokenness kept him constantly on edge. The conversation that occurred when he encountered her taking the air by the lake this afternoon, for example, had left him nearly apoplectic.

After pointing out some nearby plants she said would aid in treating gout should he ever need it, Miss Fitzhugh proceeded to fix him with that clear, direct gaze of hers and ask him whether he thought sentiment was altogether foreign to his nature.

"I beg your pardon?" Simon had replied politely, hoping he had not heard correctly.

"I merely wondered whether you are capable of delicate feelings, my lord," she explained, as a slight flush stole over her face. "I myself decided long ago that an excess of sentiment is to be shunned, but I think that some tender feeling is necessary between a husband and wife. Do you not agree?"

"Er, I suppose so." Simon eyed her dubiously.

She smiled. "I did not mean to cause discomfort, Lord Sommersby. I know that as a soldier you are not accustomed to dwelling on such matters. Now that you are to wed Felicity, however, I believe it is not inappropriate to consider them. She has some rather romantical notions about marriage."

"Does she?" Simon wondered whether he could invent

some domestic crisis to call him away from this exceedingly uncomfortable conversation. One look at Miss Fitzhugh's determined gaze, however, told him that she would not allow him to escape that easily.

Nodding, she fixed him with a penetrating look. "Felicity is not altogether unrealistic, of course. I believe she is prepared to wed in the absence of . . . of love." Simon wondered why she stumbled over the word.

"But she fully expects to grow to love her husband," Miss Fitzhugh added pointedly, "and to have that love returned."

Simon could think of no response to this. Unfortunately, Miss Fitzhugh was staring at him with the expectant air of a woman awaiting one.

"Let me be plain, my lord," she said with some asperity when he did not reply. "Are you capable of loving my cousin, or at least of treating her with tenderness? Because if you make her miserable, I shall find some way to make you regret it."

"Good God, woman!" Simon sputtered. "Do you take me for some sort of monster?"

"No, my lord," she replied quickly, coloring. "It is just that I . . ."

"That you are concerned enough about my nature to fear that I will make Miss Biddle miserable," he growled. "May I ask what prompted you to come to such a conclusion?"

Miss Fitzhugh made a great show of adjusting her crutches. Finally, she met his gaze. "I meant no offense, Lord Sommersby. It is just that as a soldier, you must have put aside sentiment so that you could—" She broke off abruptly as his brows drew together thunderously.

"So that I could kill and maim and rape and plunder? Is that what you were about to say, Miss Fitzhugh?"

"Certainly not," she replied, paling.

Simon scowled. "I have never raped a woman in my life. I have killed, and yes, I have maimed. War is like that, Miss Fitzhugh. I did not, however, enjoy it, nor do I plan to subject my wife to similar treatment."

"I know that war is difficult," she began, but he cut her off.

"Yes, it is," he said coldly. "Life and death can change in

an instant. You think I know nothing of sentiment? Well, you may be right. There is no place in battle for kindness to the enemy, Miss Fitzhugh. And it is pure folly to come to care for another person so much that you cannot see for the tears that fill your eyes when that friend is run through by the enemy's sabre. As for the loved ones who wait and worry at home, it is useless to think of them. They will recover from their loss and move on." Just as he had recovered from his own father's death.

Her eyes shone with a suspicious moisture, but Simon ignored it. "Thus you and I are in agreement," he finished. "An excess of sentiment is to be shunned at all costs."

By the time Simon recalled that her father had perished on the Peninsula, he had marched halfway back to the castle in his anger at her maddening intrusion into things she knew nothing about. But she did know, he realized. Like him, she had lost a father to war.

Hesitating, he turned. She was standing at the side of the lake, staring into the water. When she lifted her head, Simon knew he had never seen such a sorrowful expression.

With a curse, he strode back to her side. "Miss Fitzhugh," he began, awkwardly touching her shoulder. She stiffened, and a solitary tear rolled down her cheek.

He wondered how to express something he had never before put into words. "I have spent my life as a soldier, Miss Fitzhugh. I have lived with death as a daily companion and never shunned the harsh fact of death's power to rob us of all we hold dear."

Mutely, she looked at him, and Simon ached for the loss she had suffered and his own inadequacy to offer comfort. "Life is hard," he continued. "War is loss. But after a time one does not feel those things so acutely. One gets used to it, or perhaps one learns to protect oneself from the full impact of the horror."

He sighed. "I do not know whether I can make your cousin happy. I do not know whether I am capable of giving her the affection that she seeks. But I am not a cruel man, Miss Fitzhugh, nor am I unaware of a woman's needs. I will do everything within my power not to make her miserable. I am afraid that is all that I can promise."

"Thank you, my lord," she murmured, attempting a game smile but managing only half of one.

For the rest of the day that crooked smile tugged at something inside him.

Something surprisingly soft and tender.

Chapter Eight

The years had not been kind to Julian, Simon decided, studying him over the rim of his glass and recalling the youthful dedication his former colleague had demonstrated on the Peninsula. Lines of dissipation marred his bold features, and a haunted look inhabited the deep-set eyes. Simon had seen that look in the faces of wounded soldiers who no longer cared whether they lived or died. He never thought to see it in Julian LeFevre, who had always seemed immune to the frailties that beset lesser men.

When Simon had assumed the title, he discovered that he and Julian were distant relatives. The late countess, a Frenchwoman, had brought Julian to live at Sommersby after his mother—Lady Sommersby's sister—perished in the Terror. Julian's English father, a duke, had evidently shown little interest in the result of his hasty foreign marriage.

Last month, Julian had sent Simon a letter requesting permission to visit his boyhood home. He offered no explanation for his sudden interest, but then Julian had never been one to offer explanations.

"Congratulations, Simon." Julian lifted his glass in a salute. "No man of my acquaintance is more deserving of marital bliss, although I will wager it is not a love match."

Taken aback, Simon narrowed his eyes. "Why do you say that?"

"Simple. I have never known you to put personal satisfaction above duty." A slow smile spread across a mouth many would have called cruel. But the ensuing grin that exposed a gleaming set of white teeth held as much genuine mirth as Simon suspected Julian could muster.

"You are one of those men who believe duty and personal happiness go hand in hand," Julian explained. "I am willing to stake my life on the fact that you have chosen your future countess as carefully as you mapped any battle plan and that you will do your duty by her most efficiently. I fully expect you to have an heir running amok in the castle in a year or so."

Simon stiffened. Julian's comment had come unerringly close to the truth. "The breeding possibilities of the future countess are not open for discussion."

A self-mocking smile played over Julian's slashing mouth. "Sorry. The truth is, I have always envied you, Simon. You never veer from the path of righteousness, nor do you question what is your duty. You inherit an earldom, and six months later you have assured your family's future. I inherit a dukedom and cannot find any use for females except the usual ones—and those do not include bearing my sons. The last thing in the world I wish to do is perpetuate a line like mine."

Draining his glass, Simon contemplated the other man. Men of Julian's stripe made him uneasy, because they lived life carelessly without the iron controls and discipline Simon had had instilled in himself since youth. Julian was reputed to possess unquenchable thirsts for wine, women, cards, and any activity that involved unbridled pleasure. Especially noted for his exploits with the female sex, he radiated an arrogance that communicated his opinion of his own worth, along with a relentless need to have that opinion ratified by the adoration of women.

For all the man's excesses, however, Julian had been an excellent officer before the family responsibilities spawned by his father's death called him home from the war. Simon had found him a perceptive observer, a keen strategist, and a fearless leader. In the world of women he may have taken without apology, but in the world of men he gave unstintingly of himself. With his courage and cunning, he had bolstered the resolve of the greenest soldier and won the respect of the most battle-hardened professional. His bravery in facing death was unequalled, perhaps because death held no fear for a man who had exhaustively sampled life and found it wanting.

Simon wondered what had left Julian so cynical and why

the arms of death had been easier to face than those of a wife. But he did not press him. A man like Julian LeFevre would ever go his own way.

"Apology accepted," Simon said. "Perhaps now you will tell me how I may be of service. Your letter was somewhat vague. What did you wish to see in the castle? I warn you, some parts of it are in serious disrepair."

Julian walked to the hearth, where he stood in front of the roaring fire and stared into its flames. "I am searching for some papers," he murmured over his shoulder.

"Papers?" Simon frowned.

"I have reason to believe that my aunt, Lady Sommersby, had them in her possession. They belonged to my mother," Julian replied in a flat tone.

That expressionless voice and the scant information Julian provided provoked in Simon a wealth of questions, but he did not ask them. "I have come across no papers here," he said, "although I have not explored all of the castle."

"I suspect my aunt may have hidden them. Perhaps in the tunnels."

"I see." Simon knew that tunnels under the castle led to caves deep in the cliffs. Years ago, smugglers were reputed to have used them to store their booty. Simon could not imagine why the late countess had seen fit to hide important family papers there. In any case, it was not his concern.

"You are free to make use of the place." Simon set his glass down on the table with a thump and rose. "And now it is time to join my fiancée and her family."

Preoccupied with Julian's strange quest, Simon did not immediately notice anything amiss as they entered the parlor where the others had gathered.

Before he could make introductions, however, a sharp gasp followed by an almost deafening silence told him something was terribly wrong. Sir Thomas looked outraged. Miss Biddle merely appeared bewildered, but it was Miss Fitzhugh's condition that truly gave him pause.

She was staring at Julian as if she had seen a ghost. Behind him, Simon heard Julian's softly muttered oath.

"Lord Sommersby," she acknowledged. "Lord Ramsey," she added coolly, shooting Julian a look that consigned him to hell.

Simon frowned. Miss Fitzhugh might be plainspoken, but she had never struck him as frankly rude.

"Good evening, Amanda," Julian drawled in an intimate tone that took Simon aback. "It seems I have been cursed with a dukedom since last we met. I am Claridge now."

Amanda had not seen him in eight years. She waited for the old feelings of shame, humiliation, and anger to wash over her at the sight of the man who had tried to bring about her ruin and very nearly accomplished it, who had touched her so intimately in a public place as she lay spellbound, his willing slave.

He was the same. The same cruel slash of a mouth, the same contemptuous dark eyes, the same undercurrent of amusement at her expense. And yet he was not. His face bore deep lines of dissipation. His gaze was more tormented, his sharply planed features more harsh. The frankly seductive air she remembered was tinged with something that on another man she might have called desperation.

Julian had aged, but she sensed that it was not age that had changed him. Perhaps it was his own inner devils, the ones that made her realize years ago he was incapable of giving, only of taking.

What struck her most of all, however, was the manner in which standing in Lord Sommersby's shadow diminished him. She had not expected that. No one had ever cast Julian LeFevre in the shade.

Physically, the two had much in common. Both were tall and imposing, their large frames easily dominating any room. Both men filled out jackets with their broad shoulders and trim, muscular forms. The earl was half a head taller, but it was not that which gave him the edge. Rather, it was the cool authority, the unshakable control, the keenly assessing air he radiated, as if he was prepared for any eventuality. There was something solidly comforting about Lord Sommersby's effortless mastery of himself, something ineffably intriguing about the unruly red mane that suggested an inner fire beneath the steely discipline.

Indeed, Amanda waited in vain for the feelings of shame and humiliation Julian's presence should have engendered. She was startled to notice only a deepening admiration of

Lord Sommersby, who regarded her curiously as it became clear that introductions were quite unnecessary.

Julian's mouth curved into a grim smile. "Your guests and I have not seen each other for a number of years," he told the earl. "It seems that I have come at an inopportune time for my errand, Simon. Please accept my excuses. I will depart within the hour."

"No." All eyes turned toward Amanda as she spoke. "The past is in the past. I would not dream of forcing a change in your plans."

As if for confirmation, Julian's gaze went quickly to Sir Thomas, who drew himself up to his full height, though it was still considerably less than the other men's. "My niece is a grown woman who knows her own mind," Sir Thomas said, scowling. "Neither my daughter nor I wish to place her in an awkward position, but if she agrees to your remaining here, Claridge, I will not demand otherwise."

Despite her dismay at Julian's presence, Amanda shot her uncle an amused look. His response had been less than gracious, but at least he had respected her wishes. It was best to forget the embarrassing episode in her past, especially now, when the atmosphere in the castle should be one of celebrating Felicity's betrothal.

Lord Sommersby had the good manners to let the matter drop, but as he ushered them in to dinner, Amanda felt the burning speculation in that crystalline gaze.

Jeffers' ungainly backswing generated too large an action, leaving the batman off-balance and, as usual, exposed. Simon took full advantage of his vulnerability to move in and, in a swift attack, thrust the tip of his foil against the base of Jeffers's throat.

"My lord," Jeffers croaked, "I have had quite enough."

The batman's pale features fueled Simon's guilt, as he had subjected Jeffers to a particularly savage workout. Somewhat sheepishly, Simon withdrew his blade. "Sorry. I seem to be somewhat on edge tonight."

Shooting his employer a speaking look, Jeffers gathered his things. Simon could not blame the batman for being out of sorts. He himself had been in a foul mood all evening, thanks to the effect of Julian's arrival on the company and, most especially, upon Miss Fitzhugh.

That Julian and Miss Fitzhugh were well acquainted, and that it was an acquaintance that caused her awkwardness, could only mean one thing. They had had a relationship of more than passing familiarity. The atmosphere in the dining room tonight had been positively stifling. When Miss Biddle and Miss Fitzhugh left the men to their port, Sir Thomas looked daggers at Julian, who bore the disapprobation as if used to such reactions, which, Simon suspected, he was. Simon wondered how Miss Fitzhugh had become involved with such a man and what, precisely, the extent of that involvement had been.

Had Julian been responsible for the fact that she "did not take," as she had put it, during her Season? Had he been the reason she had abandoned the social whirl for a life of solitary independence? If so, that could only mean one thing.

Miss Fitzhugh had been one of Julian's conquests.

Had he seduced her? Had it been difficult? Had he found it necessary to use all of the wiles at his disposal? Or had she fallen into his arms like a ripe plum ready for the picking?

Neither possibility fit with the image he had of a strong, independent woman capable of doing for herself and gadding about on crutches as if serious injury was not a possibility she ever considered.

Dispassionately, Simon examined the tip of his foil. The button was intact, but he had beat blades with Jeffers so ferociously that his own blade had a small crack and would have to be replaced. The notion that Miss Fitzhugh was damaged goods, rather like that tiny crack in his blade, did something strange to his mental picture of her. It opened a host of possibilities that he found himself imagining in rather vivid detail—Miss Fitzhugh writhing in ecstasy on satin sheets, her hair tumbled about her shoulders in disarray, her clothing strewn about the floor, carelessly abandoned to the dictates of passion.

Miss Fitzhugh was not the sort to agree to be a man's mistress. He did not think her pride and independence would allow her to do such a thing. But perhaps it had been something spontaneous, on the seat of a closed carriage on the way home from the theater, a frantic fumbling of hands and flesh and urgent need. She did not strike him as the frantic sort, either, but who could tell? How well did any man know a woman until he had made love to her?

The image of Miss Fitzhugh's noble features enslaved to passion unsettled his pulse, and Simon frowned as he put his sword away. He had no such thoughts about Miss Biddle, whose violet eyes were truly lovely to behold but which he had scarcely bothered to look at.

Doubtless it was the impatient state in which he found himself—betrothed, but unable to claim his bride until the tedious ritual of the Season ended—that steered his thoughts away from his future bride and to the only other woman in the castle.

It was none of his business if Miss Biddle's prim chaperone had once engaged in a carnal relationship with Julian. Such liaisons were as commonplace as a stroll in the park—although he did not see how any relationship with Miss Fitzhugh could be commonplace.

Perhaps, then, there had been a true passion between them, an exchange of those delicate feelings of which she had spoken so fervently this afternoon.

That thought was the most unsettling of all. For if there had been a great passion, renewed contact between them—such as that likely over the next few days—might very well bring it to the fore again.

Would the erstwhile lovers slip through the castle corridors at night to sample new pleasures in each other's arms? Would Julian reclaim Miss Fitzhugh as his own?

A sound very like a growl rumbled deep in Simon's throat and made its way past his lips, where it erupted in a muttered profanity that caught him by surprise.

"This is excellent. I declare, Mortimer, our tenant's thoughts are warming even this drafty tower."

"Claridge was a master stroke, Isabella."

"I had nothing to do with it, but I am delighted just the same."

"Do you not think Edward is different tonight, my dear?"

"Perhaps you are right. He seems more alert. I hope he does not decide to interfere in our plan."

"Your plan, Isabella. I do not presume to have your cunning and skill."

"But you have something else, Mortimer—loyalty. I do not know where I would be without that."

"Sleeping the peaceful rest of the dead, I imagine."

"If only we can make an eternity of damnation more pleasurable, I should not mind so much being in our cursed state."

"If anyone can make damnation pleasurable, it is you, Isabella."

"Thank you, Mortimer. You are the only one who truly understands me."

Chapter Nine

"You have changed, Amanda."

So unexpected were the words whispered in her ear that Amanda teetered unsteadily on her crutches as she whirled to face the Duke of Claridge in all his dark glory.

They were alone. Sir Thomas and Lord Sommersby had gone riding, while Felicity had traipsed off to the earl's library to find yet another book of poems. Amanda had thought to spend the morning in her room resting her ankle, but it was too fine a day. Venturing beyond the confines of the oppressive stone walls, she had found a serene meadow that was just beginning to waken to spring. She had managed the walk well enough, despite her crutches.

"I do not know whether to be insulted or pleased by the fact that you did not anticipate my presence," Julian drawled.

"Neither, I imagine," Amanda said briskly.

"Then perhaps I should simply thank my good fortune to find you alone and in such an ideal setting for intimate conversation," he said with a mysterious smile that once would have set her pulse to racing.

"I cannot think that we have any reason to converse intimately after all this time," she replied, eyeing him warily.

"Do you not?" Coal-black eyes studied her. "Did you think I would make my bow last night and not exchange another word with you for the duration of my visit?"

"No," she conceded. "But I do not think our situation requires any private discussion."

"I remember a time when the opportunity for private discussion interested you a great deal."

Amanda flushed. "That was long ago. I am twenty-and-eight now, Your Grace."

"You used to call me by my given name," he said softly. "Is it so difficult to say?"

"I see no need to return to the familiarity of our former relationship."

Idly, he touched the wood of one crutch. "No, I suppose you would not. Amanda Fitzhugh does not easily forgive."

"Forgive?" Amanda eyed him in astonishment. "Is that in the nature of an apology, sir? Truly, I may faint dead away of shock."

His mouth twitched. "You wound me, madam. You were nothing if not receptive to my advances. If you would examine your own behavior, you would see how little there was in mine to give offense."

Amanda's eyes flashed indignantly. "You were a man of the world, and I so inexperienced as to be scarcely more than a child. You played on my innocence, as if I were some . . . orchestral instrument at your disposal."

His lips curled provocatively. "A very fine instrument, I should say."

"You are incorrigible," Amanda sputtered.

"I expect so," he replied with a lazy smile. "Come, now, Amanda. I freely admit that I led you quite literally down the garden path, seduction uppermost in my mind, ready to overcome any objections you might offer. My only regret about that evening is that Sir Thomas was not otherwise engaged. We encountered him at a rather inopportune moment, as I recall."

"My regrets are rather more numerous, sir." Amanda bit her lip as tears unexpectedly came to her eyes. His hand touched her shoulder.

"Let us have done with the recriminations, Amanda," he said grimly. "I accept full blame for what happened, for ruining your life, if that is what I did. But you threw a mantle of nobility over me that I did not and never have possessed."

His tone was bitter. His dark eyes looked as if they had gazed inward and witnessed something repugnant.

"You did not ruin my life," Amanda replied, surprised to realize the truth of that statement.

His gaze grew speculative. "You have indeed changed. I believe you see more with those eyes of yours now. And though I must bear the brunt of your anger, I confess that I find your maturity quite appealing."

Julian had changed, too. There was an unfamiliar vulnerability in that black gaze. What most surprised her, however, was the fact that her deepest regret lay in having allowed that long-ago disaster to carry so much power for so many years. Even though no one but the Biddles had known of her near-disgrace eight years ago, she had allowed it to become the defining event of her womanhood.

Appreciatively eyeing the burgeoning spring growth around her, Amanda savored the fact that there was so very much more to life than the past.

"You are incorrigible, Julian," she said, almost cheerfully. "But I have learned to master my passions in my old age, and there is nothing you can say that will undermine my resolve."

He did not bother to veil the hunger that leapt to his eyes. "Words are not my strong suit, Amanda. I prefer to let my actions speak for themselves."

Too late, Amanda read his intention. His sudden kiss was expertly provocative, gently insistent, and failed to increase her pulse even slightly. Amanda gave a sigh of relief as she opened her eyes and realized that the earth had not moved from its axis.

Until she saw the figure who stood a few feet away studying her with an unreadable gaze.

"Lord Sommersby," she cried, hastily stepping backward— into a rabbit hole that sent her spiraling downward. Were it not for Julian's quick arms, she would have fallen inelegantly.

The earl regarded them as they remained locked in each other's arms, and Amanda blushed in mortification. There was nothing she could say that would not make matters worse. Julian, however, had no such scruples.

"Amanda and I were renewing our old acquaintance," he said, a mischievous smile flitting over his mouth as he pretended not to see the furious look she shot him. "She seemed to be at loose ends this morning, so I thought to keep her company."

"Since you have other business here," Lord Sommersby replied in a clipped voice, "it will not be necessary for you to concern yourself with Miss Fitzhugh's entertainment, which is my responsibility as her host."

With excruciating slowness, Julian released her. "I have never found entertaining Amanda to be a burden," he drawled.

Rigidity suffused Lord Sommersby's features. When he spoke, his voice sounded unnaturally dry. "My cousin Thornton is expected back soon from a business errand. I have charged him with escorting Miss Fitzhugh, a task to which he agreed with alacrity. You need not trouble yourself further."

Thornton.

Amanda had not thought to see that drooping mustache and enigmatic gaze again. And he truly welcomed her company? Her spirits lightened at the prospect.

Lord Sommersby looked stunned, however, as if his announcement of his cousin's pending arrival surprised him as much as it did her.

He had to protect Miss Fitzhugh from Julian. Bringing back Thornton would enable him to watch her without his attention to her seeming inappropriate for a newly betrothed man. *Someone* needed to watch out for the woman. Simon could not leave her to the mercy of a man like Julian.

"Have the birds been nesting in this wig?" Simon demanded as Jeffers combed out the gray mop.

Arching a brow at his employer's sharp tone, Jeffers attempted to discipline the wig. Simon surveyed the results with a critical eye.

"Better, I suppose, but it still looks as if I have only a passing acquaintance with a comb and brush. See if you can do something with the mustache."

Simon had been out of sorts since discovering Miss Fitzhugh and Julian together. To be sure, his own interest in her was purely paternal. It was his duty to protect her. She was not up to dealing with one of the most notorious rakes in all England. As Thornton he could make certain she did not reinjure her ankle and, above all, keep her free of Julian's talons.

Simon had no doubt that, if applied to forcefully or otherwise, Julian would endeavor to be on his best behavior with Miss Fitzhugh. But Simon had no wish to call attention to his concern for her, and in any case he seriously doubted whether Julian's best behavior was anything praiseworthy. The man's predatory wiles seemed second nature.

Miss Fitzhugh needed him. The shock of seeing her in Julian's arms had prompted the sudden, brilliant notion of bringing back Thornton to attend her. To be sure, switching back and forth from Sommersby to Thornton would require some effort on his part. Perhaps he could invent some urgent business to call Sommersby away. There was no need for his presence anyway, since the matter of his future bride had been taken care of.

Jeffers fussed over the brown dimity suit, then stepped back to nod in satisfaction. Studying his reflection in the mirror, Simon decided that the somber maturity Thornton's extra years imparted was just the thing for this mission. Miss Fitzhugh would never guess he was not the earl's somber secretary, with ample years on his plate and a sober mind in his brainbox.

Simon allowed himself a smile. He had everything under control. Miss Fitzhugh would suffer no indignity while under his roof.

With a sense of freedom he had not felt in days, Simon descended the stairs in search of his guests.

"It is too bad Lord Sommersby found it necessary to investigate the disturbance himself."

Sir Thomas nodded absently at Felicity's comment. "A man cannot be too careful in these times. A disturbance can turn into a riot overnight. The earl was right to see to the matter himself. Those Luddites wreaked havoc a few years ago. Who knows how far this new rabble might take things?"

"I did not know Lord Sommersby owned a mill," Felicity said.

"The earl owns property all over England," Sir Thomas replied, admiration in his voice. "Rich as the devil he is, and very generous with the settlements, too." He cocked his head consideringly. "Now that matters are settled between you, perhaps we should return to Mayfield early. Your mother will be thrilled to hear that her hopes for you are to be realized."

Amanda held her breath as Felicity pondered this suggestion. "But the earl was quite clear that he would return soon," Felicity said. "And I am so enjoying exploring his library. Would it not be rude to go hieing back to Mayfield so soon, when he has extended his hospitality to us for the fortnight?"

"Surely he would understand your wish to share the good news with your mama," Sir Thomas replied. "I would like to see her face when I tell her that you are to receive twenty thousand pounds in pin money."

A mischievous grin spread over Felicity's lovely mouth. "Perhaps she would even wish to come to London to help me spend it. I should like to see Dr. Greenfield's face when his prize patient flies off to the mantua-maker against his express orders."

This comment produced a frown from her father. "I will not have my wife taking orders about her travel plans from the neighborhood quack."

Felicity turned to Amanda, a guilty look on her delicate features. "Perhaps we really ought to return home so that Dr. Greenfield can look at your ankle, Amanda. I did not think of that. How selfish I have been to wish to remain here merely because the earl possesses a singular library."

"I have more faith in Jeffers's skills than I do in Dr. Greenfield's," Amanda said quickly. "And Mr. Thornton has kindly offered to provide any assistance I may need."

Amanda hoped her voice sounded calm, but in truth she felt anything but. Since Mr. Thornton's arrival last night, she had felt positively giddy at the knowledge that she was free to enjoy his company without questioning—as she did with the earl—the propriety of doing so. His presence was a relief after the unsettling undercurrents between her and Lord Sommersby.

If only Mr. Thornton did not look so very much like the earl; if only that gray hair of his did not make her wonder whether it had once been the same brilliant shade of red. If only his changeable eyes did not resemble so precisely

Lord Sommersby's that Amanda was put in mind of him each time she met Mr. Thornton's gaze.

What was wrong with her? She was acting like a green miss who dreamt about every man who crossed her path. Mr. Thornton was precisely the steady, calm influence she needed to recover her sanity for this visit. Though they had seen him only briefly at dinner last night, he had inquired after her health and offered to give her a tour of the castle to take her mind off her injury. Amanda had accepted with alacrity, despite gentle taunts later from Felicity about her "suitor."

The notion that Mr. Thornton had formed an attachment for her was ridiculous. He was old enough to be her father, after all. Amanda suspected that his attention to her stemmed more from the earl's instructions to keep her occupied than from any genuine interest of his own. It would be just like Lord Sommersby to try to keep an eye on her in his absence. As it happened, Amanda planned to be considerably more active today. She had been able to put most of her weight on her leg this morning, with the result that she happily exchanged the despised crutches for the cane Jeffers provided.

Meeting Mr. Thornton at breakfast, Amanda was aware of a strange thrill rippling through her as those keen eyes noted the cane, then studied her carefully as if to determine whether she had discarded the crutches prematurely. Amanda had forgotten how penetrating that gaze could be, how it stood at odds with that disheveled mop of gray hair, and how perfectly it fit the subtle air of command that a worn suit did not diminish.

For the first time, Amanda knew a tiny moment of regret over her spinster's life. Perhaps with this gentleman she could find more than simply pleasant company. Dared she to think it? Why, after all these years alone, were her thoughts running in such a direction?

Bemused and a little ashamed, Amanda regarded Mr. Thornton over her coffee cup. The prospect that she and the earl's cousin could be more than mere acquaintances made her uneasy, especially after her disturbing reaction to the earl. Amanda had long ceased to think of herself as innocent, but now she realized how little understanding she had of the strange currents at work between the sexes.

Suddenly Mr. Thornton looked up from his plate and caught her staring. Awareness leapt to his eyes, and Amanda watched as they transformed from cool blue to a warmer green. Just as quickly, however, his gaze grew shuttered. An air of remoteness replaced the sudden electricity that sparked between them. He frowned.

"With that injury, I am not certain you ought to be undertaking something as ambitious as touring the castle, Miss Fitzhugh."

Was he trying to find an excuse to avoid spending the afternoon with her? Amanda wondered. Or was he genuinely concerned for her welfare?

"I can manage, sir. Indeed, I would welcome an opportunity to learn more about the castle's history." She hesitated, feeling uncharacteristically shy. "If you wish to reconsider, however, please do not feel any obligation to see to my entertainment. Felicity and I planned a shopping trip to the village for this morning, and we can easily extend it into the afternoon."

"I do not wish to reconsider. We shall begin in the courtyard at three o'clock." He rose. "If that is convenient, of course," he added as an afterthought.

Not waiting for her response, he left the room. Amanda frowned in exasperation. How like the men in this family to frame an invitation in the form of a command. Still, it was not so much irritation as anticipation that filled her, especially when she recalled the little jolt his touch had given her as he escorted her out onto the terrace at Mayfield that night.

Abruptly, Amanda set her cup down with a clatter and tossed her napkin onto the table. She would not make a fool of herself again. There was nothing special about Mr. Thornton. He was just a man, like any other. And she was just a woman who had no better sense than to let her mind wander in fanciful directions.

Nothing would happen between her and Mr. Thornton. Nothing at all.

Chapter Ten

Simon checked his reflection in the mirror one last time. The somber, aging Mr. Thornton looked back at him. For the first time in his life, Simon felt free. It was strange how being someone other than himself for a time could loosen the ties that bound a man to duty.

In the military or out of it, Simon had always known and done his duty. Even as a boy, he had done what he could to protect his mother and give her a better life. That he had failed then only strengthened his resolve never to fail again. As earl, his obligations lay with his lineage and his title. Miss Biddle was the perfect bride to help him fulfill his duty. He did not shun the future he had set in stone.

But he welcomed this respite, this small window of freedom during which he could become a man who had not the pressure of wealth and position to dictate his actions. For now, he was only Thornton, Miss Fitzhugh's threadbare protector. If their castle tour took hours, all the better, for it would keep her away from Julian that much longer.

Protecting Miss Fitzhugh might be his duty, but it felt like fun—pure, unfettered fun.

Simon could not remember the last time he had done anything for fun.

Strolling through Sommersby Castle was like stepping back in time. Amanda could envision the stone structure teeming with a king's army and peasants aplenty to do his bidding. And though she did not believe in ghosts, fanciful images of watchful but unseen presences plagued her as Mr. Thornton guided them deeper into the castle.

The oldest part was a sixty-foot shell keep on the north

side. When Amanda stumbled on fallen stones that cluttered the area, Mr. Thornton eyed her doubtfully.

"Perhaps we had best defer this tour until another time."

Amanda was not about to miss enjoying a carefree day without Lord Sommersby's magnetic presence. Almost giddy with freedom, she smiled. "My ankle barely pains me. I believe I could walk fifty miles today."

No answering smile made its way across Mr. Thornton's features, but Amanda did not mind. The earl's cousin was obviously not given to levity. He had made no effort to be witty or engaging or provocative, or any of the things another man might have done upon finding himself alone with an unmarried female. That was quite all right, she decided. If Mr. Thornton thought of her in any way other than as Felicity's chaperone, he would make it known in his own time. That was the way of things at his age and at hers. One did not get carried away.

Yet he did not seem to find the task of touring the castle with her unwelcome. For all his somberness, his expression had lightened this afternoon, as if he had regained a bit of his youth in their trek back through history. She was relieved when he did not pursue the matter of her ankle further.

"This part of the castle was built about the middle of the twelfth century," he said, pointing to the keep. "Stephen granted Robert Thornton the property in appreciation for his services during the civil wars."

"He fought on behalf of the king?"

Mr. Thornton nodded. "The Thorntons were notorious warriors, and it was said that whoever commanded their loyalty could claim the crown."

Amanda eyed him consideringly. "You seem to know a great deal about the castle."

"The castle's history is well known, since it was the site of Edward of Caernarvaron's murder," he replied. "My personal knowledge is not extensive, however. I came to the castle only a few months ago, when the earl inherited."

"How is it that you are related to the earl?"

Was that a flush on his face? Unlike many men, Mr. Thornton obviously did not like speaking about himself. Still, Amanda knew a small regret at his reserve. It was almost as if he did not wish to trust her with even so small a fact.

"It is one of those complicated connections," he replied vaguely. "I will not bore you with the details."

With a small, inward sigh, Amanda forced her attention back to the keep. She found herself staring at a red sandstone tower that looked as old as anything she had yet seen. "Is that where the notorious Edward met his doom?"

"Yes. Rather painfully and indelicately. Generations of Thorntons have claimed to hear his ghostly screams ringing through the castle at night."

"You will not persuade me that you believe in ghosts, sir," Amanda teased.

"Nor do I, Miss Fitzhugh," he replied. "I expect that the legend stems from popular disgust at the particularly inhumane manner of Edward's death. Reports of his ghastly suffering turned opinion against his queen, Isabella, who earned the epithet 'she-wolf of France' for deposing her husband, having him murdered, and flaunting her affair with her lover, Roger Mortimer. With such a reputation, I imagine she was fortunate to survive into old age."

Studying the ancient turrets, a feeling of unease passed over her. Amanda tried to shake it off. "And what of those dungeons you once spoke of?" she prodded. "Have they seen their share of ghostly wailing?"

"I know little about them," he said. "Legend has it that Isabella dispatched one of Edward's admirers to the dungeons when her husband refused to pay for her lavish birthday party. I believe the admirer escaped through one of the tunnels, as did some of the others who spent time in the cells over the centuries."

"Tunnels?" A thrill of excitement shot through her. "I should love to see them."

Mr. Thornton hesitated. "I would be reluctant to take you there. I am not sure they are safe."

"Are you worried on my behalf, Mr. Thornton, or yours?" Amanda challenged.

Far from producing a smile, this sally brought a grim expression to his eyes. "I understand that the Duke of Claridge is much occupied these days with searching the tunnels."

"Then I shall be happy to defer my own exploration of them until another time," Amanda said quickly.

A speculative gleam darkened his gaze, but he merely put out an arm to escort her up the path to the cliffs. For a time they walked in silence, drinking in the bracing sea air, the gulls' cries, and the waves' rhythmic roar. A strange breathlessness overwhelmed Amanda, and as much as she told herself the little hike up the path was to blame, a burgeoning anticipation within her suggested otherwise.

"The view past that ridge is one of the most extraordinary in all England—perhaps anywhere," he said quietly, pointing to a ridge a dozen or so yards ahead. "May I show it to you?"

Sea breezes ruffled Amanda's skirts as she nodded, leaning on him a bit when the uneven earth threatened her footing. Mr. Thornton possessed a steady, unflagging strength that rivaled Lord Sommersby's. Amanda could well believe that generations of Thorntons had been able warriors. Even past their prime, the men in this family radiated fortitude and competence.

There was something else Mr. Thornton shared with the earl. His strength, like Lord Sommersby's, carried a restraint that made her wonder what the Thornton men were like in battle, with their power unleashed. Each man seemed to have a keen awareness of his own might and the self-possession to control it. Yet their mercurial eyes made Amanda wonder whether the Thornton men ever lost that cool discipline.

Studying Mr. Thornton, she could not imagine that he would ever lose the steely solemnity that lent him such a remote air. As for the earl, except for that moment when he had leapt into Felicity's chamber like some barechested mythical warrior, he had never exposed the fierceness she suspected lurked beneath that civil veneer.

Amanda sighed. Why did she find the Thornton men— young and old—so fascinating? Perhaps it was the tantalizing fact that each man withheld himself a bit.

"Is your ankle bothering you?" Mr. Thornton asked, apparently taking her sigh for one of pain.

"Not at all," Amanda replied, leaning on her cane. In truth, her leg was struggling under the demands of the path's gentle ascent. But they were nearing the overlook, and she was determined to see the view, weak ankle or no.

Suddenly, she stumbled. Mr. Thornton quickly steadied her. Then her feet abruptly left the ground as he lifted her effortlessly into his arms and carried her the few remaining yards to the top of the cliff.

"I can walk well enough, sir," she protested, marveling even in her embarrassment that a man of his age managed such a task so easily.

"That may be," he conceded, avoiding her gaze, "but you have done enough for one afternoon."

Amid the pleasure of being nestled against that strong chest, Amanda was only dimly aware of reaching the overlook. The view might not have even existed, for suddenly she could not take her eyes from his face.

He set her on her feet—or rather, he tried to. In her daze, Amanda did not release her grip on his neck when he attempted to put her down. Her awkward slide down his front created a rather shocking intimacy between them.

Beneath the drooping mustache, Mr. Thornton's lips parted on a sharp intake of breath. A muscle constricted in his jaw. The hands that rested lightly around her waist stiffened, but did not relinquish her.

Deeply embarrassed, Amanda was nevertheless aware of a strange lightheadedness. There was a time and place for everything, and perhaps now was the time and place for Mr. Thornton to indicate whether he wished to deepen their acquaintance. It was no use denying that she found him attractive. Happily, he was neither betrothed to her cousin, nor a notorious rake with a past. Though they must both be mortified by the accidental intimacy, it had done no real harm. Indeed, it had loosed a rather reckless curiosity within her. As Amanda raised her gaze to his, she was half-hoping that his composed discipline had cracked.

It had not.

The mercurial eyes had gone to green, but they were as remote and unreadable as ever. And yet, and yet . . . within those depths lurked an amber spark that might have been anything, but which radiated a warmth that sent a tingling down to the very tips of her toes.

Amazing as it seemed—and she had not even dared to

think of the possibility of being kissed until this very moment—Mr Thornton's mouth lowered to hers.

Amanda felt the faint tickling of the mustache as his lips claimed hers, tentatively at first, then with increasing firmness. Closing her eyes, she allowed the kiss and the keening cry of the wind to transport her to a place unlike any she had visited with Julian LeFevre.

Dear lord! It was a world of magic—and, yes, *sentiment*—that sent her spirit soaring into territory poets had long explored but which she, Amanda Fitzhugh, had never dreamed existed. Her imagination caught flight. Her suddenly poetic heart swelled to wretched excess.

Surely they were the only people in the world to stand on this rocky precipice and feel their hearts pound in harmony with the roar of the surf and the kindred cry of a thousand gulls clamoring like souls driven to the edge of longing by one simple kiss under the brilliant sun.

Surely there had never been a moment like this one or a time when her pulse had thundered its passion so urgently. Surely there had never been another man like Mr. Thornton, with his gray hair and tired mustache and marvelous kisses that joined their lips in blazing fire.

For a sensible woman, it was an earth-shattering experience. In awe, Amanda clung to Mr. Thornton and his worn dimity as the sea winds swelled like a wordless symphony, eloquent as any of those flowery poems Felicity was so fond of.

It was as if she had discovered a woman that existed in another place, outside of the practical person she had worked so hard to become. Thinking was impossible. Touching was all that mattered, and she soaked up Mr. Thornton's touches as eagerly as a parched plant embraced the rain.

His hands roved restlessly over her, ministering to her body as expertly as the earl had once tended her wounded ankle. Perhaps age had lent him a vast amount of knowledge about such things, Amanda reflected weakly, unable to think of any other reason that his touch provoked such a burning deep inside her.

When his lips trailed down her neck, over her shoulders, and beneath the bodice that had opened under his probing

fingers, she moaned in pleasure. Helplessly, she submitted
to his caresses, offering anything he wished if he would just
satisfy this desperate desire within her.

But her moan seemed to awaken something in him. Before she could draw another faltering breath, he abruptly
stepped back to put distance between them.

Teetering, Amanda groped for her cane, which had fallen.
He thrust it into her hand and whirled away.

"Please forgive me," he said in an anguished tone. "I did
not mean to force myself on you like some animal."

"You did not force yourself on me." Amanda clutched
her cane and stared at that broad, rigid back. She wanted to
touch him, but dared not.

After a moment he turned, master of himself once more.
He cleared his throat. "I deeply regret my disregard for
your delicate sensibilities, Miss Fitzhugh."

The words sounded stilted—not at all like those of a
man's heart.

Amanda struggled to understand what had happened.
The fumbling encounter with Julian at Vauxhall had been
nothing like this—although it had provided intimations of
the terrifying secret she now discovered about herself.

In dawning despair, she realized the truth: Passion was in
her blood as surely as Mr. Thornton was standing before
her, apology and regret written on his face.

"'She-wolf!'"

*"Now, Isabella, calm yourself. It is nothing you have not
heard before."*

"Why does no one understand me, Mortimer?"

"I understand you, my dear. I always have."

"Edward never appreciated me."

"His interests lay elsewhere, Isabella."

*"I thought that after Warwick murdered Gaveston, all
that nonsense was over."*

*"It was never over, Isabella. Look what happened with
Hugh."*

*"Was it me, Mortimer? Was there something truly repul-
sive about me that he had to turn to other men for his pleasure?"*

"Edward was simply following his own nature, Isabella.

You should never have taken it personally. It had nothing to do with you."

"So you say, but no man has ever spurned me so thoroughly."

"Why dwell on what cannot be changed? You have me now."

"I am restless, Mortimer. I am tired of watching our tenant dance around the matter as if he had eternity."

"Considerable progress was made this afternoon, my dear."

"Granted. But not enough. I will warrant that at this very moment the man is putting himself through all manner of recriminations."

"What of it? You will win in the end. You always do."

"I grow weary of waiting. If we let things be, he will drape himself in that discipline in which he so prides himself and that will be the end of it. We will act tonight."

"You can only manipulate so much about a man, Isabella. In the end, we all must follow the dictates of our natures. Look at Edward."

"I am looking at him. Now that I think on it, there may be a role for Edward in all of this."

"You will never get him to agree."

"You underestimate me, Mortimer. You have forgotten about the duke."

"Claridge? What has he to do with Edward?"

"You shall see, dearest. Meanwhile, tonight we drop in on our sleeping guests."

Chapter Eleven

Simon sat up in bed. He had had the dream again, the one where carnage lay all around him, where all that remained of the brave soldiers who had plunged so valiantly into the fray of clashing swords and thundering cannons were bloody bits of flesh and bone.

During the war, the dream had been as constant a companion as death. What triggered it tonight Simon did not know, but he awoke as he always did with a desperate thirst for life. On such nights he usually roused Jeffers for a blistering bout with the foils.

Strangely, tonight there had been a woman on the battlefield. She had appeared at the edge of the cornfield, walking sadly among the broken soldiers, looking for any glimmer of life. Simon had lain among the bodies, all but dead himself.

When she came to him, she stopped. He could feel her staring at him, assessing. He wanted to cry out that he lived, that he needed her help, but he could not move nor even open his mouth to whisper his plea. Miraculously, she heard it anyway. Bending down, she touched his face so gently it might have been the wind brushing by. Her lips, so sweet they banished the pain, met his. Blood flowed in his veins again. The life force bubbled within him, reawakened by the angel's healing touch.

Reaching up, he tried to stay her progress, but she moved on. Simon struggled to his feet and lurched across the field after her. Desperate for that golden touch and life-giving breath, he did not care that he was unworthy of her. He wanted her as he had wanted nothing else.

Simon rubbed his eyes as he sat in bed and pondered the images that had pulled him from sleep. It required no special insight to see that his dreams were tormenting him for kissing Miss Fitzhugh. What a fool he had been—pretending that masquerading as Thornton would allow him to protect her from Julian, then acting like a rakehell himself. To make things more ridiculous, Julian had not shown his face all day. The only one Miss Fitzhugh needed protection from, it seemed, was himself.

The moment their lips had touched, Simon had realized how much he had wanted that kiss all along. Putting her from him had required a supreme effort. He wanted to make love to her with the wind and the salt air swirling around them. He wanted to wrap himself in merciful oblivion to anything that was not Amanda Fitzhugh.

In the guise of protecting her, he had given license to his lust.

Simon had never succumbed to passion to the exclusion of all other considerations. When he had a woman, it was a woman who wanted to be had. Never had he allowed desire to compromise honor. Honor was all a man had. That, and control. They kept a man civilized.

But what was a man to do when those things failed him?

What he must. Grimly, Simon reached for his breeches. Jeffers would not mind a little nocturnal match. Not when the sanity of his employer depended on it. He ripped open his door, determined to exorcise a few demons.

And froze.

At the other end of the corridor, a figure paused in the act of emerging from one of the bedchambers. Instinctively, Simon withdrew into the shadows. The man looked around, but did not see him. Creeping furtively down the hall, the man entered another room, presumably his own.

Shock and horror gripped Simon as he realized the identity of that slinking figure: Julian LeFevre.

The room from which he had emerged in the middle of the night was Miss Fitzhugh's.

Amanda had not been able to shake the feeling that something was amiss. Perhaps it was only that awful painting with the gory battle scene that disturbed her sleep. Perhaps it was the massive wardrobe with the burled grain that resembled sinister eyes. Or perhaps it was only her own conscience, reminding her that today she had behaved shamelessly, throwing herself on Mr. Thornton like some wanton woman of the streets.

Strangely, kissing him and feeling his hands rove over her so intimately provoked none of the fear she had felt with Julian at Vauxhall—only an exultant thrill as he led her into a world of blinding sensation.

Amanda shook her head in disgust. Apparently, her imagination was every bit as fanciful as Felicity's. For a moment on that cliff, she had allowed herself to believe that fairy tales did come true, after all.

Poor Mr. Thornton! Would she ever be able to face him again? She had virtually offered herself to him in full view of anyone who might happen by. Why?

There could be only one answer. She had deluded herself in thinking that eight years of living like a virtual hermit could control a wanton nature like hers. In truth, she had neither will nor strength to resist even so fatherly a masculine specimen as Mr. Thornton.

Was there no end to her depravity? Even now, her disgraceful imagination took flight as the moonlight caught the figures on the frieze near her bed. At first they were a perfectly respectable group of dancing lords and ladies; as she studied them, however, they began to cavort wildly and perform licentious acts.

Blinking, Amanda tried to banish the images, but others more arousing came to mind: Mr. Thornton's sensuous lips under that drooping mustache, his strong and seductive hands, a firmly muscled chest age had in no way diminished.

Could she be in love with him? That way led to disaster, for he had regretted that kiss today as deeply as he had ever regretted anything. His eyes had radiated a shocked sorrow more eloquent than any words.

Punching her pillow in angry frustration, Amanda vowed to go to him tomorrow and apologize for her actions. Somehow they would manage to avoid each other for the duration of her visit.

Gradually, her spirit calmed. Everything always seemed worse at night. Tomorrow, what had happened on the cliff would not seem so disastrous. The images that tormented her tonight would vanish, life would resume its normal character, and she would once more be a sensible woman.

No doubt the oppressive atmosphere of the castle had unsettled her. She must remember that it was only an old pile of stones, harmless and inanimate.

Before she could draw sufficient comfort from that thought, however, an abrupt creaking of hinges in her room sent her heart to her throat. In horror, Amanda watched as the doors to her wardrobe swung open.

Two hands emerged, followed by the distinctly masculine form to which they were attached. A figure stepped out of the wardrobe and into her bedchamber.

She gasped.

A slow smile spread over the man's face. As that cruel, slashing mouth curved upward, Amanda knew she was in grave danger.

No woman lying helpless in her bed had any hope for mercy from Julian LeFevre.

Sir Thomas Biddle was having a restless night. Every time he closed his eyes, disturbing images beset him. A deep uneasiness startled him awake just as sleep threatened to plunge him into what surely was to be a nightmare.

Yet when he sat up in bed, thoughts as troubling as those unsettling images plagued him. He wondered what Eloise was doing this very moment, whether she was sleeping a blameless sleep or, like him, tossing restlessly in bed.

Was she alone in that bed? He fervently hoped so. He had always told himself that his jealous misgivings stemmed from the sort of groundless fears that plagued a husband with the bad judgment to fall in love with his wife. But tonight he could not erase the tormenting image of Eloise and Dr. Greenfield locked in each other's arms with him miles away.

Sir Thomas give himself a mental shake. Eloise had always been a faithful wife. Moreover, Dr. Greenfield was a fool, and she had never taken to fools. As for the nightmare he feared he was about to have, dreams had no substance so he might as well get it over with. With a yawn, he closed his eyes in resignation.

He could almost taste Eloise's lips on his. From that first

time in his closed carriage, he had always been a slave to her kisses. She was the most passionate woman he had ever known. And yet lately she had held some of herself back. There was a remoteness in her eyes, something beyond his reach.

Now the images were growing clearer. Eloise lay languorously on the divan in her chamber, a smile upon her face, her eyes closed in pure enjoyment. Long, masculine fingers massaged her ankle, then crept to her calves to that tender spot behind her knees. When they moved up even farther, Eloise gave a purr of delight.

Opening her eyes, she smiled. Sir Thomas beamed. It was that special smile, the one reserved for him alone in the moment before their bodies joined. Pulling him closer, she fumbled with his clothing, urging him on.

Soon they were both naked. Her wild cry of exultation sent shivers of delight through him. Eloise had never seemed so passionate, so eager. Even though he knew it was a dream, the experience was as vivid as life.

Yet something was wrong. He wondered why he did not feel her under him, why he felt detached from the intimate scene as if he were watching it from a corner of the room.

And then he knew.

The man with her was not the balding baronet who had known her intimately these many years.

It was Greenfield who lay with the woman Sir Thomas had known for half a lifetime, and who had come to him so passionately in his carriage so many years ago. It was Greenfield she held in her arms, Greenfield she urged on with eager hands and helpless moans.

Greenfield. He heard the name in his ear like a whispered sigh.

Sir Thomas awoke in a cold sweat.

"Good morning, Amanda. What a happy accident to find you here."

"Accident?" Amanda stared at Julian indignantly. "This is *my* room, sir. The question is, what are you doing here?"

Knowing that he would quickly take advantage of any weakness, Amanda was pleased that her voice betrayed no anxiety at his sudden appearance in her bedchamber.

To her surprise, Julian seemed somewhat preoccupied as he pulled a kerosene lantern from the wardrobe and slowly inspected the room.

Grabbing her robe, Amanda slipped out of bed. "What in the world are you doing?" she demanded.

"Looking for something."

"At this hour? You must be mad. I insist that you leave immediately."

Julian's black gaze met hers. "There was a time when you had not the courage to defy me," he said in a taunting tone. "Or the will, I might add."

"I have no wish to dwell on past mistakes," Amanda retorted. "I will scream and wake the entire castle if you do not leave this very moment."

A distant look appeared in his eyes. "Did you know that this was once my room, Amanda?"

Warily, she shook her head.

"I have spent the day prowling the caves and tunnels. I was not certain I remembered the way to this room until I saw the door on the other side of the wardrobe."

Amanda did not know what to say. She eyed the inside of the wardrobe and the yawning tunnel opening that looked as if it went on forever. "It must have been awfully dark in there," she ventured.

"Not really. Smugglers used to store their loot in the caves, so there are quite a few sconces and lanterns." Abruptly, he turned away. "I am looking for some old family papers I think may be hidden down there."

"Family papers?" Amanda eyed him curiously.

"Mementos, really. Let us just say that I am nostalgic about the past."

Throughout their mercifully brief acquaintance, Julian had never been forthcoming about his family or history, but Amanda doubted that nostalgia had driven him back to his boyhood home. Julian never did anything that did not arise from his own selfish whims. But she did not challenge him. Her only goal was to get him out of her room.

A bitter smile distorted his features as he read her distrust. "You know," he said softly, "I never did finish what I started in the meadow."

He moved toward her, the tunnels forgotten for the moment. "Eight years ago, Amanda, you were a frightened rabbit. The years seem to have brought you a woman's awareness. Perhaps you now appreciate what we might offer each other."

Amanda stepped away. "Please leave."

"I do not think you mean that," he challenged softly.

Defiantly, she lifted her chin. "Your monstrous pride leads you astray, Julian. You had best leave now. I daresay Lord Sommersby would not like to hear that you molested one of his guests."

To her surprise, he laughed. "No. A man with Simon's stifling sense of duty would have to issue a challenge. And while I fought by his side at Salamanca, I should not like to be on the other end of his sword."

The image of Lord Sommersby poised on the balcony in Felicity's room, broadsword at the ready, brought a small answering smile to her lips. Julian noticed it instantly.

"Ah, so that is the way of things, is it? The chaperone has an eye for her charge's betrothed."

Amanda flushed. "Why must you assume that everyone has your base nature, Julian?"

"Why must you assume that I am blind?"

Crossing her arms, Amanda regarded him angrily. "If you do not leave this instant . . ."

Before she could continue, he strode toward the door, opening it so soundlessly that she suspected sneaking out of ladies' bedchambers was second nature to him.

"Let me give you some advice, Amanda," he said. "It would be futile to pin your hopes on Sommersby. The man has a dreadfully oppressive sense of honor."

A sardonic smile flicked over that slashing mouth and vanished with him in the darkened hallway.

Through narrowed eyes, Simon studied the departing figure. There could be no benign explanation for Julian's presence in Miss Fitzhugh's room. He had a mind to call the man to account here and now, but the possibility that she had entertained Julian willingly stopped him.

Yet she had this very day expressed a reluctance to visit the tunnels while Julian explored them. Why would she welcome Julian to her room under the cover of night?

If Julian had harmed her in any way, he would rip the man to pieces. First, however, he had to discover whether she was all right. He frowned. He could not simply present himself at her door and inquire whether the Duke of Claridge, with whom she shared some murky amorous history, had just had his way with her. Besides, he was supposed to be away overseeing one of his troubled mills.

It would have to be Thornton again.

Scowling, Simon threw open the bureau drawer and pulled out the infernal mustache and wig. After what happened on the cliff today, Thornton's appearance at her bedroom door would seem a brazen attempt at seduction.

And seduction was certainly not what he had in mind.

Not at all.

Chapter Twelve

The gentle tapping at her door sent panic rising in Amanda's throat. So Julian meant to try again, did he? The man was so puffed up with his own consequence that he could not conceive of a woman denying him.

Ripping off the bedcovers and throwing on her robe, Amanda ran to the hearth, picked up the poker, and strode to the door.

"I am prepared to defend myself, sirrah," she cried. "If you do not go away this instant, I shall not be responsible for the results!" Her words would not strike fear into Julian's heart, but they might give him pause.

Amanda waited for one of Julian's sardonic insults. Instead, after a prolonged silence, there came the sound of a throat clearing.

"Miss Fitzhugh?" asked a low baritone voice. "Are you all right?"

Mr. Thornton!

Relief warred with embarrassment—what must he think of the threat she had just hurled at him?

Hesitantly, Amanda opened the door. Mr. Thornton stood in his claret dressing gown, holding a small candle perilously close to that long, drooping mustache. His gray mop of hair suggested a less than restful night of sleep.

Meeting his gaze took her aback, for his eyes belied the politely inquiring tones of his voice. Indeed, they radiated a dangerous volatility that momentarily put her in mind of Julian.

"Mr. Thornton," Amanda stammered. "Yes, I am quite well." As an afterthought, she added awkwardly, "Thank you for inquiring."

His gaze flicked over her, taking in every detail from her

bare feet to the delicate lace peeking out from under her robe to the disordered state of her hair that made her wish for a nightcap.

To be sure, there was a world of difference between Julian and Mr. Thornton. Yet as she drew her robe more tightly around her, Amanda detected an unsettling spark in his eyes that resembled nothing so much as Julian's frank sensuality. Even as she noticed it, however, that intriguing spark dimmed.

"I knocked because I heard someone in the hall." He paused. "Actually, I thought I saw someone . . . in the vicinity of your door."

It was not quite an accusation, but Amanda knew he must have seen Julian leave and come to the worst possible conclusion. Would he believe her if she told him that Julian had suddenly emerged from her wardrobe, chatted briefly, then left to continue whatever nefarious pursuits drove him to wander about in the middle of the night? Probably not, but she wanted him to know that things were not the way they seemed. She took a deep breath.

"You will perhaps think this strange, sir, but Claridge did in fact just leave my room."

One brow shot skyward in silent but eloquent commentary.

"It is not like it sounds," she added quickly. "You see, he just . . . popped out of my wardrobe."

This time his look was frankly dubious.

"The back of the wardrobe seems to be an entrance to one of the tunnels," she continued, feeling more foolish by the minute. "Evidently he has been searching them for some papers." Smiling brightly, she added, "Did you know this was Julian's room as a boy?"

From his position out in the hall, Mr. Thornton peered skeptically at the wardrobe.

"Would you like to see?" she asked, desperate to persuade him that she was telling the truth, that she would never have willingly entertained Julian in her room.

Now his eyes looked anywhere but at her. "I believe I would," he said in a carefully neutral tone.

Some chaperone she was turning out to be, Amanda

thought wildly as, for the second time that night, a man stepped into her bedchamber.

Unlike Julian, Mr. Thornton undoubtedly had the best of intentions. Still, the kiss they had shared earlier had put their relationship on a rather awkward footing. As he stood a scant few feet from her bed, the air in the room seemed suddenly stifling. Amanda wondered whether he, too, was thinking of that moment out on the cliff.

As if she were wearing her most sedate walking dress, Amanda walked matter-of-factly to the wardrobe. "The back opens into the tunnel," she said, probing the rear panel in hopes of finding the entrance before Mr. Thornton concluded she had bats in her belfry.

She gave a sigh of relief as her fingers met a small groove. The thick panel swung outward, unveiling a gaping blackness beyond. Taking his candle, Mr. Thornton stepped into the yawning void. Amanda followed.

Candlelight illuminated a ceiling barely high enough for him to stand. In some places crumbling stones had fallen from the walls, but otherwise the tunnel looked in relatively good condition, considering its probable age. Amanda wondered what sort of intrigue it had seen over the years. "Have you ever explored here?" she asked.

"No. But with Claridge prowling around at night, I suppose I had best take a look." With that, he walked deeper into the tunnel. The glow of his candle faded until Amanda found herself alone in the dark.

"Mr. Thornton?" she called uneasily.

There was no response. Amanda stood motionless, undecided whether to retreat to her room, follow him into the darkness, or remain where she was.

No sounds of footsteps met her ears, no reassuring noises indicated Mr. Thornton was nearby. Since she could no longer see her own hand in front of her face, Amanda decided she must turn back. Wishing she had her cane, she edged her way toward the faint light filtering through the wardrobe from her room. Her pulse pounded nervously. When a deep voice pierced the silence, she gave a little shriek.

"Careful, Miss Fitzhugh. The footing is very uneven."

Amanda whirled. She felt rather than saw the broad chest

before her and the penetrating eyes that regarded her solemnly.

"Mr. Thornton! You gave me quite a start." Amanda took a deep, calming breath.

"Forgive me," he said quietly. "A draft put out my candle, so I had to retrace my steps. Exploration of the tunnel will have to wait for another day."

Grasping her elbow, he guided her smoothly along the darkened corridor. In the next moment, they stood in her room—she in her robe and bare feet, he in his claret dressing gown.

"Thank you for coming to investigate, Mr. Thornton," Amanda said, wondering whether he felt the bizarreness of this night as acutely as she did.

But he was studying the back panel of the wardrobe intently. "There is a deadbolt, Miss Fitzhugh. I should keep it locked so that you do not have to worry about another unexpected visit."

"I think Julian was as surprised as I when he entered my room," she replied, managing a smile. "I am sure he will not do so again."

"There is no way of predicting Claridge's actions," he said, his eyes suddenly gone to blue ice. "Unless you welcome his nocturnal visits, you should take appropriate steps to prevent them."

Anger at his implication shot through her. "I am not certain how to respond to such a statement, sir," she said coolly.

Instantly, his gaze grew shuttered. "Your relationship with the duke is none of my business, of course," he said stiffly. "I regret causing you any discomfort." He turned to go.

Panic raced through Amanda. She could not let him leave with this strained awkwardness between them. Mr. Thornton might not be one for lengthy conversation, but the kiss he had given her this afternoon had spoken volumes about the possibilities that lay between them. Those possibilities had nurtured a small hope she did not know she possessed. For the first time in eight years, she allowed herself to think of a man in such a light.

Suddenly, she wanted him to know everything.

"Mr. Thornton," she began, flushing. "Julian and I once—that is, we once had a relationship of sorts."

"It is none of my concern, Miss Fitzhugh." By his rigid posture, Amanda knew that the subject made him acutely uncomfortable. Nevertheless, she did not believe in sweeping things under the rug. She wanted no lies that might come between them, no dishonesty that might sabotage that hope. If there was one thing she had learned from the experience with Julian, it was the value of truth.

"I am not a sinful woman, only an unwise one," she blurted out. "Claridge—Lord Ramsey then—was a frequent caller during my Season eight years ago. I am afraid that I allowed his flattery to blind me to his true goal. I failed to realize that the niece of a baronet is not exactly an eligible *parti* for a man in line for a dukedom."

"Miss Fitzhugh," he protested, reddening, "there is no need to—"

"But there is," she interrupted, willing him to understand. "I nearly disgraced myself. Without the knowledge of my aunt and uncle, who were sponsoring my Season, I arranged to meet him at Vauxhall one night. I thought the idea of a walk through the garden paths most romantic, but I soon discovered he had something else in mind."

Under that mustache, a muscle tightened in Mr. Thornton's jaw. His expression remained unreadable. Before she could lose her nerve, Amanda rushed on.

"He led me down the furthermost promenade known as Lover's Walk. Foolishly, I made no protest. I was flattered that a man of Lord Ramsey's standing should wish for a few private moments with me." She studied her hands. "We came to a bench, and that is where I invited disaster. I allowed him to kiss me, and—"

"Miss Fitzhugh," he interrupted hastily, "please spare yourself this ordeal. It is not necessary, I assure you."

"But it is," Amanda protested. "Fortunately, Sir Thomas came along searching for me and discovered us there. My clothing was scandalously askew and Julian was taking extensive . . . liberties, but no real harm was done."

She broke off, biting her lip. "It was extremely mortifying, but the episode was kept quiet. I fled to the country, where I have lived ever since. Quite happily, I might add," she added somewhat defiantly.

Mr. Thornton's brows drew together like thunderclouds. "Did no one make the knave own up to his responsibility?"

"If you are referring to marriage, I could not have accepted a man of Lord Ramsey's character. Sir Thomas was torn between his obligation to demand a wedding and the obvious fact that marriage to Julian would be a trial for any woman. In the end, my uncle acceded to my wishes. I simply wanted to leave London and never return."

"And yet you are returning—as Miss Biddle's chaperone."

"With Lady Biddle indisposed, I had no other choice. Felicity needs a woman's presence."

"I will ask Claridge to leave on the morrow." Mr. Thornton's eyes glinted so fiercely that Amanda was instantly put in mind of his warrior cousin. "On the earl's behalf, that is," he added.

"That is not necessary," she insisted. "I have recently realized that over the years I allowed the episode to take on a dimension larger than itself. In truth, he can hold no power over me that I do not confer, and I have decided to grant him none. So you see, Mr. Thornton, seeing Julian again has actually been beneficial."

Eyeing her dubiously, he did not immediately respond. "Was there anything in particular," he asked at last, "that made you decide Claridge has no power over you?"

"I . . . am not sure," she said. It seemed the most natural thing in the world to be discussing such an intimate matter with Mr. Thornton in her dimly lit bedchamber. There was something extraordinarily powerful at work between them— the quickening of her pulse told her more than anything else the folly of deluding herself about that. Even if she had simply transferred to him her inappropriate attraction to the earl, the mesmerizing electricity between them was genuine.

Perhaps she had misread the regret he had expressed this afternoon after that kiss. Perhaps he only meant to convey his fear that he was rushing his fences.

"A man's character is of more importance to me than his

titles and charm, Mr. Thornton," Amanda added, shyly meeting his gaze.

"Miss Fitzhugh, there is something you should know," he began in a strained voice.

His awkwardness was truly endearing. One would almost think that he too felt shy. But before she could set him at ease, he spoke again. "I cannot tell you how deeply I regret what passed between us this afternoon. It was a grave lapse in discipline on my part. I would not for the world add to that suffering you have already endured at Claridge's hands."

Relief shot through her as she realized how worried he was that his advances had offended her. His considerateness gave her courage. Her fragile hope took wing. Yet, staring into Mr. Thornton's troubled eyes, Amanda knew she would have to take the lead.

"It is not at all the same, Mr. Thornton," she assured him. "I did not take offense." She hesitated, blushing. "If anything, I enjoyed that kiss rather too much."

When heat flared in his gaze, her pulse gave a little hop-skip.

"I am a plainspoken woman," she continued, her courage bolstered by the way his eyes suddenly went to green. "So I shall tell you that although I am not accustomed to kissing gentlemen in such a fashion, I was amazed at the . . . thoroughness of my response."

She took a deep breath. "I would not be averse to continuing our friendship, Mr. Thornton, providing any further intimacy between us could be . . . restrained until such time as our acquaintance warrants it."

Dear lord. Had she just invited an offer of marriage? That was the only way he could take her words. Incredible as it seemed, she had brazenly confessed to enjoying the sort of scandalous kiss unacceptable to all but married couples. Never had she felt so vulnerable. He must think her incapable of feminine subtlety. The world seemed to hang in the balance as she waited for his response.

Mr. Thornton looked as stunned and shocked as any man could. Yet Amanda did not think she misread the almost wistful longing in his eyes. Perhaps he, too, was eager to get to know her better, to explore whatever common ground they shared. Perhaps beneath Mr. Thornton's drooping mustache and gray hair lay the passion of a far younger man—a man who wished to know her more intimately and, above all, to repeat the experience of that kiss.

Yes, she thought as his gaze dropped to her mouth, Mr. Thornton was a man of passion. A woman did not need a great deal of experience to see that.

Anticipation made her every nerve stand on end. She smiled encouragingly.

"Miss Fitzhugh," he began, a tortured expression on his face. "I hold you in great esteem, but I cannot offer anything but my deepest regrets for what happened today. I have other . . . obligations. My intentions to you, therefore, cannot be honorable, nor can I allow our acquaintance to continue."

Amanda blinked. Her smile froze.

"I cannot but mourn my irresponsible behavior, which generated unexpected and unacceptable expectations in both of us," he added. "My actions can only be judged as heinous in view of your unfortunate experience with Claridge. I would not for the world cause you pain, nor give you reason to despise another member of my sex. But I fear that now I have no other choice. Good night, Miss Fitzhugh."

With that, he bowed deeply. Amanda stared in amazement as he turned on his heel and, without another word, left her chamber.

Her fragile hope had become an unthinkable nightmare.

Grimly eyeing the door through which he departed, Amanda hoped fervently that Mr. Thornton's sleep would be as tormented as her own.

Chapter Thirteen

Stephen Frakes cradled the worn binding in his hands and bashfully eyed his audience. Then, in a sonorous voice that wrapped around the words as lovingly as his hands cradled that old binding, he read:

> "There is a garden in her face
> Where roses and white lilies grow;
> A heavenly paradise is that place
> Wherein all pleasant fruits do flow.
> There cherries grow which none may buy,
> Till 'cherry-ripe' themselves do cry."

Felicity dabbed a handkerchief at the corner of her eye. "That was beautiful, Mr. Frakes. Though I suppose some might disdain the sentiment as excessive."

A troubled expression shadowed his deep brown eyes. "The words of a man's heart are nothing to disdain, Miss Biddle."

"No," she agreed quickly. "Oh, do continue, Mr. Frakes. I declare you have discovered my favorite poets. Though perhaps it is only the magnificent way in which you read. You have quite a gift."

Flushing, he replaced the book on the library shelf, removed another volume, then hesitated. "Are you certain that I am not keeping you from something important?"

"It is I who am keeping you from your work, Mr. Frakes," Felicity replied, her mouth pursing in concern. It was quite true. Since discovering that she and Mr. Frakes shared a mutual love of poetry, she had not been able to stop herself from visiting him daily to hear him read. His voice was not stuffy and stentorian like some orators, but rich and resonant in a way that did not overwhelm the poet's word, allowing them to shine in all their magnificence.

Perhaps she was spending too much time in Lord Sommersby's library, but the earl was away and Mr. Thornton had been occupied with Amanda. Felicity wondered if a match was in the offing in that quarter. She hoped so. Amanda did not deserve to spend the rest of her days as a spinster, no matter how willingly she pretended to embrace her fate. Happily, the Duke of Claridge had not put in an appearance for several days—although that left her father as the only other person to engage in conversation, and he had been in a brooding mood of late.

Felicity did not see why she should feel guilty for seeking out the only other person in the castle who appreciated the fine literature on Lord Sommersby's shelves. The earnest Mr. Frakes was only slightly older than herself, and he did not appear to mind her intrusions. Indeed, he seemed to welcome the break from his labors that her visits afforded. She had become so comfortable with him that she had even taken to wearing her spectacles so that they might read together. So enjoyable were these occasions that the time whirled by.

A diligent scholar, Mr. Frakes had begun arriving earlier and earlier each day to compensate for the hours he spent away from his work during her visits. Yet Felicity did not flatter herself that his interest in her went beyond their shared appreciation of literature. Everyone in the castle knew that she was betrothed to the earl; she would not do Mr. Frakes the dishonor of suspecting his interest to be anything personal.

And though Mr. Frakes was attractive enough, Lord Sommersby was the hero of her dreams, a man of imposing physical attributes, whose achievements were nigh legendary. Felicity wondered how the earl would react if he discovered how much time she spent with Mr. Frakes.

Not that Lord Sommersby had any reason to be jealous. Mr. Frakes's light brown hair was rather thin on top, even though he was not as advanced in years as Mr. Thornton, who still possessed a full mop of hair. Nor did Mr. Frakes have the earl's imposing build, but then that was to be expected of a man who spent his days inside with books and papers.

Aside from his voice, his eyes were quite the nicest thing about Mr. Frakes. Dark brown, they bore a sincere and appealing openness. Both vulnerability and courage lay in their depths, suggesting that Mr. Frakes would not be at a loss for words when it came to expressing his feelings.

The woman who merited Mr. Frakes's adoration would be very lucky, Felicity decided. She suspected he felt emotions deeply and would not shy from making them known. Even though it was not appropriate for a couple to display their ardor, Felicity suspected that whoever married Mr. Frakes would bask in his loving and passionate attention for the rest of her days.

Sighing, she adjusted her position on the divan and looked up wistfully as he began to read once more.

"What is wrong with these people?"

"If you are referring to our tenant, Isabella, it is clear that he is a man of principle."

"I have no use for a man who does not claim his pleasure where he finds it."

"But he is betrothed to another."

"I thought he would put aside his scruples when he disguised himself as Thornton again. The chaperone does not know he is the earl, so what is the harm?"

"But he knows. Not everyone plays to an audience, Isabella. Some people truly possess convictions."

"That is a ridiculous notion. Oh, Mortimer, I was so looking forward to being together again in the flesh. When she let him into her room, I thought it was just a matter of time."

"There is only so much we can do to manipulate a person's will, Isabella. Even controlling their dreams only takes us so far."

"We must persevere! Why, look how well that young scholar and the Biddle chit get on—even without our assistance. I'll warrant they are in bed before the week is out."

"Not everyone moves from friendship to carnal delight as quickly as you, my dear. But if you are so certain that the young people's attraction will blossom into passion,

why do we not inhabit their bodies instead of fretting over our tenant and his principles?"

"What? And look at that balding pate while I am savoring the first real passion in five hundred years? You must be joking. Now, our tenant is a man to truly fire one's passion. I can think of no other form I would wish to see you inhabit for our delightful interlude."

"Are you certain it is still I whom you want, Isabella? Or have you formed an attraction for our tenant?"

"Do not be ridiculous. You are the only one for me."

"Actually, there were several dozen others, as I recall."

"That was centuries ago, Mortimer. Where are they now, I ask you?"

"In a far happier state than we, my dear."

"If only Edward would rouse himself. I had hoped that Claridge would give him inspiration. But it seems that he only wishes to sit around and feel sorry for himself."

"A man does not easily forget being cooked alive on a spit, Isabella."

"I never meant for his death to be quite so painful. Do you think that if I apologized he would help us with our little plan?"

"Why should he? So you and I can enjoy each other once more? I daresay that prospect holds no appeal for him."

"But he never cared who I was with in life, Mortimer. I cannot think he minds now."

"Do not tamper with what is. Our existence, joyless as it is, could very well be worse."

"Nonsense."

"You were never one to let well enough alone, Isabella."

Amanda regarded a particularly lethal-looking stiletto hanging on the wall. One thrust of its triangular-shaped blade would make any man's plea for mercy his last. She hoped Felicity would be able to make some changes so that the castle did not resemble a medieval torture chamber.

Torture sounded rather appealing, however, when she thought of Mr. Thornton. To think that she had actually indicated her receptiveness to his suit, when all the while he had merely been toying with her. Obligations, indeed!

To be sure, he had not seemed like a dishonorable man.

He had not forced himself upon her, nor taken advantage of her momentary madness. But after a night of strange and erotic dreams in which she envisioned him cavorting daringly with a queenly beauty, Amanda was ready to believe the worst of him. Even now, the lovers' antics brought a blush to her face.

Clearly, Mr. Thornton was no better than any other reprobate. Any man who could kiss her as thoroughly as he had done yesterday, invade her bedchamber, elicit her embarrassing confession about that night in Vauxhall, and firmly reject her offer of a respectable relationship was up to no good.

The facts—that *she* had virtually initiated that kiss on the cliff, invited him into her room, and blurted out that confession—did not excuse his behavior.

Grimly, Amanda tried to envision the stiletto stuck between Mr. Thornton's ribs. Instantly, she felt ashamed. The poor man was probably not accustomed to women throwing themselves at him.

Why had she behaved so desperately, exposing her most vulnerable self, admitting that his kiss affected her profoundly? Could it be that she had not given up on wedded bliss after all? Could it be that a small part of her did believe in heroes who could sweep her off her feet?

Why had the practical, unsentimental woman she had worked so hard to become suddenly lose her capacity for reason? And why, even now amid her embarrassment and anger, did she pine for Mr. Thornton's kisses?

"I see you are studying the misericorde."

Amanda whirled as the voice intruded on her thoughts as sharply as a thrust from that lethal blade on the wall.

"Were you perhaps thinking of using it on me?" Mr. Thornton queried with a rueful smile. "I could not say that I blame you."

Towering a full head above her, he stood solemnly at her elbow. The brown dimity, unprepossessing as it was, did nothing to detract from the undeniable impact of his presence. Amanda's every nerve stood on end, as if an electric current sizzled in the air between them.

"My interest in the dagger is quite benign," she said as calmly as she could. "I was merely wondering why the earl chooses to display such barbaric weapons. It is somewhat akin to mounting the heads of one's opponents on the wall as trophies, is it not?" Feeling rather like a discarded trophy herself, Amanda could not feel the bitter tone from her voice.

He frowned. "I am sure the earl's ancestors merely intended to establish a collection that future scholars might study."

"Perhaps. But I should think scholars could study them better in a museum. Hanging here in the castle, they are childish vanities that pay homage to war and the fighting prowess of the Thornton men."

Mr. Thornton blanched. "I assure you, the present earl had no intention of creating a monument to his fighting skills."

"Then he would not find it burdensome to remove these artifacts and donate them to the museum."

Crossing her arms, Amanda met his gaze defiantly, only to shift uncomfortably as a speculative glint appeared in his eyes.

"Why do I have the feeling that it is not the earl's weaponry that truly preoccupies you?" he said softly.

Now it was Amanda's turn to pale. "I do not know what you mean."

His gaze moved to the dagger. "That stiletto you so admire was capable of a deadly thrust through mail or the gaps between armor plate."

Puzzled at his abrupt change of subject, Amanda nevertheless frowned in distaste. "So it was used to finish a man off," she concluded.

"Not necessarily. A knight who had been otherwise disarmed might use the dagger as his last defense."

"You seem to know a great deal about the collection, Mr. Thornton," Amanda observed coolly. "As much, I would say, as the earl himself."

"I have been with him for a long time," he replied, speaking more to the wall than to her.

Suddenly, he met her gaze. "There is something you should know, Miss Fitzhugh," he said, an undercurrent lending the low baritone a rippling intensity.

"If this is another confession about your 'obligations,'"

Amanda retorted, determined not to be swayed by that mesmerizing energy, "I had just as soon not hear it."

He flinched, but did not look away. "I wish to inform you that I am leaving today, as my presence here has become a burden for you." Despite her anger, Amanda could not suppress a stark sense of dismay.

"I do not like to leave you alone with Claridge," he continued, "although I expect the earl to return shortly."

"You need not worry on my account." Amanda strove for a careless tone. "Sir Thomas is here, and at all events Claridge does not concern me in the least."

Fire simmered in his gaze. "Promise me you will latch the back of your wardrobe."

"Do not trouble yourself on my behalf, Mr. Thornton. I am quite capable of handling Claridge. I have had years to think about *that* mistake." She gave him a pointed look. "It is my more recent missteps that give me pause."

Suddenly his hand, surprisingly gentle, came to rest on her shoulder. "Miss Fitzhugh," he said quietly, "there is nothing I wish more than to have yesterday undone."

The pain in his eyes surprised her. "Nothing has been done that a few good nights of sleep will not remedy." Amanda forced a smile. "Making a fool of myself is not pleasant, but it is not as though I have never done so."

"I never meant to kiss you," he said hoarsely.

"Alas, that is the difference between us, sir," she replied breezily. "For I *did* mean to kiss you."

Amanda took a rather perverse satisfaction in his stunned expression. "Good-bye, Mr. Thornton," she said. "Despite what has happened, I regret not one moment of that kiss."

As she turned on her heel, Amanda heard him emit an anguished sound. For a moment she almost pitied him. He was obviously in the throes of some deep, dark struggle.

It struck her that she did not even know his given name.

Staring at the misericorde, Simon felt its blade in his heart as surely as if Miss Fitzhugh had ripped the knife from the wall and stabbed it into his chest.

Her courage shamed him. Her forthrightness leveled him like a deadly blow. It was as if they had met on the field of battle and the strength of her character had left him mortally wounded.

Her honesty radiated like a shimmering beacon. Her frank admission about the kiss sent his soul soaring to heavenly heights even as it left him wallowing in the hellish depths of his own duplicity.

She was a woman of extraordinary courage, standing fast to her principles, yet unafraid to admit her past mistakes, her failures, her vulnerabilities. Her fearless offer of deeper friendship to Thornton humbled him, gutted his defenses, leaving him like that fifteenth-century knight with only the misericorde for salvation.

Simon reached for that lethal stiletto. Holding it in his hand, he rubbed the gleaming triangular blade over and over again until it grew as warm as his own flesh.

Control. He must regain the control that had once been as unyielding as that deadly blade.

Chapter Fourteen

What was he doing at Gloucester Cathedral, weeping over an alabaster tomb, his hands stroking the sculpted image of some medieval king?

Part of Julian's mind knew he was dreaming, but the knowledge did not bring him awake as it should have. Instead, and to his great horror, the stone image began to lose its finely chiseled lines and dissolve into something softer, more amorphous, rather . . . ghostly. The curling beard and long hair ruffled as if in a breeze—although the air felt as still as death. Julian forced himself to study the unappealing features. The king's hawklike nose imparted an avaricious air; the thin mouth and short chin lent a weakness that all his royal finery could not dispel.

Even as Julian registered those observations, the figure rose from its resting place. The tomb vanished, replaced by all-too-familiar surroundings. Now the ghostly king perched on the edge of Julian's bed.

As if they had not done so for centuries, the king's eyes opened slowly, almost painfully. A laugh slipped from those thin lips as he regarded a figure cowering in the corner of Julian's room. As Julian the dreamer stared intently into the dream, recognition slammed into him at the sight of the cringing figure groveling before the wispy form as if the ghost controlled his very destiny.

The figure was Julian LeFevre.

Julian tried to speak, to move, to do anything that might wrest control of his nightmare from the apparition. But he was as weak as a babe before that eerie, predatory stare. A feeling of impending dread seized him.

A vile grin flitted across the king's scrawny lips, displaying blackened teeth as rotted as the grave. Slowly, the figure's arms evaporated into long, wispy tendrils that floated across the room and wrapped around Julian like a vise.

Julian heard himself plead for mercy, although he suspected the word meant little to the creature who held him so lovingly. For that is what it was, he realized, a kind of lethal loving. An unearthly breeze swirled through the chamber as Julian felt his life's breath leave his chest. The wind's howling cry filled the room as the king brought his thin lips to Julian's ear and whispered.

Julian's shout of denial only made the ghost shake with laughter. A bone-chilling shriek emerged from the rotted cavity that was the royal mouth. It was the most unearthly noise Julian had ever heard.

As he awoke, an answering scream came from his own trembling lips.

"Miss Fitzhugh," Simon acknowledged gruffly.

"Lord Sommersby," she replied politely, taking a plate and beginning to fill it from the dishes at the sideboard. Was it his imagination, or did she look pale this morning? "I trust your trip went well?"

Simon felt about as comfortable as a raw recruit tossed onto the battlefield with a new Baker rifle and knuckle-bow bayonet. "Well enough, I suppose." He hesitated. "I trust my cousin was an adequate host in my absence."

Color infused her cheeks. "Mr. Thornton was most thoughtful," she replied.

"And yet I do not find him here," Simon observed casually. "He must have departed rather suddenly." Damn him for a fool, anyway. He could not resist trying to discover the damage he had wrought. Had Thornton hurt her deeply—or merely angered her? He prayed it was the latter.

Flashing sparks in her eyes reassured him. "I believe he had other obligations," she replied evenly.

Şimon looked around. No one in the dining room appeared to be listening to their conversation. A brooding Sir Thomas had scarcely bothered to acknowledge them. Julian's red-rimmed eyes bore a preoccupied and unhealthy look, as if he had spent the night in some ungodly hell. Miss Biddle had shot him a vague smile before leaving the table to find a book in his library.

Carefully, Simon cleared his throat. For some reason, that simple act drew from Miss Fitzhugh a startled look. "I would not wish to cause you embarrassment, madam," he began quietly, so as not to catch the attention of the others, "but if my cousin gave you offense, I wish to know of it."

Miss Fitzhugh regarded him strangely. "You put me very much in mind of Mr. Thornton, my lord."

Simon swallowed hard and made a mental note to be more earl-like.

"But that is neither here nor there," she added quickly. "In answer to your question, he gave no offense. I am afraid that it was rather the other way around."

Puzzled, Simon frowned. "I am certain you did not offend my cousin," he declared. "He is not the sensitive sort."

"I think you must not know Mr. Thornton very well." Miss Fitzhugh murmured, pushing the food around on her plate.

Abruptly, Sir Thomas scraped his chair back and strode from the dining room. In the same moment Julian lurched to his feet and departed, muttering darkly. Finding himself alone with her, Simon took a deep breath.

"I can see that my cousin has distressed you," he said, dishonesty compressing his vocal cords so that his voice sounded strained. "I must apologize on his behalf—"

"I found no fault with Mr. Thornton," she interjected firmly. "Frankly, my lord, I believe I frightened him away."

"Frightened him?" he echoed, startled.

Amusement suddenly transformed her features. "I know fear is a foreign concept to the Thornton men, my lord, but I daresay that any gentleman would be scared out of his wits if an avowed spinster suddenly beseeched him for kisses."

With that heart-stopping statement, she undid him.

Simon had never known anyone so unconcerned with her vanity that she willingly sacrificed her own image in the interest of telling God's honest truth.

"I-I . . . do not know what to say," he stammered.

"I imagine there is nothing to say, my lord," she replied easily. "I have been brooding about my folly, but I believe I have brooded enough. I think you may safely lay your cousin's abrupt departure at my door, and I suppose I should apologize, but in truth his absence comes as a relief."

"It does?"

Miss Fitzhugh nodded. "It was silly of me to form an attraction for Mr. Thornton. A woman of my age ought to know better. I suppose it proves that no one is immune to the follies of one's imagination." She flushed and looked away.

Simon's own imagination was running rampant. He wondered whether she felt the awareness that simmered in the space between them and begged for exploration.

Stop it, he told himself sternly. *Thornton* had explored that throbbing excitement that existed between him and Miss Fitzhugh. But Thornton was no more.

As Sommersby, he had displayed only consideration and polite rectitude in Miss Fitzhugh's presence. Oh, there had been that strangely intimate session in his study, when he had blurted out his concerns about his courtship of Miss Biddle with embarrassing candor. But he had crossed no forbidden line. His demeanor had been correct on every level.

It was Thornton, a man of sufficient years to have long ago banished a younger man's unwieldy passions, who had stared fixedly at the wardrobe in Miss Fitzhugh's chamber that night in order to avoid seeing the huge feather bed behind her. It was Thornton who had forced himself to avoid noticing the soft white lawn that peeked out from beneath her robe, Thornton who had steeled himself upon hearing of the "extensive liberties" Julian had taken that night at Vauxhall.

And it was Thornton who had wanted to make love to her until she no longer knew her own name.

Thank goodness the man had gone. He was a rogue and a liar—though to be sure he had started out as a perfectly respectable gentleman, restrained in every way. . . .

If Thornton could turn from gentleman to rogue in as much time as it took to share a kiss in the sea breeze, what might happen to his lordly cousin, who had been trying unsuccessfully these last few minutes not to imagine taking the fearless Miss Fitzhugh right here on the dining table?

Simon commanded his mind to produce the image of his

future bride, a lovely young lady with violet eyes and a heart-shaped mouth made for a man's adoration.

Alas, the notion of making love to Miss Biddle moved him not one whit. Miss Fitzhugh, on the other hand, made his pulse race blindly.

As the heat of desire inflamed his loins, Simon disciplined his ragged breathing and forced himself to swallow the coffee that tasted as bitter as loss.

"Thus times do shift, each thing his turn does hold;
    New things succeed, as former things grow old."

Felicity pondered the poignant words delivered in Mr. Frakes's resonant tones. "How sad."

Mr. Frakes eyed her quizzically. "Sad? Why say you, Miss Biddle? Change is the way of life."

"But to think that the things we enjoy have such a fleeting existence—why cannot the happy times last?"

"My dear Miss Biddle, what has you in such a melancholy state this morning? Surely you must be looking forward to the new life that awaits you." He turned toward the bookshelves. "To be a wife and a mother must be every woman's fondest wish."

Felicity smiled wistfully. "Yes, but it is also a venture into the unknown, is it not? One is never sure in leaving the old that a better future awaits."

"It is difficult to leave what one knows for something one does not," he agreed. "But we can appreciate what has been even as we greet the new with the breathless fear and excitement that is the joy of living."

"That is a beautiful sentiment, Mr. Frakes." Felicity clasped her hands and fixed him with an admiring gaze. "You have a poetic soul, sir."

Flushing, he turned toward her. "I should say rather that I have spent so many hours immersed in books that I know very little of anything else, Miss Biddle."

Felicity rose to face him. "Then perhaps there is very little else worth knowing, Mr. Frakes."

Quickly, he fumbled through the pages of the book in his hand. "I am sure Mr. Herrick has something more cheerful for us to ponder," he said nervously. "Ah, yes, here it is." He read:

> "Gather ye rosebuds while ye may,
>   Old time is still a-flying,
>   And this same flower that smiles today
>   Tomorrow will be dying."

"Oh, dear," he said, frowning. "That is not what I had in mind. Let me see if I can find something else."

"I wish you to know, Mr. Frakes," Felicity said quietly, "that sharing these times together has meant a great deal to me."

" 'Fair daffodils,' " he read loudly, " 'we weep to see you haste away so soon.' " Frustrated, he shook his head. "This will not do at all." With the look of a desperate man, he leafed frantically through the pages.

Felicity's smile grew sad as she toyed with the skirt of her sprigged muslin gown. "You always seem to know how to touch my deepest thoughts, Mr. Frakes. I do not know what I shall do without you."

"Pray, do not say so, Miss Biddle," he said, his eyes widening in alarm. "You will have a rich and full life as Lady Sommersby. You are deserving of the very best that fate can bestow on you—"

"Have you ever thought to marry, Mr. Frakes?" Felicity asked suddenly.

He began to study the shelves most intently. "I am but a scholar, Miss Biddle—a clerk, if you will, with little income and no address. I have nothing to offer a wife." He turned, and as he did, the volume of poetry slipped from his fingers.

Felicity caught the book before it fell. "You underestimate yourself," she said gently. "You have the gift of sensitivity, of understanding what it is that touches the soul. Your position in life makes no difference."

Her eyes rapidly scanned the words on the page, though she had to hold the book close because she was not wearing her spectacles. "Why look. It says right here that 'Night makes no difference 'twixt the Priest and Clerk; / Joan as my Lady is as good i' the dark.'" Coloring, she looked up. "That is not quite what I meant to say."

"I should hope not," he responded, aghast.

"The point, Mr. Frakes, is that a man's income and title are less important than the riches of his heart and soul," Felicity declared.

A wistful smile crossed his lips. "I believe it is you, Miss Biddle, who have the soul of a poet."

Felicity blushed. "I do not flatter myself that I possess any talent. But I do have a need that at times seems quite urgent to express myself in a way that others can only view as odd."

"I would not think anything you say to be odd," he declared fervently.

She smiled. "You are kind."

He regarded her steadily. "I assure you, Miss Biddle, 'kind' does not begin to describe the depth of my admiration for you."

Silently, Felicity considered his words. As her gaze plumbed his, a warmth enveloped her. Oddly, Mr. Frakes did not avert his eyes as he was wont to do.

Indeed, Felicity wondered if she was correct in discerning the heat of carefully banked fires within those somber brown eyes. Mesmerized, she simply could not do the ladylike thing and lower her gaze. Instead, as that warmth generated another sort of heat deep inside her, she recited some words that sprung suddenly to her lips:

"'You say to me-wards your affection's strong; / Pray love me little, so you love me long.'" Her lashes fluttered delicately.

"Miss Biddle," Mr. Frakes said helplessly, "I have no right, no hope, no expectation . . ."

"And I have no spectacles, sir, or I would have done this better." Felicity fumbled for the glasses in her skirt pocket and put them on. Now the words leapt out at her, and she read with great determination. "'Give me a kiss, and to that kiss a score'—"

"Miss Biddle, please do not!" he protested, but when he would have seized the book from her, Felicity laughed shyly and read on:

"'Then to that twenty, add a hundred more . . .'"

Now he did succeed in pulling the book from her hands, but Felicity continued anyway, the words long etched into her heart: "'A thousand to that hundred; / so kiss on . . .'"

"Miss Biddle," he said breathlessly. The book slipped from his fingers, and his hands crept around her waist. Then, gently, he reached upward and removed her spectacles. Soon the poet's words faded into nothingness, muffled by the exquisite touch of his lips on hers.

Felicity sighed deeply as Stephen Frakes's sweet, poetic mouth claimed hers. Her soul soared upward as the slim volume of poetry lay forgotten on the floor.

Dr. Greenfield had invaded his sleep once too often.

"I am leaving for Mayfield," Sir Thomas announced. "I shall rely on you, Amanda, to see that everything remains all that it should be. And I shall depend on you, Sommersby, to look after the ladies with the same diligence you brought to the field of battle."

Startled, they watched as Sir Thomas pushed back his chair from the dining room table.

"Father!" Felicity cried. "What is the meaning of this?"

"My presence is required at home, daughter," he replied curtly.

"Sir Thomas?" Amanda queried in concern. "Has there been word from Mayfield? Is Lady Biddle ill?"

"Not as far as I know," he replied darkly. "But when you reach my age, Amanda, you realize that life is too short to play the afternoon farmer. I will be damned if I will stand for any more nonsense."

"What nonsense?" Felicity asked. "You cannot leave us like this. I—we need you, Papa. There is much to talk about. Please do not go."

Sir Thomas tossed his napkin on the table. "I see nothing amiss in leaving you in the care of your betrothed and Amanda for a few days. I would trust both of them with my life as easily as I trust them with my daughter."

With that, Sir Thomas strode from the room, leaving the remaining occupants staring in dismay at his empty chair.

Chapter Fifteen

Submerged passions simmered in the drafts that wafted aimlessly through Sommersby Castle. A restless air permeated the halls, as if Sir Thomas's departure had cast everyone adrift without mission or method to dispel the unsettling forces that engulfed them all.

Though Felicity's feelings for Stephen Frakes ran deep, she went no more to the library, wanting first to share the state of her heart with her father. Stephen was left to find in the words of the poets a measure of comfort for the absence of his lady love.

Amanda, her diligence exacerbated by guilt over her own unsettling passions, was determined to be a better chaperone. Thus, she was frequently in the company of Felicity and Lord Sommersby, and since Felicity spent much of the time in the doldrums, Amanda was obliged to fill the awkward silence between the couple by engaging the earl in steady conversation. This he bore stoically.

Julian's bleak, tormented look might have given Amanda pause had she not been concentrating so hard on acting naturally in Lord Sommersby's presence. Considering that a few days ago she had been ready to hurl herself into Mr. Thornton's arms, Amanda could not fathom how her heart could be so fickle that she wished for the one man yet yearned for the other in equal portion. More than ever, she longed to take herself off to the comforting seclusion of her little cottage in Kent.

Simon, on the other hand, had no use for solitude. Desperate for distraction, he spent his nights in such spirited fencing with Jeffers that the batman finally swore he would not go another round if all the hounds of hells were on his heels. And so Simon remained suspended in inactivity, waiting for Sir Thomas to return and take his charges to London, where the days would lead inexorably to marriage and life would lose the restless turmoil that centered around Miss Fitzhugh's presence in his house.

Everywhere he looked, she was there, playing the proper chaperone, making certain no scandal occurred on her watch—which was highly unlikely, since the blue-deviled Miss Biddle was disinclined toward any exchange that might lead to more than a passing acquaintance with him. Simon thought his fiancée's behavior odd, but perhaps it was the way of gently bred females contemplating the wedded state.

At breakfast on the second day of Sir Thomas's absence, Felicity ventured that it would be diverting to explore the tunnels.

"Not the place for women," Julian growled, looking up with red-rimmed eyes.

Felicity ignored him. "Perhaps the duke forgets that this is to be my future home, my lord," she told Simon amiably. "At all events, I should greatly enjoy the expedition."

Although he liked the idea of doing something other than waiting idly for Sir Thomas's return, Simon hesitated. "The tunnels may be dangerous. I myself have not explored them."

"Then this is the perfect opportunity," Felicity replied, fluttering her lashes and bestowing an adoring smile on him for the first time in days.

Having seen a bit of the tunnel that night with Miss Fitzhugh, Simon knew it was in passable condition. He also knew that they would all have to go in order to chaperone each other and that he would spend yet another excruciating day pretending not to look at Miss Fitzhugh and telling himself he was only imagining that she was doing the same.

"Very well," he said, with a resigned sigh. "We will go this afternoon."

A sense of foreboding shadowed him the rest of the morning. It was as if the ancient stone walls were trying to tell him something, as if all those deadly weapons were restless after so many years of inactivity. Simon found him-

self looking over his shoulder in search of ghostly presences, even though he did not believe in such nonsense.

Walls did not talk. Rusty metal did not grow restless.
Ghosts did not exist.

*"The stage is set. How fortunate that Edward decided to
cooperate."*

"He does seem rather fond of Claridge."

*"Fond! He is positively besotted, Mortimer. He has gone to
him every night, tormenting him with those erotic dreams."*

*"Edward finds them erotic, Isabella. I am not certain
Claridge agrees."*

*"That is the beauty of it. Claridge must be beside himself
wondering what is producing all those unnatural images
that haunt his dreams."*

*"For myself, I should not like to push a man like Clar-
idge too far."*

*"Pish! That is just what we want, to drive the man beyond
his limits so that he must resolve these sudden unexpected
doubts about his manhood. With everything else that tor-
ments him, he will have to act."*

"And turn to the chaperone?"

*"Precisely. Our tenant will be furious, of course. And
anger is such an aphrodisiac! Oh, Mortimer, we will not
have to wait long—rapture shall be ours!"*

*"Truth be told, I feel uneasy about this plan of ours, my
dear. Sometimes it is best to leave well enough alone."*

"When have I ever led you astray, Mortimer?"

*"Some would call being hauled out of bed to face sum-
mary execution at Tyburn a less than fortuitous result of my
following your lead, Isabella."*

"I thought you had forgiven me that."

*"One does wonder how it would have been to live a
decade or two longer."*

"Trust me, Mortimer. It was tedious. Utterly tedious."

*"You know, Isabella, I have often wondered why, after
all we shared together, you found it necessary to be buried
with Edward's heart on your breast."*

*"I simply did not wish history to remember me as a faith-
less wife."*

"There seems little chance of you being remembered otherwise."

"Hmmph! You have never possessed my vision, Mortimer."

"God's blood!"

Amanda glanced uneasily at Julian, who had made no secret of the fact that he found her presence about as welcoming as the grave. But what choice did she have? Exploring the tunnels had seemed simple enough when all of them stepped through her wardrobe to begin the expedition—until Amanda discovered that her weak ankle would not allow her to negotiate the steep path from the upper part of the tunnel down to the caves.

Rather inconsiderately, Felicity insisted on pushing on, and so Lord Sommersby accompanied her. That left Amanda behind in the dimly lit corridor with Julian, who had taken a pickax to a section of the wall. Amanda tried not to think about how the earl and Felicity might spend the time exploring these secluded caves. Her wistful sigh brought yet another curse from Julian as he threw the ax down and eyed her in disgust.

"There is no need to sit there sighing like a martyr, Amanda," he growled as his fingers probed the area of the wall his ax had just ravaged.

"I am not . . ." she began, but his attention was on the wall and she abandoned her defense midsentence as not worth the effort.

"There used to be a hidden recess here," he said glumly, "but the years have all but obscured it—ah, here it is."

He said this last with such hopefulness, that Amanda's curiosity was caught. "What sort of family papers are you seeking?" she could not resist asking.

Julian's only response was another curse as his fingers probed the recess and found only crumbling rock.

"May I help?" Amanda ventured.

Julian leveled a contemptuous glare at her. "Spare me your altruism, Amanda. I know you wish me at Jericho, so there is no use in pretending otherwise."

"Even if that were the case, which it is not," Amanda retorted, "I have no wish to see you destroy yourself, as it seems you are intent on doing. You look as if you have not slept in days. Has anyone told you that you appear to be at your last prayers?"

"Which would give you great pleasure, I am certain," he snarled.

"You persist in thinking that I hate you, Julian, when in fact I have no feeling for you at all. You no longer affect me in the least," she added breezily.

"Is that so?"

His ominous tone sent a frisson of fear shooting up her spine. Even in the imperfect light of the lantern, she could see that something was terribly wrong with him. Rage and self-hatred subsumed whatever vulnerability she had once imagined in his eyes. Julian LeFevre looked to be a man at the end of his rope.

Uneasily, Amanda looked around. Felicity and Lord Sommersby had long moved beyond earshot. The lanterns that lit the corridor at regular intervals did nothing to stave off the sense of danger that beset the shadowy tunnel.

Julian read her discomfort. "Tell me, Amanda," he said with a silky purr, "is it just me you scorn or men in general?"

"The only men I scorn are those in the habit of taking advantage of innocent females," she replied pointedly, determined not to be cowed.

Julian's lips curled in an ugly smile. "When are you going to admit that I took no advantage you did not willingly cede? Quite simply, Amanda, you wanted me. You wanted a man." Menace flared in his eyes. "I am still a man," he added softly. "And I daresay that beneath that prim exterior, you still want me."

Slowly, he moved toward her. Amanda put her hands out in front of her. "Stop it, Julian," she commanded with a bravado she was far from feeling. "You took advantage of my innocence. There is nothing manly about that."

He flinched as if she had struck him. Suddenly, he yanked her brutally against his chest, imprisoning her arms behind her back.

"My *dear* Amanda," he said with a hiss, "I will show you the meaning of manly. And I daresay you will never forget it."

Fear sliced through her as he forced her down to the tunnel floor. Sharp rocks cut into her back, but that was the least of her concerns.

"Stop it!" she cried, but the glazed look in his eyes told her he was beyond reaching. Desperately, she flung a prayer heavenward, wondering if heaven could gain purchase in the enraged demon that was Julian LeFevre.

He made no pretense at seduction, and Amanda realized he meant to waste no time on such nonsense. This was not Vauxhall. Covering her with the full weight of his body, he pinned her to the ground, fumbling beneath her gown. She struggled against him, but her strength was nothing to his.

"Raping me will only prove your cowardice," she cried.

Julian stilled. Quickly, Amanda pressed her slender advantage. "A true man would not do this, Julian," she said in a hoarse whisper.

Too far. She had gone too far. Amanda saw it immediately in the rage that leapt anew to his eyes. "So," he growled, "you think I add cowardice to my sins?"

Pinned like a butterfly under the collector's glass, Amanda scarcely dared to breathe. But she was no helpless insect, she thought, gathering her courage around her. She had a voice. She would use it or die trying.

"Only you can be the judge of that, Julian," she flung at him.

Black pupils widened, giving her a glimpse of the hell of his soul. With a moan that might have come from the very center of that torment, he pushed himself away from her.

"Very well, Amanda—you win," he rasped. "Keep whatever virtue you still possess after all these years."

Sitting up, he put his head in his hands and began to shake as if a great pain racked him. Realizing that she could finally breathe again, Amanda hurried to repair her clothing. Her fingers shook, however, making the task extremely difficult.

Julian said not a word. Compassion gripped her as she regarded the shaking man sitting next to her. Gingerly, she placed a hand on his shoulder.

"Julian?" she asked hesitantly. "Are you all right?"

Dully, he looked up. "There is nothing wrong with me," he said in a distant voice, "that finding my mother's marriage lines will not remedy."

Confusion furrowed her brow. "Marriage lines?"

As he nodded, his sardonic gaze filled with bitter self-loathing.

"The papers—the documents you are seeking," she said with dawning awareness. "Dear lord, Julian. Is there some doubt about your . . . your legitimacy?"

Bleak confirmation lay in Julian's answering silence.

"But how—how could you inherit a dukedom if such a thing is in doubt?" Amanda persisted.

Abruptly, he rose, a self-mocking smile contorting his mouth. "There are two possible answers to that question, Amanda. One is that information questioning my lineage came to my attention after I inherited."

"Of course," she said, nodding sympathetically. "I am certain that when you find the papers, everything will be—"

"The other possibility," he interrupted, regarding her with a cynical gaze, "is that I inherited the title suspecting all along that I was a bastard—in character and name."

Amanda stared up at him. "Oh, Julian!" she gasped. Blindly she reached for his hand, though she knew her small effort did nothing to ease his plight.

"And now," he continued, his eyes stark as a moonless night, "I find that strange dreams torment me, make me doubt myself and other . . . things for the first time. I suppose that is the punishment of a man who chooses to pretend he is legitimate when he is not, to occupy a title and possess the wealth that does not belong to him."

Speechless, Amanda could only squeeze his hand in a feeble attempt at comfort. Her fear of him had vanished. Only compassion remained. She rose and gently pushed a lock of his thick black hair away from his eyes.

"What is the meaning of this?" A low baritone fractured the silence as Lord Sommersby emerged from the shadows. His penetrating gaze took in her disordered gown, wrinkled skirts, disheveled hair—and fingers that still smoothed Julian's brow.

Felicity, who had come up behind the earl, gave a shocked gasp. "Amanda!"

"Do be quiet, Felicity," she ordered in her best chaperone's voice, trying to overcome her mortification at the obvious conclusion they had drawn. "Despite what you may think, nothing is amiss."

Felicity gaped at them. Lord Sommersby merely arched a brow, betraying nothing beneath that still exterior.

When he moved toward her, Amanda felt the instinctive urge to flee, despite the fact that his cool control had not wavered. He set her gently away from Julian, then planted himself squarely in front of him.

Physically the men were of a piece. But as her gaze moved quickly from one to the other, Amanda decided that the quiet warrior with the keen eyes possessed a strength beyond anything she had seen—certainly beyond Julian's sheer brute force.

That was the difference between them, she realized. For all his physical power, Julian was weak—in spirit and heart. He would never be the man Lord Sommersby was. The earl would never take a woman against her will. Discipline, control, and perhaps even compassion ruled whatever uncivilized forces lurked within him.

"You will leave at first light," he told Julian coldly. "If I find the documents you seek, I will send them on to you."

There were no threats, no lectures, no crossing of sabres. The two men regarded each other steadily, and in that silent exchange, Julian admitted defeat. With unseeing eyes, he made his way out of the tunnel.

"The tunnel leads to a large cave where smugglers used to store their goods," Felicity explained eagerly. "Lord Sommersby says the smugglers must have had to stash their booty deep inside the cave to protect it from the high tide. It is the perfect place for us to hide!"

"Hide?" Stephen's gaze was troubled.

Felicity made an impatient sound. "Do you not see, Stephen? We shall run away. No one will find us, and when the commotion passes, we shall escape to Scotland without a care of being overtaken."

"Scotland?"

Shyly, Felicity nodded. "I did not think we possessed the funds to obtain a Special License."

"You want us to elope?" he said, aghast.

"It is terribly romantic, do you not think?" When he only

regarded her with deepening horror, she frowned. "Surely you do not wish me to marry Lord Sommersby?"

"No." Slowly he shook his head. "Of course not—especially if you do not wish it."

"I do not. It is you I love."

Sighing regretfully, he took her into his arms. "You deserve more than a mad dash to Gretna Green, my dear."

"I do not care as long as I have you," Felicity murmured.

"But think of the scandal," he protested. "What would your parents think?"

Felicity frowned. "I should not like to cause them pain, but I see no way around it. I cannot talk to Papa, since he is gone. Who knows when he might return? No, I am afraid we must take matters into our own hands."

"I cannot like this, Felicity. You deserve more than to start married life in such a way. Are you sure this is what you want? I have very little funds and little prospect of advancing beyond the status of a lowly scholar. I am afraid that is the fate of the seventh son—"

"You must tell me about your family," she interrupted, "but all I need know now is that you still want me for your wife." Her voice broke on the last, and he crushed her to him.

"I want nothing more," he reassured her. "But is there no other way? Can you not talk to the earl? Or Miss Fitzhugh? Perhaps she can help."

Felicity thought of the scene she and Lord Sommersby had come upon this afternoon between Amanda and the duke. "Amanda has her own concerns. As for Sommersby, well, I cannot think he will understand such things. I believe he has ice in his veins."

"Then he has not formed an attachment for you?"

"He has said very little to me, if you wish to know the truth of it. I do not think the man has any regard for sentiment. Or for me, either."

"Then the man is a fool," Stephen murmured as he brought their lips together.

Chapter Sixteen

Simon savored the fine French brandy like a long-lost friend, letting its pungent fragrance sting his nostrils and awaken long-dormant memories. Its soothing bite eased him into a time when everything had tasted bitter and flat and when the only scent was the pervasive odor of death.

Blood ran almost as thick as the wine back then, but victory was all that had mattered. Death stood sentry, his presence an accepted part of the landscape. Wellington rode the ridge, the allies' cockades in his hat, urging his troops on in the face of the blazing French twelve-pounders. Rifle fire, round shot—musket and grape—resounded through the hills as the enemy fell back to the plain. Under a sky darkened by battle smoke, it was impossible to tell who was friend or foe.

Fifteen thousand British gained their eternal rest in that bleak cornfield. Simon had survived to know a survivor's guilt for prevailing when worthy men had not, for killing and maiming and knowing that he would do so again without a moment's thought. But part of him had died another death that victorious day in Belgium.

War did that. The longer a man went about the business of killing, the longer that part of him capable of feeling slowly withered. The more a man killed, the more the inside of him died.

Simon had not felt anything for a very long time, except rage at the futility of measuring victory by the gallons of blood spilled and of sacrificing brave young soldiers to a tyrant's greed. He had learned to restrain his rage, but the more he did so, the more uncivilized grew his true self.

That was the only explanation he could muster now for the savageness that swept him as he sat in his study, draining some long-ago smuggler's brandy and mulling over that scene in the tunnel when Miss Fitzhugh had shown her true colors.

It was one thing to hear her tell Thornton she was not averse to his kisses—indeed, even wished to deepen the acquaintance. The part of him not horrified at provoking such a response had thrilled at the possibilities.

It was quite another thing to discover her stroking Julian's cruel brow with every appearance of having just emerged from an amorous tussle in the dust. To Miss Fitzhugh, apparently, one man was as good as the next.

Mortifying as it was to acknowledge his naiveté, Simon knew the truth when it blasted him in the face. Miss Fitzhugh's flushed features and disheveled clothing had betrayed more eloquently than any words the intimacy between her and Julian.

He had never known much about females. Despite his recent dream, no women had walked the fields where he had fought. In the hellish storm that portended Waterloo, he had slept alone under his muddy blanket of straw—and for most of the nights afterward. Simon had never cared to share his nightmares.

His mother was the only woman who had ever engendered tender feelings in him, and he had failed her miserably. The fact of his youth did not excuse his inability to protect her from poverty, degradation, death. A man did not fail those who depended upon him. A man must lead, and he must bear the burdens of leadership as best he could—without complaint, without giving in to the despair that swirled around him in the faces of raw recruits and experienced soldiers alike.

And if a man could not bear those burdens, he must at least pretend that he could. He must shield himself in the armor that kept despair at bay and prevented anyone from penetrating the stone fortress he had erected around his shriveled and aching heart.

And if he could not always keep his armor whole, he could at least drown his thoughts in the bottle of brandy Jeffers had left near his elbow.

"Lord Sommersby?" A familiar voice floated in from the hall through the door he had shut to ward off visitors.

"What is it, Miss Fitzhugh?" he growled, hoping to discourage her from stopping in.

It did not surprise him that she chose to ignore his tone and stride into his sanctuary like a Norman invader. "I must talk with you, my lord."

He eyed her coldly. "I cannot think what we have to discuss."

For a moment she hesitated—but only for a moment. Then she sank into a chair in front of his desk and sighed.

"I suppose now you think I am an unfit chaperone and a terrible example for Felicity."

Not by so much as the blink of an eye did Simon allow her to see his dismay that she dared to broach the episode that had tormented him since this afternoon.

"Your performance leaves something to be desired," he agreed, his tone condemning her as thoroughly as he condemned himself for wishing that it had been he—not Julian—alone with her in that darkened tunnel.

"What you saw, my lord, was not what it seemed." Embarrassment darkened her gaze, but he could also see a flash of anger within those expressive brown eyes.

Did she think him a fool to be persuaded that up was down and night was day? Now, he supposed, she would earnestly declare that she was not that sort of woman. He waited, steeling himself for her lies. Her next words, however, caught him by surprise.

"Julian is deeply troubled."

If he had nurtured the slightest hope that she did not care for Julian and that her behavior today had been but a momentary lapse, it vanished then and there.

"Claridge is not my concern." His gut tightened, as if a vise around his heart had constricted mercilessly. "If he is yours, Miss Fitzhugh, I suggest you go to him. I imagine he is in his room, seeing to his packing. Undoubtedly you can find your way."

Flushing at his barely veiled insult, she nevertheless managed to control her temper. "I know you overheard his remarks in the tunnel today," she said. "He is quite intent in his quest to find his parents' marriage lines. Julian is a tormented man, my lord."

"And he delights in tormenting others," Simon growled, not even trying to muster sympathy for the man.

"He is not beyond redemption." She hesitated. "Especially if you would take a hand to help him."

Simon would just as soon help a fox find the henhouse. "I have no interest in saving Julian's soul, Miss Fitzhugh. He was an excellent officer and a skilled strategist, but like many men since the war, he has lost his way." He shrugged. "The war deprived many men of the their moral compasses. It happens."

"But not to you."

"No."

Anger darkened her eyes. "Nothing disturbs that cool control of yours, does it? Nothing moves you in the least."

Arching a brow, Simon gave her a look reserved for the few hapless souls under his command who had ever possessed the temerity to challenge him.

"What of it?" he demanded, his tone as soft and deadly as the satiny patina of a polished steel blade.

"What of it?" she echoed, thunderstruck. Indignation propelled her to her feet. "You once assured me you were not cruel, Lord Sommersby, nor unaware of a woman's needs." She pointed an accusing finger at him. "But I have watched you with Felicity. You extend her no special consideration. You make no effort to get to know her, nor display any tenderness toward the young woman whose body will soon be yours to use as you please."

As her words resounded in the room, her cheeks reddened. "I can only pity my cousin for being saddled with a man of such cold temperament," she finished.

Simon barely restrained himself from reaching across the desk to shake her and declare that she understood nothing about him. Instead, he gave her a disdainful look.

"A man of my profession cannot afford to be swayed by emotion."

"You are not at war any longer, my lord," she retorted. "And a woman is not an enemy soldier."

"Has it never occurred to you, Miss Fitzhugh," he asked through gritted teeth, "that you might be mistaken in your conclusions about me?"

"There can be no mistaking the fact that you are as cold a

man as I have ever encountered, despite your earlier pledge to try to bring some affection to your marriage."

Simon raked her with a contemptuous gaze. "Given your previous encounters, any man who does not throw himself into your arms must seem cold by comparison."

Appalled, she drew herself up. "May I remind you, Lord Sommersby, that you know nothing about my 'encounters,' as you so delicately describe them?"

Verbal fencing was for fools, Simon decided, his patience at an end. He slammed his fist on the desk.

"I know what my eyes tell me," he growled, "and what you yourself have detailed of your activities in Vauxhall with that rascal Julian." His gaze strayed longingly to the bottle of brandy, hoping against hope that Miss Fitzhugh would finally see fit to let him be.

He should have known better. Anger, sharp and brilliant as a freshly honed blade, shot from her eyes.

"And I might have known that a man like you, a man of no feeling, would take advantage of the momentary weakness I had in confessing my past mistake," she sputtered. "I might have known that you would throw that humiliating incident back at me like the heartless man you are . . ."

Abruptly, she broke off. Her eyes widened as if she had seen a ghost. Her jaw gaped. "Dear lord!"

Simon ripped his gaze from the brandy bottle. "What is it now?" he demanded irritably, trying not to think of the appealing flush that agitation lent her features.

"I never . . . told you," she said slowly.

"What the devil are you talking about?"

"I never told you about that time in Vauxhall."

"What? Of course, you did." He waved a dismissive hand. "That night in your room—"

Suddenly he understood. Oh, foolish, irredeemable mistake.

"It was *Mr. Thornton* I told," she said in a dazed voice. "The night Julian emerged from my wardrobe, the night Mr. Thornton came to my room." She stared at him in horror. "It was *you*," she whispered. "*You* were Thornton."

Denial was useless. Miss Fitzhugh's accusing gaze bore all the certainty that reason, instinct, and moral indignation could provide. Simon wondered how he could have been so witless as to make such a slip. Had that scene in the tunnel today affected his concentration more than he knew?

Now she knew the truth: That he had allowed Thornton to do what honor forbade to Sommersby. That he, Simon Hannibal Thornton, Earl of Sommersby, had thoroughly kissed his betrothed's chaperone on that sun-drenched cliff. That he had wanted her, cloaked himself in a disguise to be with her, and allowed desire to supplant honor.

Too stunned to reply, Simon sat motionless at his desk. Miss Fitzhugh was not similarly incapacitated, however, and fairly flew at him across the furniture.

"So you are not so cold, after all, my lord," she taunted, shaking her finger at him. "You *do* know what it means to lose control."

Her gaze bore all the derision of a hardened general confronting a wayward soldier. "Or was that kiss on the cliff but a calculated maneuver designed to bring me to disgrace?"

Numbly, Simon shook his head in denial. "I never intended to kiss you," he said hoarsely. "I certainly intended no disgrace."

"I see. Then you merely meant to make of me a fool," she concluded. "For that is what I feel like at this very moment—a complete and utter fool."

"Miss Fitzhugh . . ." he protested.

"Oh come now, my lord," she flung at him. "Do you not think we are at 'Amanda' by now? Considering the nature of our various . . . *encounters*? And to think that I thought you more of a man than Julian."

"Do not compare me to that debauched rogue," he said evenly.

A bitter smile flitted over her mouth. "The truth is that you are no different. Both of you use women for your own twisted ends."

"I have never used a woman ill in my life," he barked, rising from his chair.

"Pray, what do you call it when you worm your way into a lady's affection, ply her with kisses, come to her room in your bedclothes . . . ?"

"Damn it, woman!" he shouted, all pretense at control at an end. "It was only a kiss!"

Silence filled the room as his words, suspended in the heavy air across the desk, robbed that clifftop kiss of its magic.

"Yes," she agreed in a flat voice, "it was only a meaningless kiss. Nothing to dwell on, to be sure. It was of so little consequence, I cannot think why I even remark upon it." She whirled away.

"Amanda."

Strangely, saying her name gave him a sudden thrill.

"Amanda," he said again, savoring the soft vowels as they slid off his tongue. He reached across the desk. His hand touched the back of her shoulder.

She flinched, her stiffly upright posture an eloquent statement of the damage his masquerade had wrought. Instantly, Simon withdrew his hand.

Shame filled him. The lie had sprung so easily to his lips. She really believed that the kiss was nothing to him.

"I did not mean to denigrate what happened between us," he said. "It was not . . ." He searched for words, but heartfelt speech had never been his strong point. "It was not meaningless," he finished helplessly.

"Oh?" She turned toward him, her eyes unnaturally bright. "Pray, what was the meaning of that kiss then, my lord? To have fun at my expense? To seduce Felicity's spinster cousin? La, what a joke that would have been!"

"I did not—" he began, but she cut him off.

"For if you did not intend those things," she added quietly, "if you did not intend ridicule or seduction, then I can only conclude one thing."

Foreboding, born of the warning sense that had saved him from many an ambush in battle, overwhelmed him. Unfortunately, Simon had no idea how to ward off whatever cannonball Miss Fitzhugh was about to shoot his way.

"I can only conclude, sir, that you could not help yourself," she continued, an unsettling glint in her eyes, "that in spite of your principles, your 'obligations,' your honor— you *wanted* me. Something about me pierced that maddeningly controlled reserve of yours and drove you to commit an unwise act—in spite of your betrothal, in spite of everything."

One of her nobly shaped brows rose disdainfully. "How

curious that you had to hide behind Thornton in order to give in to your . . . urge, let us call it. Could it be that one of England's most esteemed heroes is at heart a coward?"

Simon knew he deserved that. What he did not know was why he suddenly came around the desk and gripped her arms with the desperation of a wounded man trying to stem the seepage of his life's blood.

"Go ahead, my lord," she flung at him. "I give you leave to kiss me—again—as *yourself,* if you dare."

He had not been thinking of doing that. He had not been thinking of closing the distance between them, of enfolding her in his arms, of pulling the pins from her hair and running his hands through those silky tresses until they tumbled around her shoulders in glorious disarray. He had not been thinking of the fire that licked at his gut, or of her little gasp as her lips parted for him, or of his body's primitive and almost painful response to her womanly softness.

He had not been thinking of any of those things, but they had happened as naturally as breathing.

Something splashed onto his skin. Tears. They streamed down her face as she shook in his arms.

"Amanda," he murmured helplessly, stroking her cheeks with his fingertips.

She caught his hand, brought it fleetingly to her lips, then placed it over her heart. His own heart lurched treacherously in his chest. A groan escaped his lips. Her chin rose defiantly.

"I shall not fight you, my lord," she declared in a raw voice. "I shall hand you my virtue without the slightest struggle. I am not too proud to acknowledge that you make me abandon every principle I hold dear."

"Stop," he commanded hoarsely. "You do not know what you are saying."

"It is you, my lord, who persist in ignorance," she said softly. "You think your superior control makes you impervious to such untidy and unpredictable forces as lust."

Her lips curved in a rueful smile. "I learned long ago that I am a foolish and weak woman. I thought to hide myself away in the country and avoid facing my flaws, but it seems I was too wise by half. Neither my foolishness with Julian nor my solitary refuge prepared me for how overwhelming passion could be. Galling as it is to confess, I hereby humbly admit that you rob me of all control."

Simon did not know how his willful fingers had found the smooth skin beneath her bodice, but when she shuddered in desire as his hand closed over her breast, an ingrained discipline forced him to retreat.

As he stood with his hands balled in fists at his side, she eyed him in clear-eyed understanding. "I see that I do not have the power to force the Earl of Sommersby to lose control, my lord. Nor, I suspect, does Felicity."

She straightened her clothing. "I can also see by the look in your eyes that you mean to protect me from myself." Her lips trembled slightly as she spoke. "Your heroism hereby stands reinstated, Lord Sommersby."

Moving quickly to the door, she walked out of the room without a backward glance. For a long time Simon stared at the spot where she had been. Then, turning once more to the brandy bottle, he refilled his glass.

Julian had one eye open before Simon reached him, but he was not quick enough to prevent Simon's hand from closing over his throat.

As Simon registered the fact that Julian lay alone in bed, that Amanda had not gone to him after all, Julian regarded him with a sardonic gaze that held no surprise at this midnight invasion. Indeed, he looked as if the interruption of his sleep was not at all unusual.

"I see that mine host has come for his revenge," Julian observed softly.

Simon preferred not to examine the forces behind the restless rage that had driven him to Julian's room without so much as a candle to give warning of his presence. He shrugged.

"I had the urge to meet you at foil," Simon replied calmly, releasing his grip on Julian's throat. "I did not imagine that you would refuse."

Julian sat up in bed. "Do not take me for an idiot, Simon," he drawled. "I have seen the way you look at her. I did not think you would let this afternoon go unanswered."

"Her?" Simon echoed, frowning.

"Amanda. The woman you persist in respectfully calling

'Miss Fitzhugh' even as your eyes undress her like the lover you so desperately wish to be."

A muscle twitched in Simon's jaw. His eyes narrowed to granite slits. "Your caustic wit is useless here, Julian. All that matters is the condition of your sword arm."

Tossing aside the covers, Julian slid out of bed. Lines of exhaustion sprawled across his face, but a sardonic grin contorted his mouth.

"As a matter of fact," Julian said softly, "my sword arm is in perfect condition."

Chapter Seventeen

Jeffers gave a small prayer of thanks that he was not the one facing Major Simon Hannibal Thornton's coldly efficient sword and murderous eyes tonight.

"Corps-a-corps!" the batman warned as a missed lunge sent his employer and the Duke of Claridge into a bone-crushing embrace. Quickly, the opponents stepped back into position.

In a money fight, Jeffers would have had his blunt on the major, who could read the feint as if he had invented it and whose riposte was nigh legendary. A more calculating, controlled swordsman Jeffers had never seen. In contrast, the duke fought with the wild abandon of a man who did not care about his fate.

But when the duke executed an extraordinary double *prise-de-fer* and a graceful *ballestra,* Jeffers wondered if he had underestimated the man.

His employer handled a retreat as well as he did a lunge, however, and Jeffers watched in admiration as Simon glided backward on his left foot, then his right, about one shoe length. Then he proceeded to engage the duke in a slow, repetitive beat of blades, followed by a gentle but deep feint. The duke sneered.

"Come, man. You can do better than that," he taunted.

Unfazed, Simon continued the slow beat and feint. Again and again came the lulling motions until Julian gave a deliberately exaggerated yawn of boredom.

A lightning lunge caught him mid-yawn. With a perfect extension of the left leg, Simon scored high and inside to Julian's chest, a flawless blow that would have been lethal had the sword tip not been shielded. Then, pushing back on his right heel, Simon returned to the guard stance as quickly and fluidly as any acrobat.

Stung at suffering the indignity of a trap, Julian threw himself at Simon with an angry roar, and the match suddenly turned deadly. Locked in the lethal embrace of close-quarters fighting, the opponents' blades whirled hungrily, seeking the satisfaction of muscle and bone.

Jeffers gasped in horror. In a tight brawl, each man risked the edge of his opponent's slicing weapon. It was one thing to engage in sport with tipped foils; quite another to face the deadly length of an unprotected blade.

Neither man seemed concerned, however. Ducking deeply, Simon narrowly avoided Julian's slashing, cutover riposte. Then he whirled inward to execute a thrust that missed by a hair's breadth.

Jeffers knew the match must be stopped before disaster struck, but he dared not intervene without getting his head bitten off by his employer or sliced off by the duke's slashing sword. When a sudden grunt and a string of profanities brought the bout to a momentary halt, Jeffers saw his chance.

"Hold! Hold!" he cried as the duke touched his bleeding cheek.

Running over with his medical kit, the batman saw that Simon had also been wounded. One arm of his employer's shirt had been slashed to ribbons, and blood seeped from a wound under the gaping cloth. Fumbling with his bandages, Jeffers shook his head reproachfully.

The combatants merely scowled at him.

"I do not recall inviting you to this bout," Simon growled as Jeffers pressed a cloth to his wound.

"No, sir," Jeffers agreed, preparing another cloth pad with his free hand. "But it is fortunate that I am here, is it not?"

"Only if you can produce a bottle of brandy forthwith," Julian interjected, grimacing as Jeffers pressed the fresh cloth against his bleeding cheek.

"Make that *two* bottles," Simon snarled.

Hurriedly, Jeffers produced brandy and glasses. Each man tossed off the drink in silence. Finally, Julian spoke. "Would you like to hear about it?"

"Hear about what?" Scowling, Simon thrust his empty glass at Jeffers, who promptly refilled it.

An amused glint filled Julian's eyes as he, too, held out his glass for a refill. "About the night your Miss Fitzhugh took a turn with me on Lovers' Walk."

"No," came the terse reply.

Jeffers could not imagine how Miss Fitzhugh had come to be involved in this matter. But eyeing Simon's suddenly rigid features, he decided that the duke was on the verge of scoring a blow more stunning than any he might have achieved through the *ballestra*.

"That is unfortunate," Julian drawled softly, "for I shall tell you just the same."

Simon impaled his opponent with a look as sharp as any sabre. Good God, Jeffers thought uneasily, what a fine pickle this is.

"Our tenant handles a sword as well as you did, Mortimer."

"Well enough, I suppose."

"I thought Claridge had him that once."

"Claridge is too wild. Edward must have driven him a bit mad."

"Edward could drive anyone mad—as you would know if you had ever lived with the man."

"I have endured my share of Edward over these last few centuries, Isabella."

"With any luck, that is about to end. I have never seen Edward enjoy tormenting anyone as much as he does Claridge."

"Yes, but where does that get us?"

"Out of this castle, of course! We must stay and endure Edward's screams only as long as he remains here."

"You think he may decide to go off with Claridge? It seems unlikely."

"Not for a man subject to sweeping infatuations. I should know, Mortimer—all those years of keeping up a front while he indulged in one affair after another. Did you know that Edward passed all my beautiful wedding presents from Papa on to Gaveston? At the coronation, Gaveston

was dressed more magnificently than Edward himself. I was never so mortified in my life."

"Is that why you had Warwick murder Gaveston?"

"A queen cannot endure public embarrassment. I might have tolerated Edward's mistresses, but to have the world know that he preferred Gaveston—it was too much!"

"And here I thought you cared not a fig for public opinion."

"Sarcasm has never been your forte, Mortimer."

"Why must you always want more than you have, Isabella? Anyway, how can you be so certain that if Edward leaves the castle, we will be free?"

"Because that is the way of things. We have paid well enough for our sins—five hundred years of listening to Edward's screams. Can you imagine anything worse?"

"What if what awaits beyond these walls is worse than what we have already endured?"

"The trouble with you, Mortimer, is that you insist on looking on the dark side."

"It is a side with which I am well-acquainted Isabella, having spent so many centuries with you."

"You must have faith. Edward's fascination with Claridge will make him see that there are more enjoyable ways to pass the time than screaming at us for eternity. We will be free to float here and yon, inhabiting one fine human form after another and indulging in all manner of fleshly delights denied us for so long."

"I thought you were content to inhabit our tenant and the chaperone, when the time comes."

"They are all we have at the moment. But they are a stubborn pair, and it is taking far too long to get them together. Imagine what would happen if we were free to seek out those who do not feel so constrained."

"They did go on a bit much about that kiss."

"This era seems to be a bit stuffy, does it not? People are positively consumed with issues of honor and propriety."

"I imagine that you will find a way to change that, Isabella, should we manage to flee the confines of this castle."

"But it must happen soon, Mortimer, or I shall go mad.

Why have we not succeeded with our tenant and the chaperone? Can it be I have lost my touch?"

"You have not had the faculty of touch for centuries, Isabella."

"But I have always had the ability to inspire lustful thoughts, and thought is but precursor to deed, as you know."

"I daresay their thoughts are lustful enough, my dear. It is just that our tenant and the chaperone seem to be burdened with an excess of principle."

"That again! But her control lies in shards around her, and desire is making his nigh to unbearable. Oh, Mortimer! Soon their lust will bloom for us."

"Hold that thought, Isabella."

"Amanda, may I talk to you?"

The headache that had kept Amanda from rising with the alacrity with which she usually greeted the day pounded anew in her brain as she opened her eyes and regarded the troubled look on her cousin's face.

"If it is advice you need, Felicity, you might as well talk to those horrid weapons on the walls. I cannot think why your parents ever thought me a fit chaperone."

Felicity hesitated. "You had difficulties with Claridge in the tunnel yesterday, did you not?" When Amanda did not speak, Felicity sighed. "I thought so. It is all my fault. I should not have insisted on exploring the cave."

"No one can blame you for wishing a moment alone with your betrothed," Amanda said. "I have been your constant shadow, after all. It is only to be expected that you would take the first opportunity to go off with him."

Felicity's expression grew even more miserable. "It was not like that, Amanda. I wanted to see the caves because I thought they might provide a good hiding place."

"Hiding place?" Amanda frowned.

"I might as well tell you the whole." Felicity hesitated then rushed on: "We have decided to run away."

"Run away? You and the earl?" Amanda's jaw dropped.

"Not Lord Sommersby," Felicity corrected. "Stephen."

"Who is Stephen?"

"Mr. Frakes—the curator."

"Curator?" Amanda put her hand to her aching head.

"Dear lord, Felicity, will you please say something I can understand?"

"I suppose he is not really a curator," Felicity conceded. "He is more of a scholar. He is cataloguing the earl's books and weapons. And I mean to marry him."

Stunned, Amanda groped for the tea the maid had placed by the side of her bed earlier. The fact that it was cold barely registered. "You wish to marry a perfect stranger?"

Felicity crossed her arms over her chest. "He may be a stranger to you, Amanda, but *I* know him well enough." Her eyes took on a dreamy expression. "Indeed, I believe I know his very soul. He is a poet, a man who treasures the words of the heart and the needs of the spirit."

"Just *how* well do you know this Mr. Frakes?" Amanda asked weakly, taking a sip of the frigid tea.

"Well enough to know that I wish to spend my life with him," Felicity declared passionately. After a pause, she added, "I have told no one except you. You *do* see the difficulty?"

Amanda nearly choked on her tea. Setting the cup down with a clatter, she swept from the bed.

"Difficulty? I should say so." She gave a shaky laugh. "You are about to have a London Season, during which your betrothal to England's foremost war hero will be trumpeted before the cream of society. Meanwhile, your father has taken himself off to Mayfield, entrusting me with the task of ensuring that the proprieties are met in his absence. And now, in terms that give me no confidence as to the condition of your virtue, you inform me that you mean to marry a man I have neither heard of nor met."

Amanda threw open the wardrobe and ripped a dress from it. "Yes, Felicity," she snapped, "I see a number of difficulties, indeed I do."

Chagrined, Felicity reddened. "My virtue is intact, Amanda," she retorted angrily. "I cannot believe you would think otherwise—unless it is because you once had the bad judgment to allow Claridge to have his way and can only see men as connivers driven by base desires."

The moment the words were out, Felicity put her hand to her mouth. "Oh! I am sorry, Amanda."

Felicity could not know how close to the truth her angry words had struck, Amanda thought as a guilty flush spread over her own cheeks. Her young cousin had no idea that her trusted chaperone had virtually offered herself yet again to Thornton or Sommersby—or whoever he was— heedless of the fact that he was Felicity's betrothed.

She could not know that Amanda had fallen in love, for that was the realization that hit her in the middle of the night and kept her staring at that warlike painting opposite her bed until dawn crept in through the window and forced her to see how terribly she had wronged her cousin and family.

"Felicity," Amanda began miserably, "there is something you should know."

Instantly, Felicity was at her side. "Do not, Amanda. Do not put yourself through the ordeal of speaking about that episode with Claridge again. It is bad enough that because of me you are forced to endure the presence of that evil man here in the castle."

"Claridge is not the problem." Amanda took a deep breath. "It is Lord Sommersby."

"The *earl*?" Aghast, Felicity stared at her cousin. "Never say that Lord Sommersby forced his attentions on you! Oh, dearest—were you harmed?"

"No, no," Amanda said quickly. "It was not like that. Indeed, it was rather the other way around. You see—"

But Felicity, upon hearing that Amanda had suffered no harm, clapped her hands in glee. "Wait until Papa learns of this! He will not force me to marry a man so despicable that he tried to seduce you!"

"I beg your pardon," Amanda began indignantly.

"How wonderful!" Felicity trilled happily. "I will be free to marry Stephen."

"Stop it!" Amanda cried, firmly grasping Felicity's hand and forcing her to listen. "Lord Sommersby did not try to seduce me. It was *I* who dangled myself before him like a piece of suet before a flock of birds. To his credit, he rejected me quite honorably." She elected to omit the part about the earl's masquerade as Thornton on grounds that it would only confuse Felicity further.

Stunned, Felicity stared at her. "I do not believe it."

Amanda grimaced. "I have trouble believing it myself, but there it is, Felicity. I am a weak woman. I betrayed my cousin, my uncle's kindness, and my own good sense by throwing myself at your betrothed. How can you ever forgive me? I know I shall never forgive myself."

A look of almost morbid fascination swept Felicity's delicate features. "I cannot imagine how you could be so bold with a man like Lord Sommersby," she said in a hushed voice. "He is quite handsome, of course, but so large—and fierce. What if he—that is, what if he had not behaved honorably? Were you not afraid?"

Amanda blinked. She and Felicity obviously differed in their impressions of the earl. He had not inspired fear in her; rather, she had yearned to be folded into that fierce, manly embrace. "The point," she said firmly, "is that I behaved dishonorably."

"What of it?" Felicity grinned. "I am not going to marry the earl anyway. Oh, Amanda, do come with me now to meet Stephen. You will adore him! You must help me persuade Papa to sanction the match. Otherwise, we shall have to run away."

"But what do you know of this man?" Amanda demanded. "A man who would elope against your family's wishes could not have your best interests in mind."

"Eloping was my idea," Felicity replied. "I know that Stephen is pure of heart and noble of spirit. And that he loves me. That is enough for any marriage."

After that eloquent declaration, Amanda had not the heart to point out the more practical aspects of marriage with a penniless scholar.

"Very well," she said, sighing. "Let us go and meet this Mr. Frakes. But I do not know what will come of it. Have you thought of going to the earl and telling him everything? I am certain he would release you from your betrothal and perhaps even intervene with Sir Thomas." Privately, however, Amanda shuddered to think of Lord Sommersby's reaction to news that his efficient marriage plans had unraveled under his very nose.

Felicity's eyes widened. "I could never talk to Sommersby, Amanda. You must be the one to tell him. Or Papa can, if he returns soon. I hope it is soon. I do not think I can wait much longer."

Amanda offered a silent prayer that it would not fall to her to inform Lord Sommersby that his betrothed had fallen in love with a young man in his library.

Chapter Eighteen

When Simon walked into the parlor, he found his betrothed weeping like a watering pot. The red state of her nose and eyes suggested that she had been doing so for some time. Miss Fitzhugh stood beside her, grim-faced but dry-eyed, which presumably meant that Miss Biddle herself was the victim of whatever calamity had just occurred.

Simon imagined he was supposed to do something. Females doubtless expected their future husbands to offer comfort in such situations. He could not see what was required of him, however, as Miss Fitzhugh was doing a fine job of making soothing sounds to her cousin.

The fact that there was no obvious need for his assistance made it all the more strange when both women shot him expressions ranging from apprehension to pure horror. The latter reaction came from his fiancée, who regarded him as if he were about to loose a dozen plague-ridden rats upon the room. As for Miss Fitzhugh, Simon had never seen her show anything remotely approaching apprehension in his presence. Thus, he realized something was truly amiss.

"May I be of service?" he inquired politely, not certain how one went about dealing with female crises, as this one appeared to be.

This query caused Miss Biddle to weep more loudly into her handkerchief. Miss Fitzhugh frowned. "We must talk to Lord Sommersby sooner or later," she told her cousin in a matter-of-fact tone. "Indeed, I believe you might take this as a propitious opportunity."

Warily, Simon watched as the two women exchanged a meaningful look. Obviously they shared a secret. Secrets between females—especially these females—made him uneasy.

He had not seen Miss Fitzhugh since she had learned the truth about his masquerade and defiantly offered herself to him anyway. Simon had never known a woman capable of such forthrightness. In his experience, women were coy creatures who rarely spoke their minds and deferred to men at every turn. Simon had a difficult time reconciling his image of Miss Fitzhugh, who seemed to defer to no man, with the timid and malleable maid Julian had described in that brandy-induced talk after their fencing match.

"I cannot, of course, speak for the present state of the lady's virtue," Julian had drawled, "but she left Vauxhall that night quite chastened and as innocent as ever she had been. She has since become quite a thornback, of course. I believe she would sooner box a man's ears as allow him to kiss her."

Was he speaking of the same woman who had kissed him with such wild and inviting abandon that day on the cliff?

Simon forced his eyes away from Miss Fitzhugh's somber features to Miss Biddle's reddened ones. It struck him that it was a pity Miss Biddle was the perfect bride for him, when Miss Fitzhugh was far better suited to his temperament—not to mention his passions.

But passion was not everything, and no one knew that better than he. Men who threw themselves on their opponents' swords in the fervor of battle ended up dead, their shredded flesh rotting on the battlefield long after the smoke had cleared. There was no glory in letting passion control reason. Battles were not won with fervid exhortations and the venting of bloodthirsty urges. They required dispassionate planning and a methodical approach.

Since he had used both to arrive at the choice of Miss Biddle, he had great confidence in his decision. Miss Fitzhugh represented too many unknowns, and in one important area fell woefully short: She was very much alone in the world and no longer young; there was no guarantee that a woman like that could provide her husband with a brood of the size necessary to secure the line.

Simon was not about to let his title and lands revert to

the Crown. He had not wanted an earldom, but now that he had it, he would do his best to fulfill his duty and discipline himself to submerge the passions Miss Fitzhugh stirred in him.

Their eyes met over Miss Biddle's head. Simon sensed that her thoughts were on that heartstopping moment in his study when, except for the control he had summoned from deep inside him, they might have become lovers. She did not flinch from his gaze as he suspected many women might. And although there was now no invitation within those dark eyes, he found her simple courage strangely erotic.

Simon wondered how they would be looking at each other if he had not found it within himself to send her away. In the past, he had never experienced a moment's doubt as to the honorable course. It was only in Miss Fitzhugh's presence that honor became a tiresome burden, that desire threatened to undermine his good intentions, and that admiration endowed her with the courageous nobility of a martial queen.

Had he sunk so low that he no longer embraced the tenets that had guided him his entire life? Even if he had wished to risk the future of his family on Miss Fitzhugh's breeding abilities, it was too late. He was betrothed to Miss Biddle. A man did not break such a promise, nor fail those who depended upon him. Simon put all rebellious thoughts from his head.

"What did you wish to talk with me about?" he asked Miss Biddle, even as his gaze remained locked with Miss Fitzhugh's.

His betrothed sobbed anew. "Oh, dear," she cried, "this is unspeakable."

"It is *not* unspeakable, Felicity," Miss Fitzhugh said sternly. "Indeed, I believe you must speak it this very moment or risk having Lord Sommersby think we are both candidates for Bedlam. The man is your betrothed. You owe him an explanation."

When these ominous words penetrated his mind, Simon finally tore his gaze from Miss Fitzhugh and regarded his weeping fiancée. "Miss Biddle?" he inquired gently.

"He has gone," she blurted out.

Simon frowned. *Who* had gone? He could not imagine that Miss Biddle was in despair over the departure of Sir Thomas. Suspicion swept him. Julian had left Sommersby just this morning. Though Julian had spent most of his time at the castle searching for the papers to prove his legitimacy, Simon wondered whether he had not also managed to worm his way into Miss Biddle's affections.

"I am afraid I do not understand," he said. When Miss Biddle did not immediately enlighten him, Miss Fitzhugh eyed her cousin reproachfully.

"Felicity is referring to the young man who has been cataloguing your books and weapons," she said, pursing her lips.

Simon frowned. A vague image of an earnest young man with dark curly hair came to his mind. Since hiring the young scholar last month, he had been only dimly aware of his presence in the castle. What was the man's name, anyway? "Mr. Flake?" Simon asked, pleased that he plucked the name from out of nowhere.

"Frakes," Miss Biddle corrected tearfully. "Stephen Frakes." She blew her nose. "He was not in the library when I took Amanda to meet him. Mr. Jeffers said he had left word that he would not return to his duties at the castle."

Simon could not imagine why that statement should call forth more tears from Miss Biddle, but it did. Helplessly, he eyed Miss Fitzhugh.

"There, there, Felicity," she said.

Miss Biddle wiped her eyes. "He has abandoned me. I should have known better. You were right after all, Amanda. This is what comes from indulging in silly romantical fantasies."

Simon stared at his fiancée in dawning horror. "Do you mean to say, Miss Biddle, that you formed an . . . an *attachment* to the man I hired to organize my collection?"

He waited for a denial. None came. "I do not understand," he said at last.

"What do you not understand, Lord Sommersby?" Miss Fitzhugh snapped. "The fact that Felicity formed a compelling attraction for someone other than you, or the fact that such attractions can exist at all?"

"I understand, Miss Fitzhugh, that women are prone to

unpredictable fancies." Simon spoke slowly, with the exaggerated patience one might use with a small child. "It is the man's responsibility to assure that reason rules. That is what I am trying to do now."

"Fancies?" Steel glinted in her eyes. "There is nothing fanciful about love, my lord."

"I suppose you expect me to yield to your extensive knowledge of the subject, Miss Fitzhugh," he retorted, his patience dissipating as she pinned him with those challenging eyes. "I take leave to disagree, however. Reason must rule in human relations. What you call love is nothing but an excess of the more primitive elements of human nature. Those elements must be controlled if one is to achieve an orderly future."

Miss Biddle, he noticed, had stopped crying and was staring at them, wide-eyed. Miss Fitzhugh regarded him with something approaching incredulity.

"Reason?" she echoed. "Primitive elements?" She shook her head. "I thought that *I* had done myself a disservice by shunning sentiment for all these years but *you,* sir, are worse than I ever was."

Simon frowned. "I have had no cause to regret adherence to my principles."

"Your discipline is to be commended, of course," she replied in a voice laced with sarcasm. "Unfortunately, not everyone—especially we pitiable females—possesses your iron will. I wonder that you do not simply decide to keep to your own company for the rest of your days. Then you will never be disappointed."

"That would make it somewhat difficult to set up my nursery," Simon growled. "Unless a woman of your vast experience with such matters knows of some other way to achieve that goal—"

"Ah. We women are useful for something, it seems," she interjected dryly. "But if it is a breeding machine you want, why do you not simply hire a woman off the streets to bear your children? Undoubtedly that would be quicker and more efficient. And surely you would not have to bother giving her a Season."

"Amanda!" Miss Biddle gasped.

"Moreover, you would not have to worry about the intrusion of excessive sentiment or something as nasty and primitive as passion—"

"Amanda!" All tears were forgotten as Miss Biddle eyed her cousin in astonishment. "I have never heard you speak this way. Whatever is the matter?"

But Miss Fitzhugh was beyond reaching. Riveted, Simon watched as she shot him a final disdainful glare and swept from the parlor like a queen who had just savaged her mortal enemy.

And indeed, he did feel savaged. Ripped to shreds by a woman who did not know how to mince words. He had no doubt that if Amanda Fitzhugh had possessed a sabre, she would have run him through with it.

Fury rose in his veins, demanding that he follow her this very moment and force her to explain why a woman who had offered herself to him so breathlessly just last night now disdained him so completely. He would sweep her into his arms and force her to admit that she did not disdain him, that she wanted him as much as he wanted her.

The uncivilized side of him wanted her, that is—the side capable of primitive urges. Simon had always been able to restrain those urges. It was only now, as he eyed the door through which Miss Fitzhugh had so recently passed that he felt that loss of control that was becoming so familiar in her presence. His fists clenched at his side. He would not go after her. He would not.

"Lord Sommersby?"

The quiet, tentative voice of his betrothed dimly penetrated his brain. He turned and saw Miss Biddle staring at him uncertainly. *His betrothed.* Simon took a deep breath.

"Miss Biddle," he acknowledged calmly, pleased that he had managed to bring himself under control, "I fear I have been insensitive. Perhaps you would care to start anew and tell me about this Mr. . . . Frakes, is it?"

She nodded. Simon cleared his throat, feeling his way into unfamiliar territory. Warily, he eyed his fiancée's tearstained face, hoping she was not going to cry again.

He coughed. "I gather that the two of you have, ah, became somewhat . . . close?"

At that, Miss Biddle burst into tears anew. As she buried her face in her now-soggy handkerchief, Simon wondered how he had ever thought the task of securing a bride to be a simple, straightforward mission.

Waterloo had never seemed so inviting.

Lady Biddle shook her head and for the sixth time that morning eyed her husband in tight-lipped disapproval. "I cannot imagine why you left Felicity and Amanda in that castle with two unmarried men, one a known rake. Think of the scandal if this became common knowledge!"

"I trust that it will not become common knowledge," Sir Thomas snapped, weary of the harangue that had begun upon his arrival in Mayfield and had continued steadily since they left home yesterday. He suspected his wife had chosen to attack him to cover her discomfort at the scene he had interrupted in her sitting room and which they had yet to discuss. "Besides," he added churlishly, "Felicity has Amanda as her chaperone."

Lady Biddle rolled her eyes. "And who, pray, is to chaperone Amanda and protect her from that horrid Claridge? Can you answer that?"

Sir Thomas frowned. "Why would Amanda need a chaperone? Did you not tell me she was beyond all that? She has been a spinster for years, after all."

"But she is still an unmarried woman. And Claridge has already demonstrated the fact that he desires her. I do not know why you took it into your head to leave the girls at that man's mercy while you came to see about my ankle. I was in perfectly good hands with Dr. Greenfield."

"I daresay," Sir Thomas muttered.

Lady Biddle cast him a curious look. "You were very rude to him, you know."

That, he decided, was too much to bear. "It is my right," he said evenly, "to be rude to any man whom I discover in my wife's private sitting room caressing her foot as if it were the answer to all his prayers."

A coughing fit suddenly seized his wife. Sir Thomas glared at her, unable to decide whether she was sputtering in laughter or indignation. When she could speak, her voice bore a melodious tone that sounded suspiciously like the former. "Richard was only examining my foot, dear. He is a doctor, after all."

"Doctor or no, 'Richard' was fondling your foot as rapturously as I have seen any man touch a woman," Sir Thomas growled. "And you were not attended by a maid at the time." He glared at her. "Do you think me an utter fool, Eloise? I should have killed him on the spot. Now I suppose it will have to wait until we return."

Lady Biddle paled, all hint of amusement gone from her face. As the carriage rounded a curve, she clutched the seat nervously. "Thomas," she said uneasily, "I think we should talk about this."

"Talk?" He eyed her scornfully. "How much talking did you manage with the good doctor?"

"It was not like that," she insisted. "Perhaps he is overly attentive, but Richard—Dr. Greenfield—only has my best interests in mind. He truly *adores* healing. . . ."

Her voice trailed off as her husband eyed her with cold fury. "Let me be plain, Eloise. After we pluck the girls from that moldy castle and rescue them from the potential scandal that no doubt accrues from my abysmal lapse in judgment, we shall go forthwith to London, where you yourself shall see to the matter of Felicity's Season. I will not have the responsibility of launching our youngest fobbed off on Amanda simply because Felicity's mother prefers the hands of the neighborhood quack."

He ignored her shocked gasp. "Furthermore, I do not now—nor ever—intend to share my wife with another man. If that condition is too much for you to abide by, I shall not scruple to send a divorce petition to Parliament."

"Thomas!" she cried, but he continued as if he had not heard her.

"Any notoriety that might result," he said, "is preferable in my view to spending the remainder of my days wondering if my wife was playing me for a fool."

"I have never been unfaithful to you," she protested. "Never have I given you cause to make such accusations!"

Sir Thomas leveled a skeptical gaze at her. "Think again, Eloise. Think back to that little scene I stumbled on two days ago in your room. Think about the good doctor's 'healing' hands, about that predatory look in his eye and that rapturous smile on his face."

His voice dropped. "What do you imagine would have

happened had I not arrived when I did? Can you tell me that, Eloise?"

The acknowledgment in her eyes was painful to see. Lady Biddle bowed her head. "I did not think about that, Thomas."

"No?" His gaze was frankly challenging. "I think you did, my dear. I think you sent me away to Sommersby with the girls because you wanted to find out what would happen. And you almost did find out, but for my untimely arrival." A cynical smile distorted his mouth. "Tell me, Eloise, do you regret that it went unfinished?"

Silently she shook her head. A single tear rolled down her cheek, but it was followed by no heart-rending sobs. His wife had never resorted to such cowardly female tactics and for that, Sir Thomas guessed, he should have been thankful. At the moment, however, he felt anything but. He wanted only to shake her and force her to tell him why he was not husband enough for her.

Sommersby Castle rose on the near horizon, however. With a heavy sigh, Sir Thomas turned his thoughts away from the woman at his side and toward whatever disastrous situation awaited within those ancient stone walls.

Chapter Nineteen

Amanda knew she had to leave. Almost overnight, her contented spinster's existence had been shattered by a man who did not even suspect he had turned her world upside down.

That Felicity imagined herself infatuated with Stephen Frakes changed nothing, for Amanda suspected her cousin would come to her senses once the full import of Mr. Frakes's departure settled in. The feckless young man had obviously preyed on Felicity's romantic illusions, then prudently taken himself off after considering the consequences of dallying with Lord Sommersby's betrothed.

Amanda had no doubt that Lord Sommersby still considered himself bound to Felicity. He was a man who honored his commitments, who would not be swayed from his course by something as irrational as anger or jealousy. Lord Sommersby was a man of reason.

Reason. Amanda had come to despise that word, for it constantly reminded her of her own failings. As much as she endeavored to learn from past mistakes and purge herself of irrational thoughts and deeds, she still came up short. Had she made so little progress since Vauxhall? Had she learned nothing at all in eight years?

Precious little, it seemed. Her every sense tingled in the earl's presence. She could not even speak to him without wondering what thoughts lay behind that enigmatic gaze. Tearing her eyes from his demanded enormous effort.

What was it that drew her? To be sure, Lord Sommersby cut an imposing figure in his claret kerseymere, buff trousers, and burnished Hussars—but even in Thornton's poorly cut dimity, gray hair, and drooping mustache, he had fairly taken her breath away.

Perhaps it was his character that made him so compelling. Reserve and modesty were remarkable in a man of his achievements, discipline and restraint incongruous in a man of such wealth and fame. Doubtless even in battle, he retained his poise. Amanda could not envision him charging wildly into the fray, hacking at the enemy with a crazed cry. He would be cool, assessing, and deadly.

Did the man never lose control? Did he never fall prey to the passions that besieged lesser mortals? Amanda sighed. She would never find out, not while she still possessed a shred of honor.

And yet, she yearned to shake his iron discipline, to push beyond his steely control and touch something in the man that would respond to the woman in her.

She would write to Lady Biddle and tell her she could not accompany Felicity to London. Her aunt would be displeased, but Amanda had no other choice. She did not have Lord Sommersby's discipline. She had become a woman out of control.

With a heavy sigh, she began to compose the letter to her aunt.

"Edward looks miserable."

"He always does, Isabella."

"This is different. It is because Claridge has left, I am sure of it. It is only a matter of time before Edward hies after him and we will be free at last!"

"Free to do what, do you imagine?"

"Free to wander England with abandon, choosing comely humans to inhabit and savor the delights of the flesh that have been denied us for so long."

"You will pardon me if I retain some skepticism, my dear. I cannot think that it will be that simple."

"Pah! With Edward gone, there will be nothing to chain us to this miserable castle. But before we go, we will finish the business with our tenant and the chaperone."

"How? Our tenant seems unable to shake his resolve."

"He is suffering, Mortimer. That is what is important."

"The man is a soldier, Isabella. He can endure a little suffering."

"You have not taken the chaperone into account."

"But she means to leave."

"Does she? We shall see about that."

"What are you planning, Isabella?"

"Mortimer, dear, happiness will soon be ours."

Felicity did not usually nap during the day, but today's ordeal had been too much. Huddling under the bed covers, she closed her eyes against the devastating discoveries she had made.

Stephen did not love her—otherwise, he would have stayed to face Lord Sommersby and her father. That revelation was bad enough, but Felicity had discovered something almost as shocking.

Amanda was in love with Lord Sommersby.

How else to explain her cousin's strange behavior today? How else to account for her reckless defense of love, her wild temper, and that amazing confession about offering herself to Lord Sommersby? How else to explain the way Amanda looked at the earl and—wonder of wonders—the way he looked at her?

Just this afternoon, however, the earl had renewed his promise of marriage, claiming that Felicity's rash behavior with Stephen had not altered his commitment. Felicity suspected that honor, not affection, lay behind his decision to remain bound to her. But although Lord Sommersby had been very kind, she felt no more for him than she would a kindly stranger.

It was Amanda who loved Lord Sommersby, Amanda who deserved her chance at happiness after so many years of spinsterhood. But she would never take it as long as Felicity and the earl were betrothed.

Felicity's head ached from trying to think of a solution to this conundrum. Perhaps if she slept for a while, the answer would come to her. Sighing, Felicity allowed the soothing darkness behind her eyelids to overtake her.

Ghostly images flitted through her dreams. A strangely dressed couple in ancient clothing began to act out a scene in which two lovers consummated their undying passion.

It was a rather scandalous dream, but when Felicity awoke, she had a smile on her face. Now she knew precisely what to do.

*   *   *

"What do you mean she is missing?" Lady Biddle stared incredulously at Amanda.

"She had retired to her room to rest," Amanda explained unhappily. "When I went to fetch her for dinner, she was gone."

Sir Thomas frowned. "'Tis a rather large place, this castle. Can you be certain that she is not here?"

"No." Lord Sommersby looked grim, and Amanda could not blame him. They had only had time to search the living quarters when Sir Thomas and Lady Biddle had unexpectedly arrived. If Felicity had taken it into her head to explore the farther reaches of the castle, who knew where she might be? Perhaps one of the crumbling stone walls had fallen on her. Now night was upon them and something had to be done.

Sir Thomas evidently had the same thought. "This is your castle, Sommersby, and I judge that you have the best shot of finding her within these walls. I will ride out and search the countryside."

"Jeffers will go with you," the earl said tersely, doubtless as aware as Amanda of what could happen to an unescorted young woman on the roads at night.

"I do not understand," Lady Biddle said, bewildered. "Why would Felicity have run away?"

Amanda exchanged glances with Lord Sommersby. Perhaps this was not the time to tell Felicity's parents about Stephen Frakes. On the other hand, it was probably the only explanation that made sense. Amanda knew that he was leaving the decision up to her. She could see little choice except to tell the Biddles everything.

"Felicity suffered a disappointment today," she began. "I am not certain she would wish to have the matter discussed like this, but I think unhappiness must be at the heart of her disappearance."

Lady Biddle eyed her in confusion. "Disappointment? Unhappiness? Amanda, whatever are you saying?" Her eyes widened suddenly. "Never say that monster Claridge insinuated himself with Felicity!" She rounded on her husband. "This is precisely what I feared when you left so rashly, Thomas. I do not see how you could have done such a foolish—"

"Claridge left early this morning," Lord Sommersby interjected. "He had nothing to do with Miss Biddle's state."

"'State?'" Sir Thomas frowned. "Just exactly what has been going on here? Sommersby? Amanda?"

Amanda sighed. "Felicity formed an attachment for a young man in the earl's employ."

"Dear lord!" Lady Biddle gasped. "A *servant*?"

"Mr. Frakes is a young scholar I hired to catalog my library and weapons collection," Lord Sommersby explained.

Inadvertently, Lady Biddle's gaze wandered to the lethal-looking devices that hung from the walls of the Great Hall. "I see," was her tight-lipped response.

"I assume responsibility for being less than diligent in my chaperone duties," Amanda said quickly. "I was so intent on keeping Felicity and the earl company that I paid no heed to the occasions when she took herself off alone."

Sorrowfully, she eyed her aunt and uncle. "I gather she spent a great deal of time in the library with Mr. Frakes. I have no reason to believe that anything untoward occurred. Nevertheless, I was remiss in my duties."

Sir Thomas's frown deepened into a scowl. "Did this reprobate go off with my daughter?" he demanded.

"No. At least not initially," Lord Sommersby replied. "Jeffers said Mr. Frakes departed on his own, leaving word that he did not expect to return."

"My poor baby," Lady Biddle murmured, shaking her head. "To have her eyes opened to the natures of men so soon."

Sir Thomas glowered at his wife, then spoke to the earl. "You say she was distraught?"

When Lord Sommersby hesitated, Amanda touched her uncle's hand. "It seems so, sir, but I pray that when she has had time to consider the matter, things will not seem so dire. Lord Sommersby was quite understanding about the entire matter."

The baronet's countenance darkened. "A man ought not be 'understanding' when another poaches on his territory."

"Thomas!" his wife said reprovingly. "There is no sense

taking Lord Sommersby to task. None of this was his doing."

"No, indeed," Amanda agreed unhappily. "I take full responsibility."

"I bear the blame," the earl said in a clipped voice. "I am afraid I was not very attentive."

Sir Thomas threw his hands up in disgust. "Who the devil were you attending to, if not my daughter?"

Frowning, the earl opened his mouth to speak, but Sir Thomas cut him off. "Never mind. Time is wasting. Felicity could be anywhere. Sommersby, you and Amanda will search the castle. Your man and I will be off immediately."

"But what about me, Thomas?" Lady Biddle asked worriedly. "Surely there is something *I* can do?"

Her husband shot her a black look. "You can contemplate how to better instruct your daughter as to the 'natures of men'—since it appears that you have become something of an expert."

Lady Biddle's lips thinned, but she did not say a word. Amanda eyed her uncle in surprise, never having heard him speak harshly to or about his wife.

Looking decidedly grim, Lord Sommersby grabbed her elbow none too gently. Wordlessly, Amanda followed him into the bowels of the castle.

"I do not think Felicity would have come up here." Worriedly, Miss Fitzhugh eyed the forbidding tower.

With an impatient shrug, Simon pushed open the door. It did not give easily, leading him to doubt that a delicate young lady such as Miss Biddle could have opened it. Still, it was worth a search. They had looked almost everywhere else. "Do not tell me you put any stock in those old stories," he said gruffly, when she hesitated on the threshold.

"What stories?" Her voice held a faint note of apprehension.

In spite of his black mood, Simon found himself admiring the way their arduous search had dislodged that primly arranged hair and sent errant tresses tumbling down around her shoulders. Her nose bore a faint but charming smudge that she must have acquired in one of the dustier rooms.

"'Tis rumored to be haunted by the ghosts of Edward II

and his queen, Isabella of France," he said, noting the ripple of uneasiness that swept her features. It seemed that the self-possessed Miss Fitzhugh was not entirely immune to superstition. "Her lover, Roger Mortimer, is supposed to reside here as well."

"Oh, yes. Now I recall. Mr. Thor . . . you told me the story earlier."

Being reminded of his reprehensible masquerade did nothing for Simon's already dour mood. And while the prospect of entering a haunted death chamber did not bother him, the idea of unsettling her gave him a perverse pleasure.

"Edward died in this very tower," he said, entering the room. Simon's candle illuminated a cobwebbed ceiling and rotting beams that looked to be an ideal perch for bats, who no doubt hung from them during the day. An ornately carved chair, its cushions long gone to dust, served as the only furniture.

"I see." She did not look as if she wanted to hear more, but Simon could not resist the ungentlemanly desire to repay her for some of the agony she had cost him.

"A heated iron spit was thrust into him," he said in a matter-of-fact tone. "'Tis said that the dying king's screams were heard throughout the castle for hours."

Her sharp gasp made him instantly ashamed. "Dear lord," she said faintly, sagging against the wall.

Regret filled him as he moved quickly to her side, offering his hand for support. "I am sorry. That was poorly done of me."

"Perhaps war has inured you to heinous acts, my lord, but I confess that contemplating that poor man's horrible death makes me ill. Who could have done such a thing?"

"His devoted wife and her lover," Simon said dryly. "After Edward deprived Isabella of her estates and bestowed them on a court favorite, she left for France and raised an army with Mortimer. They deposed Edward in favor of his son and imprisoned the king here."

She looked around the musty little room and shivered.

"'Tis said that as punishment the ghosts of Isabella and Mortimer must remain in the castle for all time, listening to Edward's screams." Simon paused. "'Tis only a silly legend, of course," he added reassuringly. "Shall we move on?"

A cold draft blew by them. Simon fought the sudden urge to warm her in his arms.

"Isabella must have been a vengeful woman," she commented. A sudden, sharp gust whipped her hair into her face, and she recoiled at the sting.

Simon had to restrain himself from smoothing the hair back from her cheeks. "It is said that she did not care for Edward's tendency to bestow his affection and her wealth on court favorites," he replied.

"I do not imagine that it was unusual for a king to have mistresses," Miss Fitzhugh said as she tucked an errant tendril behind her ear.

Simon cleared his throat. "I believe the king's favorites were not precisely, ah, female."

A deep flush spread across her features. "Isabella must have been deeply distressed to lose her husband's affections in such a manner."

"Insulted, more likely," he said, fascinated with the way that flush warmed her cheeks. "The king made no pretense of holding her in affection."

"How ironic that they—and Mortimer—are joined together in eternity."

Simon eyed her in surprise. "You speak as though you believe in our ghostly trio."

"I believe that there are forces at work in our lives that we do not always understand. I would never have called them ghosts, but I would never have imagined my actions of the last few days, either." Her expression grew somber. "I have no choice but to conclude that I know very little about the world and perhaps even less about myself."

That dark, bottomless gaze held his as she continued. "I apologize for my intemperate words earlier today, my lord. I do not know what has come over me lately."

Her honestly wrapped around some heretofore unknown place deep within him. In that moment, Simon knew how little his admiration for Amanda Fitzhugh had to do with her physical charms. It was her mature grace and strength of character that truly captivated him. In acknowledging her flaws, in apologizing for a dishonorable passion, she embraced a fearless humanity that in no way diminished her.

The stark sound of the tower door creaking on its hinges brought him back to the present. He forced himself to recall the mission at hand: to find his fiancée.

With a sigh, Simon clutched his candle and led them out into the hall. A moan like the wailing of all souls blew through the tower, whipped by the wind and the emptiness of the little chamber behind them.

Chapter Twenty

The more Amanda thought about it, the more convinced she became that Felicity had taken to the tunnels. Had not her cousin envisioned the cave as a temporary hideaway in the event of her elopement? With Felicity's sense of drama, it would be just like her to seclude herself in the love nest she meant to have had with Stephen Frakes. Amanda suspected they would find her cousin this very night, nursing a broken heart in what was to have been their underground bower.

How could Felicity form a heart-wrenching affection for Mr. Frakes in so short a time? But then, she reasoned, Lord Sommersby had made an indelible imprint on her own emotions. Perhaps time meant nothing set against the yearnings of the human heart.

Yearnings and love were not necessarily the same, as she had discovered years ago and as Felicity was learning now. To avoid a lifetime of misery, her cousin must set aside her yearnings, as Amanda had learned to do.

And yet, as Amanda stood contemplating the door to her wardrobe, she heard an internal voice taunting as useless her efforts to set aside her feelings for Lord Sommersby.

Part of her fervently hoped that when she and the earl searched the tunnel, Felicity would be waiting for them, ready to give up her childish behavior and return to her betrothed. The other part of her wanted only to walk with Lord Sommersby in those dimly lit corridors, feel that strangely relentless bond between them, and pray that Stephen Frakes returned to claim Felicity as his bride.

The knock at her bedroom door was polite, firm, and purposeful. Lord Sommersby had given her time to refresh herself and, like the meticulous officer he was, appeared promptly at the appointed hour.

Amanda opened the door. His lantern illuminated the chiseled planes of his face, the firm jaw, the pupils that initially widened, but quickly retreated into a familiar blankness that told her no hidden passion could possibly lurk behind that flat gaze.

Another woman might have nurtured the fragile hope that those secluded tunnels they were about to explore would awaken the wild warrior who slept within that rigid bearing. But by now, Amanda could read that cool, controlled gaze. The Earl of Sommersby would never submit to a desire that would taint the honor he bore so relentlessly on his broad shoulders.

Hope shriveled in her breast.

Simon tried not to stare at the big four-poster bed that dominated Amanda Fitzhugh's chamber. Once before he had carried her to that bed, albeit under vastly different circumstances. He could still envision her in the dressing gown she had worn the night she had injured her ankle. Though her hair was now pinned back neatly, his mind saw that silky curtain falling loose around her shoulders as he cradled her in his arms. And though her ankle had largely healed, he could still envision her wince as his fingers explored that smooth, bare limb.

With a start, he realized his thoughts had wandered far afield. Forcing his gaze away from hers, he surveyed their supplies, taking approving note of the extra candles she had assembled. By the time he turned to her once more, he possessed the discipline to throw her a briskly impersonal glance and growl a terse order to stay by his side.

Wordlessly, she nodded, and Simon suppressed a twinge of guilt. She was not one of his men, and he ought not to treat her so.

"Let me go first," he said gruffly. "It would not do for you to injure yourself again."

"No," she agreed quietly.

When he stepped into the wardrobe, he was amazed to see that the panel affording entrance to the tunnel had not been secured. "I thought you were going to bolt that shut," he said, frowning.

"I daresay no one is plotting to invade my chamber." She

seemed surprised by the notion. "Claridge has gone, and I know of no one else who would even contemplate such a thing."

There was no need to confess that he had more than once imagined invading her chamber himself. He spoke quickly to cover his embarrassment. "Yes, well, who knows what creatures reside in the caves? Bats, snakes, perhaps even bears. I should not think you would wish to risk exposing yourself—"

"Lord Sommersby," she interrupted, eyeing him in sudden amusement, "neither bat nor snake has the power to open that door. And if you truly thought a bear prowled these caves, I daresay you would not take us farther."

In the face of her impeccable logic, Simon could only proceed into the tunnel, feeling like a babbling fool. But as he turned to assist her into the darkened corridor, all amusement vanished from her face. Her step was tentative, uneasy. Simon wondered whether her ankle pained her. Though she no longer used her cane, he began to suspect she had abandoned it prematurely. The thought of having to carry her if her ankle gave out unnerved him. Simon tried to put that possibility aside and concentrate on the mission at hand.

As they walked through the tunnel, Simon held the lantern while she lit the candles in the wall sconces the smugglers had installed, replacing those that needed it. Soon they approached the cavern he and Miss Biddle had explored the day Miss Fitzhugh had remained behind with Julian. Something bitter rose in his mouth at the memory of the way in which she had tenderly stroked Julian's brow.

Grateful for the uneven footing that suddenly distracted him, Simon grasped her about the waist to lift her over a few precarious spots. The intimate knowledge he gained from this exercise—that she did not wear a corset—sent an almost unbearable desire knifing through his gut.

Anything was bearable, he reminded himself. One merely walled the pain up inside and went on.

Duty, honor, obligation. As he led Miss Fitzhugh through the narrowing stone corridor, inhaling her scent, contemplating her curious combination of strength and vulnerability, he recited these words to himself. They would keep the anguish at bay. They always had.

Once, as he eased them through a particularly narrow part of the tunnel, his arm inadvertently brushed her breast, and she inhaled sharply. He debated whether to apologize, then reasoned that to speak of it would embarrass her further and acknowledge something between them that should best go unacknowledged. In the end, he decided to say nothing, and was relieved when they emerged at last into the spacious cavern.

There, on a moldy pallet sat his betrothed. A dozen candles blazed on the walls. A small knapsack and other supplies rested beside her. Miss Biddle had obviously been prepared for an extensive stay.

"Good evening, Amanda, Lord Sommersby," she said gaily, seemingly unsurprised to see them. "Or is it good morning? One cannot tell night from day in this place."

"Felicity!" Miss Fitzhugh cried. "What are you about?"

"Why must I be 'about' anything, Amanda?" Miss Biddle frowned. "I should think it perfectly acceptable for a lady to slip away by herself to do some thinking."

"We have been looking everywhere for you," Miss Fitzhugh declared. "Your parents are here. They know all about Mr. Frakes."

A shadow crossed Miss Biddle's delicate features. "Mama must be beside herself thinking that I have done something rash." She smiled apologetically. "I suppose I have been very foolish."

Miss Fitzhugh eyed her cousin in relief. "It is wonderful to hear you say so, dear. Lord Sommersby will make you an inestimable husband. I am glad to see you have put that other episode behind you."

Rising, Miss Biddle smoothed her skirts. "I quite agree, Amanda. The earl will make an excellent husband."

Simon did not particularly like being talked about as if he were some inanimate rock formation to be remarked upon. He stepped forward. "Miss Biddle, nothing that has happened has diminished my respect and admiration for you," he said, knowing that that much, at least, was true. "You have made me very happy by agreeing to be my bride." More difficulty with that one, but his duty was clear.

Miss Biddle beamed. "Then it is all settled. Shall we return to the castle?"

As they made their way back through the tunnel, Simon had the distinct feeling he was missing something. His betrothed bore no resemblance to the young lady who had been so distraught over Frakes's disappearance. She chatted gaily, nonchalantly making amusing small talk as if they strolled sedately in the park. He supposed he should be glad that the whole thing was settled so quickly, but something nagged at him, nevertheless.

Finally they reached the entrance to the wardrobe. Miss Biddle suddenly frowned.

"Oh, dear! My necklace is gone! I must have dropped it somewhere along the way." Her mouth pursed charmingly. "My lord, would you be so kind as to try to locate it?"

The last thing Simon wanted to do was to prolong this expedition, but he could hardly expect her to go back for it. "What does it look like?" he asked, suppressing a sigh.

"What? Oh, it is a small gold locket. It was a present from my mother, and I am greatly attached to it."

Simon frowned. A small locket could easily languish in some tiny crevice out of range of the lantern's glow. He might be here all night and never find the thing.

"I am afraid I do not recall the necklace you mean, Felicity." Miss Fitzhugh's brow furrowed.

Miss Biddle looked shocked. "You cannot have forgotten it, Amanda," she said reproachfully.

Leaving the ladies to dispute the matter between themselves, Simon started back into the tunnel. In the next instant, he heard the solid thump of a door closing. Turning, he saw Miss Fitzhugh standing quite alone, wearing a look of consternation.

"Felicity!" she cried. "What is the meaning of this?"

Laughter sounded from within the wardrobe, where Miss Biddle had evidently gone to. "You will understand when you read my note, Amanda," came the faint, but amused, reply.

As Simon's gaze shot from the solid back of the wardrobe

to Miss Fitzhugh, they heard the distant sound of the heavy bolt being drawn.

Miss Biddle had locked them in the tunnel.

Suddenly, he realized what had nagged at him. Miss Biddle had left her knapsack and supplies back in the cavern.

Fear swept through him, the kind of raw, primitive fear every soldier faces when he enters a new battle realizing it may be his last. Simon's fear had nothing to do with being trapped in a tunnel at night with whatever wild creatures prowled the caves. It was born of the awareness between him and Miss Fitzhugh that suddenly blazed like banked fires stirred to new life.

He tried to discipline his thoughts toward the task at hand. They would have to conserve their supplies while they found an escape route. It was a simple exercise in basic survival. He had done it a thousand times.

But not with Amanda Fitzhugh. They would have to huddle together for warmth, as well as eat and possibly sleep together. They might as well be tethered to each other. His control was facing its greatest battle yet.

In that moment, Simon recognized the limits of his own discipline. He felt like the weariest soldier on earth.

"Felicity!" Lady Biddle sat up in bed, rubbed her eyes, and stared at her youngest daughter.

"Good morning, Mother. I trust you had a pleasant journey." Guilt at the lines of worry on her mother's face did not dampen Felicity's spirits. Indeed, she felt positively buoyant. If ever two people were meant for each other, it was Amanda and Lord Sommersby.

"Where have you been, child?" Lady Biddle demanded. "And where is this . . . librarian of yours?"

A sharp pain of loss punctured her high spirits. Felicity took a deep breath and met her mother's gaze. "Mr. Frakes is gone. But I am grateful for the opportunity to have known him, for it has opened my eyes to an important truth."

"What, pray, would that be?" Lady Biddle demanded.

Felicity settled herself on the edge of her mother's bed and sighed. "That I cannot dictate the needs of my heart."

Lady Biddle frowned in disapproval. "I do not know why your father allowed you to study literature at that school for young ladies. It ruined your eyesight and left you with a lot of foolish notions."

"Is it foolish to wish to spend the rest of one's life with the man one loves, Mama?"

There was a long pause. "To desire such a thing is natural, I suppose, at your age," Lady Biddle conceded. "To expect it, however, is foolish."

"But you and Papa gained your hearts' desire. For years I have envied that special spark between you two. It is obvious that you feel great affection for each other."

"Relationships do not always sustain themselves at a feverish peak," Lady Biddle replied, looking away. "You are better off marrying someone appropriate, not a penniless librarian who recites poetry."

"How did you know that Stephen loves poetry?" Felicity asked in surprise.

Her mother allowed herself a smile. "My dear, I cannot imagine that it would be otherwise in a man who has claimed your heart."

"I will not marry Lord Sommersby."

Lady Biddle arched a brow. "I take it that the earl has no use for sonnets?" she said dryly.

"It is not that," Felicity said. "I cannot marry a man for whom I have no passionate feelings. Do you understand?"

Recalling some of the more lustful aspects of her own courtship, Lady Biddle colored. "I do indeed," she murmured. "But passion does not always last."

Felicity did not miss the troubled look in her mother's eyes. "All is not well between you and Papa?" she ventured.

"Felicity!" Lady Biddle said sternly. "The state of relations between your father and me is not your concern."

"Dr. Greenfield," Felicity intoned with a knowing expression.

"What about him?" Lady Biddle grew rigid.

Felicity hesitated. "Have you not seen how the man is besotted with you? He is always hanging about, ostensibly to check on your health. When you turned your ankle and required his tending, he was nigh to ecstatic."

Lady Biddle's gaze grew troubled. "I did not realize that the situation was so obvious," she said quietly.

"If I have noticed it, you can be sure Papa has," Felicity replied. "Indeed, I believe he turns positively green when the man's name is mentioned. That is how I knew Papa was lying when he counseled me to marry for suitability, instead of love."

"Lying?" Lady Biddle echoed, startled.

"Why, yes, Mama. Papa is thoroughly in love with you, you know." A dreamy look inhabited her violet gaze. "You are fortunate to have what so many yearn for."

Tears welled in Lady Biddle's eyes. "I have been so foolish—and lonely. I did not want to face the fact that the last of my chicks was leaving the nest. With your sisters established in their own households, they have no need for me, and soon you—"

"Not so, Mama," Felicity protested. "We will always need you."

"Your father has been away in London so much," Lady Biddle continued, dabbing her eyes with a lace handkerchief. "Richard's attentions made me feel young again. And, I suppose, they kept me from worrying about whether there might be . . . someone else that kept Thomas away so much."

Felicity's eyes widened. "Oh, Mama! I am sure that Papa does not have a mistress!"

Lady Biddle colored. "What a thoroughly inappropriate subject to discuss with one's daughter," she said, blowing her nose.

"It is all right, Mama," Felicity said sadly. "My knowledge of the world has recently expanded."

Lady Biddle gasped. "Felicity! Never say you let this young man take liberties—"

"Stephen was the perfect gentleman," Felicity assured her. "Sometimes I wish it had been otherwise," she added with a wistful sigh. "I do not believe that love should be denied just because society says that it is proper to wait until marriage."

Felicity expected this confession to produce another shocked gasp from her mother. To her surprise, Lady Biddle merely smiled. "You know, dear," she said softly, "I see a great deal of myself in you."

Shyly, Felicity clasped her mother's hand, feeling closer

to her than she had in some time. It was a relief to have everything out in the open. Or *almost* everything, she amended.

"Where is Papa?" Felicity asked cautiously.

"Out scouring the countryside for you. I expect he will be back soon. He will be overjoyed to know that you are unharmed. As will Amanda." Lady Biddle started. "Oh, my! I had forgotten about Amanda. She and Lord Sommersby have been searching the castle. We must let them know you are back—where *were* you anyway, dear?"

Felicity regarded her mother with wide, innocent eyes. "Merely reading in a quiet place I discovered recently. You know, Mama, I do not think we ought to try to locate Amanda and the earl. The castle has so many rooms, we should never find them. I am certain they will be back in good time."

"But they may search all night," Lady Biddle protested. "And in all that dust and draft, too. Amanda may catch her death."

Felicity smiled reassuringly. "Lord Sommersby is nothing if not capable, Mama. I am certain that Amanda is in good hands."

Chapter Twenty-one

Bewildered, Amanda held the letter Felicity had hurriedly thrust into her hands before darting inside the wardrobe. Lord Sommersby said nothing, but his bleak expression made his thoughts abundantly clear.

"I cannot account for Felicity's actions, my lord. Perhaps she is playing a prank and will soon free us."

"I suspect not, Miss Fitzhugh," he replied grimly. "Shall we return to the cavern and decipher her note? I believe she has left us ample light."

Following him through the winding corridors into the spacious cavern, Amanda saw that Felicity had indeed left dozens of extra candles, her knapsack, and even a blanket. Opening the knapsack, she discovered it contained cheese, fruit, a crusty loaf of bread, a bottle of wine, and two glasses. Confused, Amanda stared at the supplies. Had Felicity been planning to meet Stephen after all?

Lord Sommersby spread the blanket over a flat rock and gestured for her to sit. Placing the lantern on a slab above them, he eyed her expectantly. "Would you care to read the letter now?"

With great trepidation, Amanda opened the missive and stared at Felicity's neat, round handwriting. Her eyes widened as she read the first few lines to herself.

"Aloud, if you please," Lord Sommersby commanded.

Coughing awkwardly, Amanda fingered the pages. "My lord," she began, "I do not think—"

"Read it, Miss Fitzhugh. I have a suspicion that this concerns both of us."

His implacable gaze told her there was no use arguing. With a sigh, Amanda read aloud: " 'Dear Amanda: Please do not be angry with me. You and Lord Sommersby are so estranged from sentiment that nothing short of forced imprisonment would erode the barriers between you.' "

Her face turned scarlet. Amanda felt the earl's eyes burning into her. With deep apprehension, she read on: " 'Forgive me, my lord, for choosing this cowardly way to tell you that I cannot marry you.' "

Amanda gasped. Mutely she tried to hand him the pages. It was obvious that the note was too personal to read aloud.

"Continue, please," Lord Sommersby ordered coolly.

Swallowing hard, Amanda took a deep breath and continued: " 'My heart belongs to another, and though he has gone away, I find myself incapable of being the devoted bride you so deserve. I cannot marry without love.' "

Dear Lord, Amanda thought, wishing she were anywhere else. She risked a sidelong look at the earl. His face seemed to have turned to stone. "Do you wish me to continue?" she asked quietly.

"Yes."

She took a deep breath. " 'You see, I have discovered the secret that you and Amanda hold so close to your breasts.' "

"I do not know what this is about, my lord," she stammered uneasily, "but I should warn you that my cousin is known for her fanciful imagination."

"Read on, Miss Fitzhugh."

The atmosphere in the cavern had become oppressive. Amanda forced her attention back to the pages. "Very well," she said, praying her voice did not waver.

" 'Knowing that it is not fashionable for a husband and wife to sit in each other's pocket, I was prepared to accept a cordial marriage in hopes that deeper feelings would follow. But Stephen claimed my heart, and I can settle for nothing less than a true meeting of our souls—however long it takes.' " Amanda frowned. Far from abandoning her hopes for Mr. Frakes, Felicity had intensified her feelings, thereby inviting more pain.

" 'In discovering true love,' " she read on, " 'I also realized that I was not the only one in its throes. And so, I send you both this gift—to quote Mr. Jonson—"Not so much honoring thee as giving it a hope that there it could not withered be." ' "

Confused, Amanda pondered her cousin's words. She

might have known Felicity would draw inspiration from the poets, although what "gift" she referred to was a mystery.

Not, apparently, to Lord Sommersby. Amanda met his gaze and noted an unsettling, but knowing, light within those enigmatic depths.

Surreptitiously eyeing the knapsack, wine bottle, candles, and worn pallet, Amanda had a horrible thought. This was the spot Felicity had chosen for her romantic hideaway with Mr. Frakes. Was this the "gift" of which her letter spoke? Had she planned all along to trap them with her ruse about the locket?

"I am not sure I care to read the rest of this," Amanda said, feeling suddenly ill.

Deftly, Lord Sommersby plucked the pages from her hand. "I have always found it best to confront a crisis head-on," he advised calmly, "as delay tends to cause one to imagine a far worse outcome."

It was hard to see how the outcome could be much worse than what she was presently imagining. Shifting uncomfortably on the rock, Amanda listened as the earl took over the reading.

" 'And so, here is my gift to you and Lord Sommersby—' " His rich baritone echoed off the cavern walls as he paused ominously, then read distinctly: "—'a night in this cavern.' "

The sudden, panicked galloping of Amanda's pulse left her hopelessly short of breath. As she stared at him in horror, Lord Sommersby merely read on, his resonant voice warming to the topic.

" 'I have tried to foresee everything you might need. I daresay both of you will come to your senses quickly. At all events, you will be so thoroughly compromised by tomorrow that you will have no choice but to marry. Please do not think harshly of me. Remember: "Nought venture nought have." Yours is a match made in heaven. Now you have my blessing, and one night to discover the truth.' "

Amanda could almost hear Felicity's pleased sigh as she wrote those final word and envisioned the romance her rash act would spark. How could her cousin do such a thing? Did she really mean to lock them away for an entire night in each other's company?

"I do not know what to say, my lord," Amanda stammered. "I am certain my cousin did not mean for us to . . . to . . ." Her voice trailed off.

"To become lovers?" he finished, one brow arching skyward. "On the contrary, Miss Fitzhugh, I believe she most certainly did."

Mortified, Amanda shut her eyes, wondering how to extricate herself from this disaster. Lord Sommersby must be filled with disgust, thinking her so desperate for a husband that her cousin must pull an outrageous prank to secure one for her.

Yet only a coward would sit here with her eyes closed, hoping the cavern floor would suddenly swallow her whole. With renewed determination, she finally met his gaze.

"My lord," she began miserably, "I am sorry."

Without a sign that there was anything out of the ordinary, Lord Sommersby rose and calmly extended his hand. "You will join me, I assume, in trying to find another way out?"

Amanda sighed in relief. He did not take Felicity's scheming seriously. He meant to see that they escaped from this untenable situation. "Oh, yes!" she declared as he helped her to her feet.

"The other side of the cavern must lead to the cliff face," he said. "I have never explored the sea opening, but I believe we have sufficient candles to light our way."

Thank goodness he was such a pragmatic man. She might have known that he would not fall apart in a crisis. Amanda felt silly for panicking. Of course there had to be an outside entrance to the caves. They would find it and be back in the castle before anyone discovered their absence. Feeling the weight of disaster lifted from her shoulders, Amanda picked up a supply of candles and followed him.

The more they walked, the more she allowed herself to relax and appreciate the beauty nature had wrought. Stately stone columns thrust upward from the cavern floor and down from the vaulted ceiling nature formed millions of years ago. Some of the formations resembled flowing draperies, their rippling curves frozen in the path the water had taken. In places, water still trickled over the walls, forming dark pools that could have been a few inches deep or many feet.

Grateful for the candles that lit their way, Amanda remarked upon the serviceable wall sconces.

"The smugglers left nothing to chance," Lord Sommersby replied as he led them into one of the narrower alleys off the main cathedral. "According to Julian, freetraders still used the caves as recently as a few years ago. That is why the tunnels are in such good repair."

"I suppose he spent a great deal of time here as a boy," Amanda observed.

"I suppose."

"It is too bad that Julian left the castle before completing the search for his mother's marriage lines," she said.

Was it her imagination, or did those broad shoulders stiffen? "I take it he did not make his good-byes to you," Lord Sommersby said quietly.

"No," she replied, surprised.

There was a prolonged silence. "Then he did not tell you that we fought."

"Fought?" Stunned, Amanda tried to imagine Lord Sommersby and Julian in hand-to-hand combat. "Over what, pray?"

Whatever response he made was lost as he disappeared around a sudden turn in the tunnel. Amanda hurried after him and crashed abruptly into that rock-solid chest. Instantly, his arms went around her for support.

For a few breathless moments he regarded her silently. Finally, he set her gently from him. "You told me once that no one called Julian to accounts for that night in Vauxhall."

"No," Amanda replied, puzzled. "I did not wish it."

"Well, now the thing has been done," he said simply, turning and resuming his steady pace.

Gasping in shock, she scrambled after him. "Do you mean to say, my lord," she demanded, "that you fought with Julian over *me*?"

"It was not a battle to the death, Miss Fitzhugh," he said dryly, "only a rather spirited fencing bout."

"Still . . . I do not understand," she said, breathless from the effort of keeping up with him.

"Nor did I at the time," he muttered. "It is only now that certain things are becoming more clear."

And with that cryptic statement, Amanda supposed she would have to make do, for he was already pressing ahead. One further thought made her hurry after him.

"Was anyone hurt?" she demanded. "I warn you, sir—I do not hold with bloodshed."

"Fencing is a very civilized sport, Miss Fitzhugh," he replied blandly over his shoulder. "Occasional wounds are unusual and, in any case, largely insignificant."

"You did not answer the question," Amanda persisted. "Nor have you told me how this duel came about."

"It was not a duel."

Exasperated, Amanda sighed. "Then what would you call it?"

So abruptly did he stop in mid-stride that Amanda almost crashed into him again. "I prefer not to discuss this further," he said in a clipped voice.

"And I would prefer not to be hurrying after you in this tunnel as if it were a race."

"My dear Miss Fitzhugh, it *is* a race." He frowned impatiently. "And if I do not miss my guess, we are within moments of discovering whether we have won or lost."

As Amanda stared in confusion, he strode rapidly past the rippling rock formations that in this part of the cave gradually gave way to smoother stone. Suddenly she noticed a salty taste in the air. To her joy, a stiff sea breeze and a thunderous crashing of waves signaled that they were almost free of the confines of the cave.

"Thank goodness!" She heaved a sigh of relief. "I can almost taste the sea."

Strangely, Lord Sommersby did not share her elation. "The sea is near," he confirmed. "*Too* near."

Squinting to pick up the faint outline of the cave opening, Amanda saw with dawning horror what he must have suspected earlier. Angry seawater swirled at the entrance, creeping toward them like giant fingers. Frothy foam lent the encroaching ocean a restless agitation, as if it meant to gobble everything in its path.

"The tide," she said slowly, as the full implication of their plight came to her, "is coming in."

"Yes."

Pools of water had already collected in some of the lower impressions in the ground. "The high-water line seems to be about here." He pointed to a spot on the wall even with his waist.

"How far inside will the water come?" With a sinking feeling, Amanda realized that she already knew the answer.

"Far enough so that we will have to return to the cavern. We cannot get out this way."

Something wet chilled her feet. She looked down to discover frothy tentacles already lapping at her toes. "Will we be safe back there?"

"I am certain the tide does not reach that far in," he replied. "As to the other dangers facing us as the result of Miss Biddle's plan, I cannot say."

Grimly he met her gaze. "It seems that we are destined to spend the night in your cousin's romantic bower after all."

It was well after midnight when Sir Thomas opened the door to his wife's chamber, weariness and defeat etched in the lines of his face. He and Jeffers had searched every inch of the countryside around the castle and every public place in the village itself. No one had seen a young lady meeting Felicity's description. On a desperate whim, he had returned to the castle in hopes that Lord Sommersby and Amanda had discovered his daughter, but the earl and his niece were nowhere to be found.

All in all, it had been a discouraging night. Worry sat heavily on his shoulders, along with the inescapable knowledge that he had been neither an adequate father nor husband. When Eloise greeted him with word that Felicity was sleeping safely in her chamber, he nearly collapsed from relief.

"Thank God!" He sank onto the featherbed beside her.

"Apparently Felicity took herself off somewhere in the castle to think things out a bit," Lady Biddle said. "I believe that young man touched her more deeply than we imagined. She declares herself in love with him."

Sir Thomas glowered. "A penniless librarian who cannot stay to face her father? 'Tis a poor candidate for love. It is best that he fled. She will get over him eventually."

"I would not be too sure of that," she murmured. "Love is a very powerful force."

Sir Thomas shot his wife a sidelong glance. Instantly, his mind gave him the image of Dr. Richard Greenfield, as he had looked caressing her foot not two days ago. "And sometimes love is but an illusion," he growled.

"I have no illusion about the fact that I have never been in love with anyone but you, Thomas," she said quietly.

Startled, Sir Thomas studied his wife. There was a vulnerability about her features he had not seen in some time. As much as he tried to suppress it, a quiet hope surged within him.

"Eloise?" he asked uncertainly.

Lady Biddle sighed. "You have been very busy, Thomas. London has seen more of you than I have."

"Arranging the financing for the rubber plantation in Jamaica has taken a great deal of time," he said, feeling inexplicably awkward. He rushed on. "Once the venture is under way, I expect to realize a handy profit. It will leave us both well-fixed for our later years, and if anything happens to me, you—"

"I thought you had a mistress."

Sir Thomas's jaw dropped. A strangled sound emerged from deep in his throat.

"I know that is the way of men," his wife continued, "but I was lonely, nevertheless. I no longer have the beauty of my youth. Richard's admiration made me feel . . . desired." Her voice caught in her throat.

Tentatively, she reached for him, her gaze pleading. "Nothing happened between us, Thomas. It has always been you."

It was as if the weight of a thousand rubber plantations had been lifted from his shoulders. Moved beyond speech, Sir Thomas pulled his wife into his arms.

"I have not been the best husband," he said, stroking the silky hair that had lost only a bit of its fiery lustre. "But I have never stopped desiring you, Eloise. Or loving you. I have been away too much, but I only had your financial future in mind."

He looked directly into her eyes. "There is no other woman for me. I have always been faithful to you."

A tear rolled down her cheek, a cheek that to him looked as soft and dewy as the day he had met her twenty-five years ago. "Truly?" she asked tremulously.

"Truly."

She closed her eyes. For a while she did not say anything. Finally, her long lashes fluttered open. "I do not know if Felicity still wishes to have a Season," she said shyly, "but I would like to come with you to London while you conduct your business."

Sir Thomas enveloped her in an embrace that was all the more delightful for the fact that he knew every curve, every aspect of the way she fitted into his arms. Her heart beat rapidly against his, betraying her passion. Suddenly he felt young again. That scandalous carriage ride had happened only yesterday, and he was filled with the wonder of a man in love for the very first time.

"I would like that very much," he whispered against her ear. "Perhaps we could even drive to Richmond in a closed carriage some lovely afternoon."

"Thomas!" Lady Biddle said reprovingly, though her eyes sparkled.

"We shall be terribly unfashionable, you know," he added mischievously. "Society does not expect husbands and wives to hang on each other's sleeves."

Defiant sparks shot from her eyes. "The devil with society's expectations."

It had been too long since his wife had displayed such spirit. "The devil, eh? My dear, I believe this castle has had a marked affect on your temperament."

"Are you complaining?" Parting her lips slightly, she blew a warm and tantalizing breath into her husband's ear.

"Never," he swore, groaning helplessly as he covered her mouth with his.

Chapter Twenty-two

Simon contemplated the rock cathedral around him, stuffing his hands into his pockets as he imagined Napoleon must have done before urging his troops on at Waterloo. Napoleon had no idea he was about to send thirty thousand Frenchmen to their doom; Simon, on the other hand, could sense his own impending disaster.

God save the world from women who took matters into their own hands. To be sure, Simon would just as soon not have a wife who constantly mooned over one of his former employees. Still, he could not approve of the drastic steps Miss Biddle had taken to extricate herself from her betrothal and foist upon him a bride of her own choosing.

There was no getting around the fact that Miss Fitzhugh did not meet his qualifications for a wife. Regardless of how much he admired her appealing forthrightness, unadorned beauty, and innate nobility, a woman of her years might never produce the heirs to safeguard his family's heritage.

Simon ventured a sidelong look at Miss Fitzhugh, who was busying herself with exploring a rock slide near the worn pallet. Who knew if she even wanted children? He might ask her, of course, but that would be unforgivably crude, given their current situation.

Would they become lovers this night? Could he control the desire that surged through him whenever he thought of the possibility? It scarcely mattered, for Miss Fitzhugh would be irredeemably compromised no matter what happened. Either way, he was staring at his future wife.

And she was staring back. Gradually, Simon registered the fact that Miss Fitzhugh had ceased her exploration and was regarding him gravely with those velvet eyes, as if she had something important to say.

"This is not the first time my reputation has been jeopardized," she said matter-of-factly.

Simon scowled. "You are referring, of course, to that episode in Vauxhall." Damned if he cared to hear about that again. The image of her and Julian cavorting amid the bushes summoned a host of violent impulses that did nothing for his self-discipline.

She nodded. "At the time, I did not wish to marry a man of weak character. My resolve is just as strong now."

Simon stiffened. "My conduct toward you has not been exemplary, but I scarcely think it warrants a judgment of moral turpitude—"

"I am not disparaging your character, my lord," she interrupted. "I merely wished to make the point that I shall not do something against my nature simply to rescue my reputation."

She sighed heavily, but her gaze never wavered. "What I am trying to say, Lord Sommersby, is that I refuse to force you into marriage—" She hesitated, then added, "Whatever comes of our stay here."

Had he heard correctly? Was this simply a show of bravado? Simon immediately rejected that notion. From the defiant tilt of her chin and the determined set of her mouth, he judged Miss Fitzhugh to be quite serious. Moreover, her eyes glinted with the steel of someone prepared to fight to the death for her principles.

It was a noble, but futile, gesture. Simon was not about to allow a woman to fight his battles, nor would he hide behind a woman's skirts. He would not shun his obligation to her. Still, her earnest offer hit him squarely in his gut, in that soft and tender place whose existence frightened him.

War had taught him that a wise man accepted fear and learned from it. Simon felt immeasurably humbled by the woman before him who was bravely prepared to face the future alone, irreparably compromised as a result of this night.

"I will not allow you to sacrifice yourself and your reputation, Miss Fitzhugh."

A mulish glint darkened her gaze. "I am most resolved on this subject, Lord Sommersby."

"As am I, Miss Fitzhugh."

Only the steady trickle of water somewhere in the cavern filled the sudden silence. Finally, she leveled a steady gaze at him. "Then it seems we are at loggerheads."

"Perhaps. I would prefer to call it a *phrase d'armes.*" At her puzzled frown, he added, "'Tis simply a period of continuous fencing."

Abruptly her lashes obscured those pools of dark velvet as she lowered her gaze. "And how does such a period end, my lord?"

The steady trickling sound seemed to synchronize with his heartbeat, which Simon could swear was loud enough to carry back to the castle. "When there is a break in play," he replied, aware of a strange new excitement in the air between them.

"Would you care to take such a break, Miss Fitzhugh?" he added quietly. "To set our dispute aside for a time? I cannot think we will enjoy the next hours while constantly at odds."

She eyed him uncertainly. "Very well, sir. But I warn you, I am not very good at small talk."

Warmth spread through him like wildfire. Or perhaps it was not wildfire, but an inner fire he had heretofore known only in battle, a fire capable of carrying a man beyond his imagined limits.

"Neither am I," he murmured, moving toward her.

"This will be heaven, Mortimer."

"Hush, Isabella! Do not say that word."

"Pah! We are beyond reach now."

"The last time I thought myself beyond the reach of justice, I was snatched from your arms and marched naked to Tyburn."

"Well, you cannot blame me for that! Who would have imagined that my treacherous son would have his guards invade his mother's bedchamber?"

"The point, dearest Isabella, is that one can never be too sure that one has escaped retribution for one's deeds."

"I weary of your lectures, Mortimer. Edward is nowhere to be seen, and our tenant is mere minutes away from savoring carnal delight with the chaperone. The time is ripe to inhabit their human shells."

"May I remind you that you never liked caves, dear?"

"Five hundred years is a long time, Mortimer. I am willing to risk a bit of damp discomfort in exchange for sampling the joys of the flesh once more with you."

"Are you sure you know how to go about inhabiting a human?"

"How difficult can it be?"

"Something tells me that our tenant and the chaperone are not ordinary humans."

"Well, we are not ordinary ghosts—are we?"

"There has never been anything ordinary about you, dearest."

"Thank you, Mortimer. Shall we join them now? Oh, listen. I made a little pun. How clever!"

"Wit was never your strong suit, Isabella."

"There is no need to be insulting. Mind your tongue, Mortimer."

"If I had such an appendage, you can be sure I would guard it well."

"That is all about to change."

"If you say so, dearest."

Amanda sighed as Lord Sommersby's mouth descended to hers. Their lips met gently at first, then more insistently. The kiss suddenly catapulted her mind back to that cliff with Mr. Thornton, when the warmth of the sun and the salty sea spray had awakened her senses as if for the very first time.

No sun or sea penetrated this far into the cave, but her skin basked in the escalating warmth between them. Amanda was glad it was Lord Sommersby—not Mr. Thornton—who kissed her in this underground bower, so that there could be no pretense, no artifice, no illusions about the moment they shared.

His arms, a warrior's arms, slid around her. Strong and solid, they nestled her against his broad chest with a fierce tenderness that held her captive even as it beseeched her to flee. When he lifted his head, Amanda could see anguish and tightly controlled desire reflected in his eyes, where cool blue seas warred with encroaching green fire.

"My lord," she murmured weakly, "I confess I have no desire for small talk."

"Nor do I."

An underlying roughness in his tone reminded her that he was above all a man of war, capable of violence and accustomed to leading soldiers into the fearsome unknown of combat. Amanda realized that she had yearned to see that warrior again ever since that night in Felicity's room, yearned to break the shackles of that steely discipline. Shameless though it might be, longing trembled in her very bones.

What Julian LeFevre had dimly awakened in her so long ago was as nothing to the intense craving she felt for this man. Despite her proper spinster's habits that shunned every untidy passion, Amanda realized that she did not care what happened beyond this night. She did not care that she would doubtless live the rest of her life an object of scandal. She cared only for the strong arms that enfolded her and the churning green eyes that held hers, waiting for her to speak the words that would give him permission to continue.

Even in passion, it seemed, he was a model of restraint. "Are you always so honorable, my lord?" she asked a bit wistfully.

He frowned. "What do you mean?" There was a strained note in his voice.

"You do not mean to press yourself upon me any more than I allow, do you?"

The shudder that shook that imposing frame was barely noticeable, but it gave Amanda hope. "I would be less than a gentleman if I answered other than in the negative," he replied carefully.

"And you are always a gentleman, I suppose." Amanda sighed heavily. "My lord, I must tell you something quite frankly. If it lowers your opinion of me, I cannot help it."

His expression formed itself into one of stoic resolve. "I would not dream of stifling your nature, Miss Fitzhugh."

Was she imagining it, or did that polite baritone hold a hint of amusement? But no, his expression was impassive, the look of a man accustomed to schooling himself to patience, to studying the battle plan before rushing into the fray. Amanda took a deep breath.

"I do not wish you to be the gentleman, Lord Sommersby."

He did not reply, but the sudden rigidity of his features suggested that he held himself tightly in check.

"I do not wish you to exercise any of those honorable qualities that have no doubt guided you all of your days," she continued firmly. "In short, my lord, I very much wish to be ravished."

A choking sound emerged from somewhere within him.

"I know you have it in you, my lord," Amanda added sternly. "I would go to my grave swearing that there is a beast in you that struggles to be free."

"*A beast?*" He looked at her as if she were mad.

Amanda nodded. They stared at each other as the dripping water nearby beat a steady cadence.

"Restraint is a good thing, my lord," she whispered. "The world would be nothing but chaos without it. But love demands that some restraints be cast aside."

"Love?" He frowned. "I do not know what you mean."

"Perhaps you can learn, my lord. Perhaps you can even consider whether Felicity was correct about us. I shall not force you into marriage, but I shall ask you to ponder that."

Looking slightly dazed, he shook his head. "I have found the heart a poor guide. A dispassionate outlook on life is necessary to keep a man whole."

"We are not at war, my lord," Amanda responded quietly. "Are you afraid to look into your soul and discover that there may be a feeling there some might call love?"

"Call it anything you wish." There was a slightly desperate edge to his voice. "That does not make it so."

"No," she agreed, shyly toying with a lock of his fiery hair.

Slowly her fingertips began to trace the outline of his jaw. The muscles in his face strained with tension, and Amanda sensed the steely discipline that controlled every fiber of him. Gently, she brushed her fingers over his lips, which parted involuntarily at her touch. Smoothing that dusky flesh, she marveled that the lips of a man of such strength could seem so expressively vulnerable.

Instinct alone guided her as she took his hand and blew a gentle breath across the ends of his tapered fingers.

With a great shudder and a savage growl, he reached for her, the veneer of his discipline shattered. Roughly, desperately, his mouth claimed hers. Each of her nerve endings felt the raw, delicious scraping of his chin as his lips moved lower, generating a tide of wild abandon within her as he nibbled at her neck, her ears, her shoulders. When his hand closed over her breast, Amanda gave a little moan of desire that brought from him another growl.

"You see, my lord?" she murmured breathlessly, floating on a wave of helpless delight. "Sometimes a little chaos is necessary."

"Amanda," he snarled, "be quiet."

Chapter Twenty-three

An enemy—cold, implacable, ruthless, deadly.

Unseen.

Simon's fingers flew instinctively to his waist for the scabbard he had not worn in months. Though he felt neither scabbard nor sabre, to his great surprise the ancient broadsword suddenly appeared in his hand, its heavy weight no burden, only an invincible extension of his fighting arm.

Whirling to face his foe, he saw a hazy form dimly outlined against gray, unearthly fog. Simon's senses, which moments ago had sung with the fire of desire, fell strangely silent, save for the sense of smell. He inhaled deeply. His nostrils brought him the familiar, musty damp of the cave along with a new, fetid odor.

Oddly, he possessed no awareness of his own body. He seemed to be as formless as the enemy and curiously light-headed.

Where was Amanda? Only moments ago he had held her in his arms, lost himself in her bottomless brown eyes and gentle strength. Now he beheld only the intruder's obscure outline. Had this menace—whoever he was—stolen her?

"Amanda!" he called in a hoarse cry.

Another voice, vaguely feminine, answered. "Oh, darling. He is magnificent! Those muscles, that fire—do hurry!"

"Ah, but it seems our tenant has decided to be difficult," answered a new voice, straining from exertion.

"Oh, come now, Mortimer. No man can best you with a sword," responded the first with a snakelike hiss.

"Have you told our tenant that?" came the labored reply. A split second later, a sudden blow left Simon reeling.

Where was Amanda? Who were these menacing spirits who struck with such deadly, invisible force?

For a brief moment, Simon's senses came alive again. His gut felt as if a thousand cannons had exploded in him. His head ached as if someone had pounded it with a spike. His vision blurred, and suddenly he was viewing his body from the cavern's vaulted ceiling, looking down on himself and the woman who clung to him.

Amanda.

Not Amanda—though she looked like Amanda.

Kissing him—no, not him. A man who looked like him.

Simon's every instinct tensed for battle. But how did one fight the unseen foes who had invaded their forms? He felt utterly lost.

Suddenly there was another presence beside him, hovering near the ceiling, radiating the fire of life. This spirit was distinctly feminine. Like him, she held a sword. Raising it aloft in a militant salute, she emanated a regal strength forged in some long-ago battle.

And then he knew—that it was Amanda at his side, that he would follow her into death, if need be, that life held no meaning without this woman.

With a warlike cry, Simon clutched his sword and swooped down from the ceiling onto that foreign form that was him and not him. Amanda followed, crying out her own declaration of war, her wispy robes flowing out behind her like angel's wings.

Never had his strength seemed so invincible. Never had any sword handled so effortlessly. The clashing of swords rang through the cavern as he and his love fought side by side with the strength of thousands of lovers before them.

When Simon once more began to feel the ache of his own muscles and the tensing of his own flesh, hope exploded within him like a beacon of light.

"Amanda," he murmured.

"Kiss me, Simon," he heard her reply.

Was it truly Amanda who had spoken? He did not know, for at that moment, his foe assailed him from behind. Simon whirled. With all the strength he possessed, he brought the great broadsword crashing down upon his enemy.

Then he felt Amanda's lips on his.

* * *

In the stone cathedral created by nature's glorious art, Simon discovered frightening forces within him.

Awed by Amanda's bravery, humbled by her passion, he bowed to those forces as he had never bowed to anything in his life. His insides shook with desire and pleading. He felt strangely disjointed, like a man who had just slipped the bonds of a powerful dream. He tried to remember what had momentarily distracted him, but his mind gave him only a vague image of the ancient broadsword and some forgotten battle. Had it been a fleeting dream? Or only his own fears given a life beyond themselves?"

No words came to her lips, but her eyes spoke louder than cannons. She was his.

Like a man with a mortal wound, Simon ached for relief from the stabbing passion and need. Her bodice fell away under his feverish hands, her skin burned under his touch. He could not make himself go slowly in deference to her innocence. Once acknowledged, once unleashed, his wild passion would not be denied.

As her eyes sent him the wordless message of her heart, Simon looked into his own heart and discovered to his amazement that there was something there after all. And in the moment that she gave herself to him, he wondered how he had lived this long without allowing her to touch his soul so sweetly.

Never, in all the dangers he had braved, had he risked handing another person his need, his hopes, his dreams—all that made him human and vulnerable. Yet he found that he could not give Amanda his body without also giving her those things. She drew all from him but gave them back, uninhibited and unafraid, with the nobility of a queen.

No walls, no barriers, no hesitation marked their love-making. The worn little pallet on which he spread his coat and worshipped her with his longing became the center of his entire existence. Awed by a vulnerability that matched his own, he offered her all that he had.

Afterward, he lay with his arms around her, lacking the words to tell her of his feelings. So new, so fragile was this happiness within him, that he was loath to speak for fear of breaking the spell. But Amanda had no such reticence, and her words made him realize how truly vulnerable he was.

"I was right," she said, sounding awed. "You are a beast."

Guilt shattered his burgeoning joy. In unleashing his uncivilized nature, he had gone too far and too fast for a woman of gentle sensibility. No matter how willingly she had met his passion, she could not have been prepared for the full force of it. Amanda might possess rare courage, but he ought to have reined himself in. A man in whom conquering was bred to the bone should never have loosed his unbridled lust on a delicate female.

"Forgive me," he rasped, for the first time ashamed of his physical prowess. He had always known his own strength, always known that it was the ultimate weapon he possessed. But he had always had himself under control. Until now.

"I will not." Her deliciously swollen mouth curved upward, and her husky tone sent new spasms of desire through him. "Nor will I allow you to leave this cave without showing me that beast again."

His spirit soared as understanding of her gentle humor dawned, only to come crashing down again when a solitary tear rolled down her cheek.

"Amanda?" he prodded. "Did I injure you?"

"'Tis but a tear of wonder," she assured him through a wry smile. "Love is more beautiful than I dreamed. I did not think I had those dreams, the kind that Felicity has. But I did. Thank you for showing me the truth."

Love. Simon gazed at the stone ceiling. They had shared the most intimate experience a man and woman can, and they would marry soon—he would insist on that. She had spoken of love and had a right to expect that he would speak of it, too. Yet the words stuck in his throat, and something else came out—bald, unadorned truth.

"My father died in war," he said in a distant voice. "I fully expected to die in the same manner. When I inherited this cursed title, I swore that even if battle claimed me, there would be children to continue the line and help my widow carry on. Not one child, you understand, but many. A family. I was twelve when my father died, and my young strength was all that stood between my mother and poverty and degradation. It was not enough."

"I see." Sympathy filled her eyes.

"No," he returned bleakly, "you do not. The truth, Amanda, is that I failed to protect her."

She shook her head. "You were just a boy."

"And she was just a woman. Beauty was the only asset she possessed besides the small boarding house. The boarders she took in were an unruly lot. Once I came home from selling her pies on the street to find her lying in a pool of blood, her skirts up around her waist."

Amanda gasped and reached for his hand.

"She had been raped and beaten." He tried not to see that sight again, but he knew his mind would never forget. "She was never the same. Her beauty disappeared almost overnight. The next winter she died from consumption."

"It was not your fault," she said softly.

For a moment he accepted the solace she offered, allowed himself to savor the touch of her fingers. Then, feeling as cold and remote as the stone around them, he withdrew his hand and shook his head in self-disgust.

"I failed her," he growled. "Hell, I could not even protect her in her own house."

"Simon . . ."

"I was good at war, you know," he said, ruthlessly banishing her efforts to console him. "Wellington used me to draw up battle plans, to sneak behind the lines and learn what I could about the Corsican's plans. I did that very well."

Despair forced him to continue, even though he knew it would hurt her. "Everything centered around the mission, around duty. Like a damned fool, I thought I could arrange the matter of my marriage in the same way I formulated battle plans. I went about the process methodically. I chose a well-bred young lady who could give my offspring a genteel upbringing and the education I myself did not obtain until well into my adulthood."

He met her gaze. "And who seemed likely to give me many children."

She had no trouble following his thoughts. "With her large family, Felicity must have seemed the perfect bride."

He saw that she was near tears. Not tears of wonder or happiness. Not this time.

"Amanda," he murmured, wondering how he could have been so stupid.

She managed a weak smile. "I have no brothers or sisters. And I am no longer young. In short, I am not a very good bet as a breeder. You must be practical, my lord. If Felicity will not marry you, you must find another woman with the same qualifications."

"No." He nearly shouted his denial. "I thought I could protect myself from the hurt of failing those who needed me. But now I realize war also taught me that even the most thorough planning can bring death, destruction, failure. There are no guarantees for anything in life."

She lowered her gaze. "I suppose not."

Gently, Simon touched her chin, forcing her to look at him. "I thought to control my fate by denying that part of me that could be hurt. Like you, Amanda, I did not know I had dreams. You made me see that I did. And that you are the answer to those dreams."

"But I am only one, Simon," she said, tears spilling onto her cheeks.

"And I am only one. Whether we have children or no, we will have each other."

Tremulously, she searched his face. "I will not force you into marriage," she said at last.

"No," he agreed, smiling. "We will force each other."

The joy in her eyes shattered the stone fortress around his heart. Suddenly, words were no longer difficult. In a rush they spilled from him, as if they had been there all along merely waiting for those walls to fall.

"I love you, Amanda."

Silently, she pondered his declaration. "I believe Felicity was right," she responded at last.

"That we were meant for each other?"

Tilting her head, she appeared to consider the matter gravely. "That even practical sorts like us are capable of growing to appreciate sentiment in our old age."

A grin swept his face, but as she continued to stare at him, Simon suddenly felt wretchedly unsure of himself, like the greenest youth. He cleared his throat. "Does that mean that you return my, ah, regard?"

She frowned. "Did I neglect to say so?"

"Amanda," he groaned, "if it is your intent to torment me . . ."

"It is not," she assured him. "'Tis just that I love two men, my lord."

"Two?" A sudden fury filled him. "I will not share you with Julian. If it takes another duel or ten duels, I will force him to relinquish his claim."

"So you admit it was a duel after all?" She eyed him thoughtfully.

"Amanda," he growled in a warning tone.

"'Tis not Julian but another gentleman," she said softly. "I believe you know him. And I do not think you could best him in any duel."

Bleak, blinding anger filled him. "Oh?"

Her gentle laughter took him aback. "I am terribly sorry for teasing you. I only referred to Mr. Thornton."

"Thornton!" Simon barked. Relief warred with embarrassment. He was not accustomed to this new intensity, this raw feeling for her that turned him into a vulnerable mass of nerves. He coughed awkwardly, trying to regain his poise. "Rather a somber sort, was he not?"

She nodded. "But he kisses quite as nicely as you."

"Now that is a challenge no soldier can resist," he murmured, bringing his lips to hers.

"Beast," she declared, and sighed contentedly.

"God's teeth, Mortimer, these humans are impossible!"

"My sentiments precisely."

"Love is to blame. Were our humans consumed only by lust, we would have had a chance. Who could have guessed that our tenant was capable of such feelings?"

"Or such strength, curse it all."

"It is so unfair, Mortimer. I have never felt so defeated in my life. I could not worm myself into so much as an earlobe of that chaperone. In another life, I think she must have been one of those warring Romans."

"I had equal difficulty with our tenant, dear."

"I was prepared to settle for the Biddles—indeed, they

do seem a lusty sort. But that was no good, either, for they are just as besotted."

"With Edward gone, perhaps this would be a good time to follow your plan and leave this castle to seek our pleasure elsewhere. There are many humans in the world concerned only with lust."

"I suppose. But I was rather fond of our tenant."

"A little too fond, if you ask me, Isabella."

"I do not recall doing so, Mortimer."

"What is that ungodly sound?"

"Mortimer, no! Could it be? It cannot!"

An unearthly groan swept through the tower.

"Edward!"

"It seems the prodigal has returned."

"Now we are trapped here forever!"

"It is not the end of the world, love."

"Speak for yourself, Mortimer."

Amanda stared at her aunt. "What do you mean Mr. Frakes has returned?"

Lady Biddle beamed. "That nice young man traveled on foot for two days to seek his father's permission to wed Felicity. Do you not think that romantic?"

Stunned, Amanda could only nod in agreement.

"They are in the parlor now with Sir Thomas," Lady Biddle said with a pleased smile. "I believe Thomas is satisfied with Stephen's ability to provide for Felicity. It seems that he is the seventh son of an earl, and while he possesses no great fortune, his father has given him a small farm. Felicity is delighted, of course."

"And you have no objection?" Amanda ventured.

"Her sisters married brilliantly, and I confess that a farmer's wife is not exactly what I had in mind for her. But after seeing how happy she is, I cannot bring myself to object. Love will win in the end, you know," she added, pointedly eyeing the couple before her.

And they were quite an eyeful, Amanda conceded, for by the time Felicity had remembered to unlock the back of the wardrobe, they had passed all night and much of the next morning in each other's arms. It had been rather daunting to find Sir Thomas and Lady Biddle waiting in Amanda's room as they emerged from the wardrobe with wrinkled clothing and telltale blushes. But Sir Thomas had merely eyed them sternly and said he trusted that the earl had a special license in his pocket. Now, she and Simon stood with her aunt studying the Great Hall as a possible site for their wedding ceremony.

"I am sorry Julian has left," Amanda said.

Simon frowned. "Forgive me if I do not share your regret," he said dryly.

"I would like to thank him for his letter." Amanda withdrew a piece of paper from her skirt pocket. "I found it under a corner of the rug in my room. He must have slipped it under the door when he left, only it caught under the carpet and I did not notice it until today."

Over her shoulder, Simon regarded Julian's large black scrawl with suspicion. "Would you care to share the contents?" he said coolly.

Amanda smiled mischievously. "If that is jealousy I hear in your voice, my lord, I hope this will soothe it." She handed him the note. Warily, Simon began to read it.

Dear Amanda [Julian wrote]— *Allow me to wish you happy, for I can see that it is only a matter of time before Simon discovers his feelings for you. I only hope he does not allow his rectitude to stand in the way, for if I do not miss my guess, Miss Biddle has other fish to fry. (I trust you have not, in fact, learned to master your passions as you insisted that day in the meadow.)*

Amanda blushed, but Simon's countenance darkened at the memory of finding her in Julian's arms that day. Resolutely, he returned his attention to the letter.

I have taken myself off. The immediate resolution of my lineage is somehow less important than the silencing of the inner demons that have long plagued me, and which seem louder here at Sommersby. I regret giving you offense—recently and in the past—not with my lecherous behavior so much as the fact that you did not enjoy it. Undoubtedly, Simon will succeed where I could not. Yours, Julian LeFevre.

Simon glowered. "If you are even thinking about inviting this man to our wedding, Amanda, I will be most displeased."

"Actually," she said, flushing, "I was at that very moment thinking of our time in the cave and how you had, er, 'succeeded' when Claridge had not."

"I see," he said, a smile hovering about his lips as the devilish fire in his eyes warmed her to the tips of her toes.

Lady Biddle arched a brow, then sighed. "I believe I shall go look for Sir Thomas." A faint blush stole over her cheeks. "He has pestered the children long enough."

Simon and Amanda exchanged glances as Lady Biddle left the room. "Do you suppose it will still be like that with us after we have been married for twenty-five years?" Amanda said wistfully.

Simon drew her closer. "I cannot imagine otherwise," he replied, nuzzling her earlobe.

"There is just one thing," Amanda said, studying the various weapons suspended on the walls—until his wandering hands made that task impossible. "Do you think you will be able to do without so many lethal weapons around the castle? I find them rather unsettling."

"Do you?" he murmured as his mouth trailed butterfly kisses up the side of her neck.

Flames of desire ignited within her. "The war is over, you know," she noted breathlessly.

Folding her against his chest, Simon stroked her hair, his gentle touch betraying nothing of the violent desire Amanda could feel in his uneven breathing. Restraint radiated from every pore of his body. She sighed wistfully.

But suddenly, he lifted her into his arms with the speed and force of a man who has reached his limits. His warlike gaze radiated green fire.

"Yes, it is over," he agreed hoarsely. "And to the victor, 'tis said, belong the spoils."

Like a savage warrior claiming his prize, Simon carried her up the stairs to his room.

Epilogue

"I cannot bear it, Mortimer."

"Edward does seem to be in rare form tonight."

"The screams! The ungodly screams! They are worse than ever. This is truly hell!"

"I wish you would not say that word, Isabella. I fear you tempt fate."

"What of it? Nothing could be worse than this!"

"I disagree, my dear. For all the inconvenience we suffer, it is only Edward we must endure. I imagine the fires of hell are a great deal worse."

"Hah! Hell would be a pleasure compared to this place. At least there would be others like us. . . ."

"Isabella! Do not speak so!"

"After all these years you still fear your shadow, Mortimer. . . ."

"I have no shadow to fear, my dear."

"Do not play word games with me. You know, Mortimer, I am beginning to weary of you. I think I should like to see if hell has more to offer."

"I fear you would regret it, my dear."

"Never! I challenge all of the powers that be to show me this place called hell. I daresay it is a paradise of sinful delights."

"Isabella, hush!"

"Sinful delights! Do you hear me, Mortimer? I have not had one moment of pleasurable sin in five hundred years. I deserve something for that. I want what I deserve! I demand it!"

A fiercely spiraling wind suddenly whirled through the tower, bringing a flash of lightning and an ominous roll of thunder. For a moment the little tower was alight as it had never been. Then the blustering gale vanished, leaving behind only an eerie silence.

"*Isabella?*"

There was no response.

Mortimer's wistful sigh drifted over the vaulted ceiling. Slowly, his solitary moan was joined by another that gradually escalated into a familiar screech.

"*Still here, Edward? Yes, I can hear that you are. One can be thankful for a little constancy, at any rate. Have I ever told you how much I admire your voice? No? Well, perhaps now would be a good time, although I imagine we shall have a great deal of time together over the centuries. Yes, together. What? Why, Edward, I never realized that you cared.*"

Author's Note

History portrays Edward of Caenarvon as the weak-willed son of the outstanding English king of the Middle Ages, Edward I. Edward II grew up a lonely lad who longed for companions of his own age and sex. Among his favorites was Piers Gaveston, a vain and sarcastic man who offended many, including Edward's wife, Isabella of France, daughter of two sovereigns and the sister of three kings. For their marriage in 1308, Isabella brought with her a vast portion from her father and a magnificent trousseau, much of which Edward promptly passed to Gaveston. Gaveston held sway over the king until the Earl of Warwick had the courtier kidnapped and murdered in 1312.

The king's new favorite, Hugh le Despenser, induced Edward to deprive Isabella of her estates in 1324. The next year she left for France and, with her lover Roger Mortimer, raised an army against her husband. Edward was deposed in favor of his son and confined to Berkeley Castle. (Sommersby Castle is my own invention.)

By all accounts, Edward's end in 1327 was ghastly. Heavy feather beds or possibly a table were employed to hold him down while a hot spit was thrust into him and twisted until he died. At the coronation of her son, Edward III, Isabella shed hypocritical tears for her husband, but popular disgust at the manner of his death turned opinion against the ruthless queen.

Edward III had Mortimer literally ripped from Isabella's arms at Nottingham Castle and taken to Tyburn, where he became the first person executed there. Isabella died in 1358 and was buried in London's Grey Friars Church, where Mortimer had been entombed years earlier. Carrying her hypocrisy even to the grave, notes historian Agnes Strickland, Isabella "was buried with the heart of her murdered husband on her breast."